TREASON'S REWARD

Annay Dawson

Treason's Reward

Annay Dawson

Published by Lulu.com
Copyright ©2009 Annay Dawson
ISBN: 978-0-557-05684-2

Other Novels by Annay Dawson

Shadows of the Past

Hidden Promises

Prologue

About five years ago. . .

"Damn. What in the hell was that?" Bobby said in anger, not really expecting an answer. He was just walking into the shower stall in the men's locker room next to Ward. Ward had already thrown off his mud-encrusted clothes and gone into the showers to try and remove the layers that still clung to him. Ward had trained with these men before and their reaction to the mini training mission they had just been on was interesting.

"Is she some sort of freak?" Bobby continued as the spray hit him and the mud began to puddle at the base of the stall.

"They said she was good when we set up the training mission," Ward put his head under the water and closed his eyes. He had been planning this since he had put in for a transfer to the Phoenix office. Part of it had been curiosity, part of it just another way to meet up with her again, but he hadn't bothered to tell Bobby, his best friend or comrade, that. Closing his eyes and placing his face back under the water he could clearly picture her. He couldn't help but smile at the outcome of this training session. It didn't surprise him that he had a good helping of admiration for her either. She had beaten them thoroughly. Her performance during the training session had not been anything less than extraordinary. Nothing he hadn't expected after he had looked at her file, after all they were PED agents. All of them worked for a little known governmental department or agency known as the Paranormal Enforcement Department, or 'PED' for short. In the department it was their job to provide protection, detection, and deception. Jan, as well as others, were part of a grand experiment that had started back in the 1960's and never ended like it was supposed to have. As in the last ten to fifteen years they had been discovered through bogus psychology experiments in colleges. Then they were slowly and carefully drafted into a lifetime of service for the department. All of these agents could read minds, and they were partnered with a handler to keep them loyal to the job. They were also well trained in all types of areas to make them virtually unstoppable.

No one could yet beat her time in assembling a firearm in pitch-blackness. It was pure pleasure to watch as she moved through terrain that was best left to swamp creatures. She then switched her weapon under live fire. She had allowed him to watch all of this through her mind. It was only toward the end when they had tried to block each other that the true strength of her talents had shined. She had been the only mind reader he had ever met that could pick off a trained blocker in pitch-blackness. He was hoping he would get a chance to ask her about that.

"Yah, but how did she find us in all that mess and pitch black conditions? She picked us off as if we were standing in the middle of open field at noon. I couldn't even read that she was anywhere around," Bobby vigorously rubbed shampoo into his matted hair, "Could you read her?"

"Genetic freak, that's what she is," the only other man on the mission made his comment as he got into the showers. The training mission had included just the four of them, Jan had been set up as the one they had to capture and bring in. One woman had bested all of them, and egos were now hurting, all except for Ward's.

"We're all genetic freaks if you want to get down to the nitty gritty and no, had no clue she was even around," he wished he could have said the last part with more conviction. Since the first time he had seen her in the office, he had never stopped feeling her when she was around him.

It had only been a quick glance at first, but then something had compelled him to look her way again. His eyes had been captured by her intense stare. It began innocently but he had stared a moment too long, and then their eyes had locked. It had only been for a minute, but that minute had changed him forever. Her eyes had invited him to get to know her back then, but he hadn't even gotten a chance to talk with her. He had looked in her files, when no one was watching, to learn everything he could about her. Ward was no stranger to computers and could break into any system that existed including his own department. A skill he had shared with no one within the department. He liked the idea that he could have any information he wanted, whenever he wanted. In college he trained to be a doctor, but found that he had a way with computers as well once he had joined the department. He saw no reason not to use it.

What he found in her records was impressive. She had been undercover a number of times according to her files, a lot of dangerous assignments. Each time had ended with the successful completion of her mission and the capture of the suspect. Nothing surprising there, that's what they did for a living. Her training session's scores had been excellent, and in some cases they had exceeded the scores and standards of the others in this as well as many other departments.

As for her mind reading abilities, only a few readers were truly in her league. In fact, his score on the ESP tests and hers were almost identical, but she certainly had discovered something that he hadn't. Digging a little deeper, he had found that the recent assessments of their mind reading skills were comparable, and their accuracy levels were off the charts. As he continued to read the file he discovered that his range for an accurate read was a bit farther and he was able to break past mental blocks a little easier according to the scores, but that might be the only differences between their abilities. They were well matched and at the top of their field. The more he learned about her, the more he wanted to learn about her. She was a psychology major, and had a minor in languages. She had joined up right out of college and there were no messy family situations that had to be dealt with. Like all of them she was a loner. She had never had a partner change in the department and her operations base had always been the Phoenix office. He had hoped that this training mission would be an opening to get to actually talk with her. All he knew right now were the dull facts that they put in her file, and he was pretty sure there was nothing dull about her.

"Did you see her time on the blind assembly?" Bobby let out a whistle, "That woman has good hands," Bobby put his head back under the water to rinse off the remaining mix of mud and shampoo.

"Shot the hell out of your record," Ward walked out of the showers and wrapped the towel around his waist as he went over to his locker. How good the woman's hands were not the only things Ward was interested in. But he kept those thoughts closely guarded.

It was never a good thing in a room of mind readers to let them see just who peaked your interest, whether it was business or pleasure. Right now Ward wasn't even sure which it was, but he knew he was going to find out. She had made him think and feel things he never thought were possible.

"Want to get a coffee and some breakfast?" Bobby asked as he walked back to where he had stored his street clothes before the training session. Ward was already dressed and zipping up his bag.

"Love to, but already have plans," or at least he hoped he did. If he was right, Jan was about to leave the women's locker room.

"Hope she's worth it bro," was all Bobby had time to say before Ward walked out. Ward should have known he would see through to his real motives.

Chapter 1

Years Later…

Jan awoke suddenly and completely in the middle of the night to the ringing of the phone on the pillow beside her. It wasn't a surprise, she had gone to bed expecting the call to come in and she was awake in seconds. In one fluid motion she had answered the secured cell phone placing it next to her ear by the second ring.

"'Lo," she pushed up on the pillows letting the sheet pool around her waist.

"What are you wearing?" The voice was low, deep, and very familiar. Ward only had a few moments and he wasn't going to waste it on small talk. He missed being near her; being in her head.

"Nothing but a smile. How's the weather there?" Jan could care less about the weather. They used the word weather instead of the word mission. It was standard procedure, even if the line was secure they couldn't, wouldn't, take any chances.

It had been about a week and a half ago when Ward had gotten an e-mail from an old friend that worked at another government agency. Over the years, Ward had only given his e-mail to those who he could truly trust, and who might need his help. They were the ones that gave him jobs that other agencies didn't want. The e-mail had simply said, *I need your help on this one. In this situation, I only want to work with the best*, and Ward was the best. He had signed it only as, *Golightly*.

They had been teamed together many times years ago and knew each other well. He was one of a small number of people that Ward trusted and called friend and even brother. Ward sent only a one line e-mail back, *Call me*, with a phone number. Two days later Ward received his call. Jan knew of him but had never had the pleasure to work with him.

Jack Golightly had needed another person whom he could trust to help set up a semi-legal surveillance operation on a developing group in South America. If that had been the only thing he needed he would have called the agency, but there was more. There was another problem he only hinted about to Ward as they spoke. Ward's skills as a technological expert, and his ability to be on the outside of the system were exactly what Jack had needed to set up his surveillance on both the group and his agency team. His current field partner on this assignment was adequate, it was farther up the grapevine that he was worried about. He assured Ward that it would only require a week or more of unfavorable conditions. The location of this assignment was in and around Iquitos where rain was the normal weather this time of year and sun was the oddity. What he didn't have to tell Ward was that it would also be handy to have a mind reader to go into the different situations where placing a bug, or checking on teammates, could be difficult, or impossible, for anyone else. Jack had promised more information when and if Ward went down there.

After a brief discussion with Jan, Ward had taken off to Peru to help out. Jan had stayed behind to monitor another developing problem that they had been watching for the last two weeks. They were about to take action on it if no one else picked it up. As it turned out the FBI had picked it up three days after Ward left, leaving them out of the picture, and Jan with nothing to do.

"There doesn't seem to be much of a change in the weather down here. It's fairly clear and I should be headed back in a few days as long as the weather balloons hold. There have been no other hints at inclement weather," he just needed to make sure no one found the equipment he had gotten into the homes, and that it monitored what they needed. Ward had also not seen anything that could confirm Jack's suspicions, either in the main office in Lima, the branch in Iquitos, or the people around him here. He also knew that if Jack suspected it then it most likely existed, but he couldn't hang around forever. That was dangerous too.

It had not stopped raining for days. He had crawled through some of the worst swamps he had seen in a while to set up this monitoring station. They now sat concealed by a camouflage tarp that was a makeshift shelter, the rain hammered down on them, the mud slid and pooled beneath their feet. The generator created just enough power to keep the monitoring equipment going; they couldn't risk running any type of heater and didn't have enough power for it anyway. He had been living off rations and whatever Jack brought back from the forest to their shelter, which was far better than the rations they had been provided. It had been exactly one week since Ward had seen a shower and the mud on his clothes and skin had begun to feel like a part of his body even though he had made a couple of trips to the waterfall about half a mile from where he was right now. This had brought about the old memories of the first time he had ever trained with Jan so many years ago. Those memories always held mixed feelings as they also contained memories of another agent he once considered his best friend, as close to a brother as one got in this business of subterfuge and mayhem. Once he left the department he had discovered just whom he could call friend.

"Good. The weather has cleared here, but it's getting a little cold," Jan leaned up against the pillows and relaxed. Being in danger was part of who they were, but she was always glad to know that the danger was minimal. When they married they never promised each other their tomorrows, only their todays. The future held no guarantees.

"Looking at the forecast here, I see a warm front coming your way soon. In fact it will get very hot," Ward glanced at his watch knowing that he would have to end his phone call in less than two minutes.

"It's been down right boring. Nothing coming over the wire for us," no jobs were coming in from their other sources. There was nothing he needed to get back for besides her. She had been watching for another job, but all seemed too quiet. Jan was watching the bedside clock, and knew that their time was almost up, "I've even considered going shopping."

"That bad huh?" Ward knew that Jan thought shopping was a form of torture, the worst kind in her books. "If you feel the need to go, at least get something I will enjoy."

"That might make the trip worthwhile. Something red and small," she could almost see his face as she thought she heard the catch in his breath, "Watch your back."

"Will do," his voice just beginning to recover, "Will call again at the set time. Hopefully it will be to tell you I'm on my way. Will have to see what information Jack's bringing me. He'll be here in about five minutes. By the way, do me a favor and start checking out some of the names of the people connected with this mission. I'm getting a strange feeling but can't pin it to anyone," he gave her a list of names quickly, including Jack's. Jan committed each name to memory. Ward paused, "Love ya." It was funny, they had spent years in this line of work learning not to make these complicated relationship connections with others, but it felt natural and even good to have someone waiting for him to get back.

"Love ya," and she placed the phone back on his pillow before getting up to go to the computer. No time like now to get started since she wasn't going to go back to sleep anytime soon.

Ward put down the phone and put his attention back on to the radio transmitter. Everything had been taped, and nothing had happened that was noteworthy. He was pretty sure he wasn't here for this though. The usual conversations had taken place, nothing that would have confirmed or denied suspicions about any type of illegal activity they were looking or not looking for. He had suspected the obvious, drug running, but they had found none of that. Jack had only hinted that the CIA had suspected the new group of smuggling something. Once Ward had arrived, he learned that it may have actually been a new terrorist cell developing. Ward now understood why Jack had never mentioned it over the phone or the e-mail. Even on secure channels terrorism wasn't discussed out loud. Just what they were up to was their job to discover. He had to wonder just who the terrorists were that Jack was looking for. Ward felt a presence coming toward the outpost. He didn't move from his place as it was only Jack that he felt. The last time that Jack had been up to see him had been a day and a half ago. He had promised to bring some computer equipment this time so that Ward could do a little more digging on his own. The flap to the tent flew open and rain spattered the small area as Jack made his way in.

"Had Toby run those pictures through the computer that you got, and came up with a big fat zero," Jack stood a few inches taller than Ward and had about twenty-five more pounds of muscle on him. He was also caked with mud from the knees down. His hair was black and even wet it hung loosely around his face and ears curling slightly. His facial features had an angular look. They were strong and set, like they had been chiseled out of stone and his muscled frame matched the hard set of his face. He had been born and raised in the West, and was part Native American. He had worked with the CIA for the last fifteen years; most of that being in South

America where his looks let him fit in like a native. Jack had his raincoat covering a bag that he was carrying. Quickly he shed his camo raincoat in the farthest corner to keep the water and mud away from the equipment. Droplets of water fell all over the corner and splattered the makeshift wall but somehow he missed the sensitive equipment that Ward had set up. Ward moved only one side of the headphones away from his ears. It was the same way he had talked with Jan just a few minutes ago.

"Did they check the other databases?" He asked the question, but Ward already knew the answer.

"They don't have access to the ones you want checked. Why do you think I called you in? Just for your pretty face, or might it be the fact that I think you like sitting here getting a full spa mud treatment down here in this little paradise of mine?" Jack took the headphones off of Ward's head, and handed him a waterproof bag about the size of a small suitcase. "We have this for a couple of days, and then they will figure out that it's missing. What you want to do after that is up to you?" Jack was unsure of just how much Ward would want to or need to bend the rules.

"Does it ever stop raining here this time of year?" it was a rhetorical question as Ward had already pulled the specs on the area and knew that to be called a tropical rain forest it had to get a lot of rain, over two hundred fifty millimeters a month on average, more in some months during the wet season. That would leave about two dry days as Ward calculated it. Ward took the case and wiped away the mud from the zippers, "There's been nothing new happening in there since we started to listen. Are you sure we're barking up the right tree?" Ward then began to open the bag right beside the radio set up on what space was left of the small camp table.

"It stops raining one Tuesday in December I think. As for the right tree, that odd feeling I get, is getting odder as this job gets older." Ward knew that only part of what Jack had said was true. Jack had had an odd feeling for a long time about this job, but he hadn't shared all his suspicions with anyone yet. Ward had only worked to pick up on a couple of random thoughts, but Jack hadn't been up here long enough yet to get past his blocks to see through to the real problem. What Ward knew was that Jack wanted him to go on his own feelings, and not Jack's. If they both felt it then it meant that he wasn't crazy after all.

Ward took out the laptop and put up the antenna to connect to the worldwide web via a satellite that was just in range. It was also time to put his mental antennas up to see if he could finally break through just a corner of Jack's blockades. His fingers flew over the keys as he logged on to the different databases looking for names or descriptions to match the people who were occupying the house about a mile down the road, and his mind started to do what it did best.

He checked the intelligence sights of the major countries first and came up with nothing. Even the United States had minimal to no information on this group. Each name he tried had come up blank or with information that included about only the last two years on each person's life. He assumed that this was a cover, a badly created one, but a cover the same. With each miss his fingers got faster and his temper hotter. Jack sat and intensely listened at the machine, hearing nothing that would have caused any alarm. Ward had gotten through part of his defenses, but not enough to get any names. A traitor was all the information he could ferret out of Jack's head. Ward switched satellites and entered the Brazilian intelligence sight. After typing in the first two names he again found nothing but uncreative underdone covers there. Each cover consisted of a name, a credit card with a five hundred dollar limit, and history of no more than two years that he could find. It wasn't until he typed in the last name that he got a hit.

This guy, or his cover, had a record. He had been picked up once for robbery, and had given a different name than was on his documents. The smile on Ward's face began to lift just a little at the corners. It may not have been a false name at all. If they had been building their covers, giving that name would have caused problems. Ward had to assume that he may have given them his real name but didn't have any documentation to support it; after all, the name could just be another alias. With little to go on, Ward started to enter the new name into the databases again. This time, he came up with all sorts of hits, and one from Russia that made him sit up and take notice.

The screen just rolled on and on. There were pages of information on this person. He read carefully through parts of the file, and when he got to the bottom he noticed there was another name attached to the file. As he read the name he suddenly sensed other minds moving in quickly. The thoughts hadn't been there a moment ago or maybe he had been lax, because he thought they were too far out in the wilderness. There were at least three men, with semiautomatic rifles. None were close enough yet for Ward to get a good look through any of their eyes; he could only read their general thoughts. That was enough for him though. His voice dropped very low, and his words were carefully measured before he said them.

"Anything change in the house?" The way Ward's voice sounded made every muscle in Jack's body tense. Ward could see his jaw clench. Without saying a word he shook his head no but never looked in Ward's direction, "Then we have unexpected guests. We have about two minutes before they catch sight of the tent, about five before we either confront them or leave. Want to tell me that something you've been hiding from me now?"

Jack turned to look at Ward, and it was if all Ward's suspicions had been confirmed. No words were exchanged as Ward looked through what Jack was thinking at a rapid pace. Jack knew enough to allow him to have all the access he wanted right now; it would make what time they did have much more efficient. Ward could now clearly see the possibilities of all of it in his mind, and what he had just discovered on the computer could only be a beginning to confirm it. He had all the information he needed to start a deeper search, so Ward hit the save keys on the keyboard putting all the information he had just located on the hard drive. Ward cleared the computer screen and with a couple quick snaps of screws he pulled the hard drive out of the laptop. Jack had already gotten up and went over to the side of the tent to grab the emergency packs and a couple of rain jackets. Ward slipped the hard drive into the survival pack in a place where water wouldn't get in, "I know a way out of here where we won't be found. Leave the rest and let's go."

Jan went over the names in her head, only one of which she knew, and that was Jack's. The CIA routinely ran checks on people but rarely got the same information Ward did. As a matter of courtesy they didn't routinely hack into other databases. Jan also believed that it might also be a matter of arrogance on the agency's part as well. Not being able to sleep now, Jan grabbed her robe that lay at the bottom of the bed and walked into the living room where the computer sat in the corner. To look at, the computer looked like many other personal computers that were in many other homes all over the world. What was inside of it was what mattered in this case. The processor was fast, the gigs high, but that wasn't what made it special. What made it special was it contained the access codes to many of the intelligence agencies around the world. If one would happen to change, then the computer itself would randomly decipher it. A special program Ward had written himself. If red flags began to go off the computer would disengage before it was tracked, and then Ward would do his magic and break the code manually. All in all, a system that rivaled most espionage systems, and he could break into most of them. Jan flipped the switch and walked into the small kitchen to make a cup of coffee as the computer booted up.

The small espresso pot sat on the stove ready to go. Jan tossed in two scoops of coffee and turned on the burner, listening for the familiar clicking of the automatic lighter of the burner. She inhaled the smell of the coffee as it brewed and the aroma did more to wake up her senses than the caffeine in the coffee would. She walked over and took out the milk from the refrigerator. After a few moments she turned off the stove, grabbed the cup on the counter, and poured a cup of coffee then added just a touch of milk. The milk was swallowed up by the blackness of the brew. As she stood in the small kitchen sipping her coffee she started to put two and two together getting the same number that Ward had come up with before he left.

Jack had called him in to do some computer and surveillance work supposedly, but there had been something else to it. Ward had heard it in his voice. She stared at the cup on the counter and wondered just what, or who, Jack was really looking for. Ward had given her a list of five names to look up, two which were field agents already assigned to the area. She decided to check the agents out last, as he would already have done an extensive background check on them. The other three names would be of the people they were watching.

She would look for discrepancies in information gathered on any of them, in any database. That would take time. She would also need to check entries and exits from almost any country that could harbor drug lords, gunrunners, white slavers, and terrorists. That would mean almost every country. It would be a long task, but one that he probably couldn't take on right at the moment due to the nature of his living conditions. In twenty-four hours he would try and contact her again and he would have whatever information she had ready. Two minutes later she picked up the cup and walked over to the computer. Sitting at the keyboard she started her search in the

CIA computers looking for any information or anomalies on the first three names. As each profile popped up Jan carefully saved them, in order to compare them to the others that she would later dig up.

Two hours after starting her search she had found nothing out of the ordinary on two of the three people. Storing all the information to the hard drive, she started the search on the third person. Jan stretched and realized just how much work was going into these background checks. Her coffee was now cold and the sun was rising as the first rays entered the room. The central computers had nothing on this one either so Jan again started the long process to look through databases that were located in other countries. She kept the search specialized as there were only a few things that they really could be looking for. When she tried the Middle-Eastern entry and exit records from different countries she began to get hits. This could mean one of many things, not too many that were good, and Jan was not the type to jump to conclusions, she needed proof. She started a new file on the one named Sal Seital. Each hit she got that was related to Mr. Seital was stored and cataloged by color as to the number of times of entry or exit. What she got was a little less than proof but more than nothing.

The gentleman in question, Sal Seital, had entered into Libya more than once. He had entered at least four times and Jan highlighted the dates. She ran the other names through the same database. Setting up the computer to automatically run all the aliases she had found had been easy to do. It would take another fifteen minutes, so she readied the next list. For fun she would run the list of agents through as well.

Another person on the list, the agent assigned to Jack at the moment, had also been recorded as having two entries into Libya as well. Without Ward, Jan could only guess at what was going on. There were reasons for field agents to be entering countries such as Libya, but similar entry and exit dates brought him under a bit more suspicion. If he had had Sal under surveillance for a while then it would be natural, but there was always a possibility that natural was not the case. Jan began to get a strange feeling again. She saved that data into Sal's folder, knowing that the connection was there, but not sure just what the connection was. By now her coffee had gotten old and cold. The sun was peeking in the windows. Getting up from the computer she moved to where she could see the sunlight. Knowing the feeling of impending doom was beginning to grow again she moved toward the balcony and began her normal Tai Chi routine. Keeping body and mind working together were especially important with her skills. Sometimes twenty to thirty minutes of Tai Chi could help clear her thoughts and focus her energies on the correct path. What she feared most was the options that were now darting through her head. Some of the explanations were logical, some a little less. Worse yet, if what she had read showed signs of the agent and Sal working together, then Ward and Jack could be in real trouble and there would be nothing she could do to warn them for almost another twenty four hours.

Chapter 2

Jack and Ward moved almost silently through the thick jungle and were now about two hundred yards from the tent. There had been no way or time to cover their tracks and Ward wasn't worried about it yet. Jack was an expert at living out here in the jungle and they would lead them far enough away from the cave Ward had discovered a couple days ago. That was if they chose to follow. The general gloom of the day and the steady rainfall would make it hard to track them through the dense part of the forest. The camouflage rain ponchos they wore only added to the illusion of being a part of the forest, not just visitors. Large tropical leaves growing from all types of plants made the going slower than either had wanted it to be.

Being careful not to break any stalks of the plants they were moving through, and barely disturbing the swarms of bugs that inhabited this part of the forest, Jack carefully followed in Ward's tracks to make it look as if only one person had gone this way. Training and survival skills had taken over; random thought was just a luxury that he couldn't afford at the moment. As Jack followed Ward, his eyes scanned every aspect of the forest for clues they might have left as to how many men had walked through here. Ward quickly turned and looked Jack straight in the eye. Then just as quickly he flattened himself into the mud and various decaying leaves on the ground. Jack stopped dead in his tracks. Even though Jack was no mind reader, he had known and trusted Ward's skills in that area too many times to count and threw himself to the ground as well only milliseconds after Ward had. The mud quickly covered his face and they both turned their heads slightly sideways just to be able to breath. The mud began to seep around them and make them as much a part of the forest as the trees and vines. The rain drenched smells of moss and rotting leaves mixed unpleasantly in their nostrils.

Jack had dropped just in time.   The sounds of automatic gunfire filled the forest just over the ridge. Birds, monkeys, and other unidentifiable animals cried out from fear as they tried to escape the unnatural sounds disturbing the rhythm of their world. The deafening sounds beat down on them from all around and it seemed that the auditory assault would last forever. Both men waited on the ground, focused and well trained for situations just like this. They counted off the time of the gunfire to help determine the type of weapon and number of rounds. It may have seemed to last forever but in reality it only lasted about thirty seconds. In the silence that followed Ward and Jack again counted off the time silently in their heads from the sound of the last shot. Both of them knew it would take less than a minute to reload and begin to fire again, if they were the true targets then it wouldn't just end at the tent.

Jack patiently waited for the signal to move again from Ward. It was quiet for a full three minutes, and that was when Ward let his mind fully travel back over the ridge. From what Ward could tell they had not entered the tent yet. They were just shredding it with the gunfire. Ward easily got into and read one of their minds.   He discovered that another man was signaling for the shooting to stop and pointing toward the tent. This would draw the fire away from them for only a couple of minutes. When they found out that they hadn't killed them they would come after them again. They were the goal. The other men's faces were not clear, but yet Ward was sure he had not seen any of them before. Their energy patterns were unrecognizable to him. Probably hired thugs with any luck. Then they entered the tent. Ward stretched out his left arm to reach out and tap Jack's shoulder.   With that simple action, and no words, Ward then started to move again with Jack closing in behind him. It was nearly impossible to hide all the signs that a person had passed this way and if they had a good tracker with them it would be hopeless. They only had a few minutes head start on them at most and it would take all of that and a little more to get into the safe cave.

They quickly approached the bank of the river that wound its way through the deepest parts of the forest. The river was swollen and brown with the run off from the fresh rain and the wash of mud from the forest. The bank was steep but not impossible to traverse. At first Jack thought they might move along the river and as Ward plunged six feet down the side of the bank and into the water Jack followed in the same path covering himself with mud and pushing more of it into the river on top of Ward. Ward ignored the flood of mud and began to walk back the way they came with the current of the river. They moved at a steady pace, hip deep, pack held above the rushing water, they could hear the movement of people deep in the forest. The sounds were not so much of people but of the animals that were disturbed by the intrusion of outsiders into their world. Ward and Jack moved through the forest as if they were one of the animals, keeping the disturbances to a minimum. They had slithered and weaved silently through the underbrush as they went so as not to bother the animals.

Ward could feel the concern Jack had about being in the river, and pushed on. He knew about the animals in the jungle and the ones that could inhabit the rivers. Ward did not want to meet up with any of these creatures either. But he wanted a face off with these men even less. What he did know was that their assailants wouldn't even try to navigate the river even though they had come into the forest. It was a gamble, but with the fast moving current and with what was ahead, Ward felt fairly safe. Predators, be they land or water creatures, rarely hunted in the faster waters.

It wasn't safe to talk yet, any foreign noise would easily be heard, and Ward could tell that their tracks had bought them a little time so far. Ward shifted himself closer to the bank of the river. He had never approached the set of waterfalls from this direction before, and the closer they got the more treacherous the river became. The water was running faster, and the bottom was much slimier making it hard to keep their footing. Ward started to look for a place to climb back out of the river. If he could find a rocky outcrop then it would be easier to leave no trace of where they went. It was unlikely that their adversaries knew of the small cave located behind the largest set of waterfalls. It had just been luck that Ward had found it. He had started to look for a safe hideaway earlier in the week in case he would need it. He had found it as he did some rock climbing for fun by the falls, but he had only approached it from the bottom. It was large enough to accommodate one man comfortably or two uncomfortably. Just then Ward saw what he was looking for, a small but stable rock formation jutting up from the middle of the waterfall. There was a problem though, the way the water was rushing around it made it nearly inaccessible without risking life and limb. Ward could see the question in Jack's mind and he turned and braced himself against the swift current. Reaching out with his mind he could not see any of their followers near, which meant that for the moment they would not be heard.

"Think you're up to this?" It was less of a question and more of a challenge. "There's a cave just about three feet below the falls and about thirty feet above the bottom. If we go in we will lose them for good."

"I'll ask later how you found this, let's go," Jack moved as easily through the swift current as Ward until the water began to reach just above their waists. It became more difficult to keep their footing stable and both knew that to reach the rocks would take a massive effort. The foliage in the forest had become thicker, but the river had widened out and made them a bit more visible to anyone from the bank, if they could get over the edge it would be better for them. They were only standing three feet apart, but Jack could see that Ward was having problems keeping his footing on the slippery bottom of the river. As the water rushed through his legs and past his waist, Jack let a little doubt pass through his mind and then threw caution to the wind.

"We'll have to go together," Ward took the pack from his back and secured the openings. The pack itself was waterproof although he rarely allowed it to prove itself. Jack handed his pack over and Ward undid the straps that held the packs to their backs. Ignoring the feel of the rushing cool water Ward hooked the backpacks together, fashioning them and their straps into a makeshift rope. Handing back the one side of the strap to Jack, they both tied the strap into a handle and placed opposite hands through the opening. They were now secured together by the packs. With the packs tied together and the width of their bodies it had now tripled their length. With a nod, they both continued slowly toward the rocks, straddling the span as best as they could while the force of the water took advantage of their added width. Jack was closest to the bank and Ward was farther out in the water. As they went deeper and deeper they both knew what was going to happen next. Without a word, they both leaned forward and let the water take away their footing, propelling them toward the rock face at an increasing speed. The years of training and swimming with Jan proved useful now for Ward and made his reactions automatic. They spread out their arms and legs to increase the mass the water needed to move. This would mean a slight difference in their speed and direction but it could mean the difference between broken or bruised bones. It would also give them precious milliseconds more to get a hold of the rocks they needed before plummeting down the falls. The only things visible now were the two heads above the water and the packs that tied them together. Moving at an ever-increasing speed the damage the rocks could do to the human body now seemed to magnify. All conscious thoughts were pushed to the back as the fight for survival awakened the most primitive instincts in them both and the adrenaline surged through their veins blocking out all other thoughts.

It was with a sickening thud that they both hit the rocks split seconds after the packs had caught. The makeshift rope made from the packs had held together as they were thrown over the edge and was effectively anchoring them to the rocks as the water rushed past them trying to pull them with it. Ward and Jack had turned their bodies in time to keep their heads from being smashed on the rocks, but using their bodies to shield their heads allowed for their bodies to take the full force of it. Taking only seconds they assessed the condition of their now bruised, but not broken bones. Looking at each other for only a split second they scrambled along the side of the rocks ignoring the pain shooting through them. With a speed he did not feel, Ward moved over the edge of the rock and noticed that they would be able to carefully climb down and maneuver their way under the falls and back into the cave.

Jack was behind him quickly and without further conversation they were on their way to the cave. Ward pulled the packs free and into the cave on top of Jack. It was only when they were safely in the cave that Jack ventured to talk about what was on his mind.

"Remind me again that I don't want to ever go hiking with you," propped up against the cool slimy walls of the cave they both could relax now and let their bodies rest, "Just how did you find this place?"

"Luck, and I needed a good shower," their voices were strained with the force of what they had just gone through, yet they kept them low and barely audible over the constant rush of the falls. Ward was amazed that they fit so well in this cave. It was actually a little bigger than he remembered. His muscles tightened and relaxed automatically as he surveyed their surroundings. On the side of Jack's shirt a red spot was beginning to grow. It wasn't growing too fast so neither of them were worried about dealing with it quickly. Ward pulled one pack to him and opened it up. He was looking for the hard drive he had stored in there only thirty minutes before. It, more than Jack's wound, would need to be checked first. He could pull all the information again, if they didn't catch it directly on the rock. If they had to the work could be done again, but Ward never relished redoing work he had already done.

Pulling it out, he breathed a sigh of relief. The drive had made it through, untouched by the pounding they had given it. Ward dug deeper in the bag looking for his medical kit now. As his fingers got to the bottom he confirmed another suspicion. The phone he had been using to contact Jan and to make satellite connections was now laying in pieces in the bottom of the bag. He pulled out what was left of the keypad and showed Jack.

"That could have been us you know," Jack sighed. He had trusted Ward and with good reason. Both were good at what they did and both of them knew the risk.

Their tracks had been covered well, and they were assured that by walking in the river they had left no trace of which direction they had gone.   If the group of assassins happened upon the waterfall, the height and speed of the water would have them believing that no one could have survived the fall without major injury or death. They both also knew it was only a matter of sheer luck that they didn't mirror the looks of the phone. Relaxation took over to a point as these thoughts settled in. Jack tried to shift his position a bit and winced from the pain. Ward wasn't in much better shape, but he had avoided any major injury. He moved toward Jack and unzipped his emergency medical kit.

"Move the arm," Jack complied knowing that it would be impossible to stop Ward when he used that tone of voice and hoping to get a bit of relief from the cut itself. Upon opening Jack's shirt Ward discovered a gouge about six inches long and almost an inch deep. From what he could see there was very little deep muscle tissue damage to it. To fix it right would take suturing the muscle as well as the skin though. If the conditions were better he would have cleaned and sutured it closed right there. Right now he would have to settle for his second choice. He cleaned the wound, "I think you might have gotten a bit too close to that rock."

"You think," Jack said it through clenched teeth. Ward continued to work on the wound. It wasn't as if he was ignoring the pain he was causing Jack; there was just nothing he could do about it. He pulled out the surgical glue he always had in the pack and tape. The glue was better on smaller areas, but quicker in general. Not being sure when they would have to move again, Ward took the option of quicker. It took him only a few more minutes before he was finished taping over the glue to add strength to the area.

"That should hold, but it won't be pretty," and Jack buttoned up his shirt as Ward moved back against the wall. Ward pulled out a syringe and a small plastic packet and started to fill it.

"I don't need anything for the pain," Jack's voice was firm and he held out a hand to stop Ward.

"I'm not giving you pain meds, that wouldn't be wise right now if we have to move suddenly, but you might have run into some tiny gremlins that could make you really sick. Especially out here, and I don't plan on carrying you out," Ward had always made it his business to know the medical backgrounds of anyone he worked with. He knew that Jack was not allergic to the antibiotic he was loading in the syringe now. Jack relaxed again and let his hand drop. "So, fill me in."

"Short version," Jack ignored the prick of the needle, "I think someone on the inside is working with the group we were watching. That's why I called you in, I needed someone I could trust and depend on."

"Gathered that," he quickly jabbed the needle into Jack's arm. "Have any clues to who it is and what they are doing?" Ward had come to the same conclusion from information he had read from Jack's mind.

"No. Every time I tried to get more information I have been put off or steered in another direction. The case officer located here right now I don't know if I trust. His record is clean, I've checked it a dozen times, and I saw you do the same. Something about him just seems wrong to me. If we had more time I would have had you read him properly. Right now, I wouldn't rely on him," Jack knew that the only one who really knew he had the house under some type of surveillance was Nathan Moore, the case officer. If the people in the house hadn't initiated the attack then that left only one other person.

"Did anyone follow you up the hill at anytime?" Ward knew the answer but they had to go over all the information and dissect it as best they could right now in order to plan the next steps.

"No. You?" Jack had to ask the obvious as well. If Ward had been out of the tent a couple of times then he might have been seen.

"Never saw or felt anyone. That leaves just a couple of

people on our list, and until we can contact my people again I think we will stay away from yours," Ward leaned out the opening of the cave to search for minds again. After being satisfied that there were none around, he looked back at Jack. "Know another way out of this neck of the woods and back to civilization?"

"First, is there another way out of the penthouse here than the way we came in?"

"Only the obvious," Ward grinned.

"I hope it's easier than what we just did."

"Only slightly," rock climbing had always been a passion for Ward and although Jack had been trained in it Ward could tell that it wasn't his favorite sport. "With the tape and the glue you should hold together fine," he wasn't going to let on that he wasn't really relishing the idea of the climb down. He had banged himself up pretty good and the strain was going to cause quite a bit of pain for him as well.

"It's a two day walk out of here if we can make it to the small village nearby," Jack stopped for a moment.

"If not?"

"If they are watching the village, then we are looking at around four days to get into Iquitos by foot, maybe five." Jack's mind was going over the area that he knew and had grown to love over the years. He had spent many furloughs out here with local guides getting to know the rain forest and all of its wonders. It also allowed him an intimate knowledge of just where the edges of legal and illegal society stood, "There is one more choice." Everything he had learned over the years would be put to good use during the next few days as they worked their way out of the jungle,

"Then you call it. Do we stay here tonight or try to move out?"

Chapter 3

Jan finished her Tai Chi routine and sat down on the couch facing the ocean. It had helped a bit to work through the routine. She still knew that there was something she wasn't figuring out though. Picking up the cell phone she called up to the Garcia's and asked them to get her Monster ready, the only vehicle she drove down here.

The Garcia family lived in the main house and took care of the hidden apartment that Jan and Ward lived in when they were in Mexico. Ward and Jan actually owned the house and the apartment. Ward had saved the Garcias' son years before and had given him a second chance, a new life, and the house to live in. In exchange for living in the house the Garcias maintained the property so that Ward and Jan could live in the cozy hidden apartment below the large main house undetected. It was a good arrangement and the son had turned around and was now in a relationship that would soon turn into something more permanent. Over the years they had become family; the only family Ward and Jan had now.

The Monster was another story altogether. When they had established their home in the Baja they had also purchased a vehicle to use here. It had been tweaked and modified by one of Ward's specialists. It had soon become known as the Monster. The old Jeep Cherokee was once white, but it had had a long hard life and was covered with dings and peeling paint. There was a three inch high checkerboard pattern that ringed the entire vehicle, and the top of it was painted black. When Jan and Ward had seen it, they bought it right away. It had more potential than problems, and just down the way there was a man who could solve the Monster's problems as well as make the few special changes needed just for them. The name had come with the upgrades to the vehicle. It had soon become Jan's favorite vehicle to drive, and the only one she drove in the Baja.

Senor Garcia assured her it would be ready to go in about fifteen minutes. Jan ended the call and placed the phone in her purse beside her gun. The purse was black leather and backpack style. It contained a quick change of clothes and a small, but adequate make-up kit for anything she might need. Jan ran a brush through her brown hair and pulled it into a ponytail. She slipped into a pair of jean shorts and a white tee-shirt. She slipped on a good pair of running shoes and was ready to go. Walking out the door and closing it carefully behind her, she walked up the outside stairs that kept their apartment hidden from view. The stairs opened onto a small patio area that was covered with climbing plants and fragrant bushes. Each time she walked through here she was amazed they never spent more time on this beautiful patio, but she knew that their true love had been, and always would be the beach, the air, and the ocean.

Jan went through the door that hid their own private world and out to the dirt area where some of the cars had been parked for years. They were over grown with the local grasses and weeds, rusted and falling apart. Walking toward the main house she saw that, as promised, Senor Garcia stood waiting with the keys to the Monster. Smiling she took the keys from him. He smiled back at her and said what he always said before they left to go anywhere, "Via con Dios," which meant go with God, and gave her a kiss on the cheek. Jan was sure that he said a silent prayer every time they left. She gave him back a peck on the cheek like she would have given a father before turning toward the vehicle. They never told the Garcias when they went out on missions or when they were just going on a trip, day or otherwise. It seemed one way to worry them just a bit less. Jan smiled warmly at Senor Garcia and climbed into the Monster. As she drove out of the drive she looked in the rearview mirror in time to see him walk toward the house shaking his head.

Jan rolled the window down and let the wind blow through the vehicle. It was only a thirty minute drive to the nearest town north of where they lived. The road wove along the coastline. The waves breaking along the rocky edges could easily be heard as she drove. The smell of the ocean teased her and invited her to dive into it. Glancing at her watch she planned to be back to the house in about three hours, just in time for an early afternoon swim. Now though, it was time to concentrate on the facts as well as find a little something that might encourage Ward to be home a bit sooner.

Thinking about the files she had just read she couldn't find any links to anything that would draw suspicion. Libya seemed to be the only link but that was easily explained away. He could have been following him as part of an assignment, which would have also led them to South America. So, now Jan was left with finding just what needle Ward was looking for. The only thing she was focused on now was the fact that they were still missing pieces, the pieces that put the puzzle together in a nice neat package. When she got back she would go back on to the net and collect information from sources not so reliable. Going fishing wasn't her strongest skill, but she was getting used to it since becoming a free agent herself.

She pulled into the town of Rosarito. It was a tourist town down by the beach, with a small but substantial settlement farther up on the hill. When she came shopping for anything she always came here. It was less active than the town of Tijuana. It was close and it had almost everything they would need. The cover was also much better. Because the town was usually filled with tourists they were always hidden, and never looked out of place. They could choose to become natives or just tourists out for the day. No one really took any notice of them at all.

Jan pulled up and parked on the street. Getting out she locked up the Monster and started to amble down the sidewalk watching the people around her. It was habit and it kept her skills sharp. Jan tried never to be too intrusive, but it was hard not to practice the skills she was taught especially with this many minds open around her. There was nothing unusual on the minds of the people around her except the wild times of the night before, and even these thoughts were quiet for most people. Rosarito was a nice place, and even a good spot for families, but it was also a place where college kids got away for the weekend from San Diego. Jan kept ambling down the sidewalk and passed the normal curio shops that tourists would enter. They carried the same items, blankets, hats, fake flowers, and various other sundries. Jan stopped in front of a curio store a couple blocks down from where she parked. She looked in the window and noticed the nice pieces of jewelry in the window. There were many people who were craftsmen in their own rights when it came to semiprecious metals and stones here in Mexico. In the window was a rather pretty little necklace on a simple silver chain with a brilliant red pendant that hung from the end of it. She had promised Ward something small and red. Wearing that and nothing more might just be what she was looking for.

Five minutes later she walked out of the store wearing the pendant around her neck. Later that night when he called again it was the only thing she planned on wearing. She looked up and down the street and decided that she would walk a little bit more before going home. After she passed a couple more shops she began to feel a bit uncomfortable. She looked around with her mind again keeping her eyes carefully on the shop windows; nothing seemed out of the ordinary. The couple nearest her was there on their honeymoon. She could feel the love they had for each other and for a moment it left an empty spot inside of Jan. Pushing that thought away she continued to search the minds of the other people around her. It was the normal, college students who had partied too much the night before and families that were looking around in awe of their surroundings, or for a bargain to take back to great aunt whoever back in the states. But the feeling that something was wrong wasn't going away. With each step Jan took it just got stronger. Now focused only on what was causing this feeling of distress she began to look closer at the minds around her trying to find the path that would lead to the source. It wasn't until her mind touched another mind that was cold and hard that her mind instinctively recoiled as a shiver ran up her spine. She knew this mind so well that it left her empty and cold, and even terrified as her face visibly paled. Quickly pulling in her mind and using only her eyes she blocked all of her thoughts. She was now visually searching for the owner of this mind that she knew all too intimately. She pushed away the feelings of being a hunted animal that just barely touching his mind had left in her and made herself practice a calm she didn't feel. Just about ten feet in front of her was a small coffee shop she had been to before. Slipping inside she ordered a hot mocha cappuccino. The window of the shop allowed Jan to look around unnoticed to most people on the street. She had carefully closed all aspects of her mind to try and keep him from seeing her, and she hoped and prayed that it wasn't already too late. Picking up the cup of coffee that had been prepared for her, she sat inside the darkened shop still scrutinizing the street. She knew he was there; it was now just a cat and mouse game of who was going to find who first.

The restaurant across the street was where the empty

feelings had come from, a mind she never thought she would feel again. He was evil, and had stripped her of her thoughts and memories once, leaving her to die a slow painful death only a shell of what she had been. It had been Ward's continued care that had brought back the memories and the person that he had so nearly destroyed. She had hoped that he would never again touch her thoughts, her mind, or her being. Jan knew that it was his mind, but was not sure if he had had time to see hers. A small tremor passed through her hands as she thought about what was to come. Tracking a mind reader was going to be so very different to everything she had ever learned. Whatever happened, she needed to keep him from feeling her mind, and that would be nearly impossible.

Waiting she sipped away at the coffee until she saw what she had feared most. A tall man, well built and well dressed walked out of the restaurant across the street. A couple of women glanced in his direction acknowledging his good looks. His calm manor hid the power of his mind and his body, but even with the nonchalant air to his walk, men naturally moved out of his way. The sunglasses didn't hide his identity from Jan. She knew that it was Bobby leaving that restaurant. Bobby was the only other mind reader to ever orchestrate his own demise to leave the department for his own selfish reasons.

Bobby and Ward had been partners, friends, and even as close as brothers at one time. Something had happened on the last mission that they had been assigned to and served together on. Whether they had been set up or what had really happened, Ward had never told her. What little she did know was that they had been captured, tortured, and later experimented on. To escape the brutal torture Bobby had caved and allowed himself to become one of them. Ward hadn't ever broken, and Jan wasn't sure why. Bobby later framed Ward, feigned his own death nearly killing Ward as well to escape the department. In the end he left Ward holding the bag so to say.

Suddenly another man caught Jan's attention as he left the restaurant and walked in the opposite direction. By the way he was dressed, in slacks and a crisp white shirt, and the secondary glance toward Bobby, Jan knew that they had just met. Taking the small, but powerful, digital camera out of her bag she quickly snapped a picture of each man. One picture was to try to identify the person Bobby had been with, the other to prove that Bobby was still alive if anyone would listen. She watched them slowly walk away from each other. Bobby sold his services to the highest bidder not letting the morality of it spoil the bounty for him. Somehow his moral fiber had ultimately rotted, but she didn't have time to debate that. There was a choice to make, either she followed Bobby or she followed the other man. If she read the stranger's mind it would be easier to decide, but if she read his mind she could risk being discovered by Bobby. The risk was decidedly worth it. A quick look into the man's mind let her know that he was headed back over the border, and that would leave her with very little to go on if she did, or could follow him across. He wasn't purchasing a service from Bobby; he had just received money from him in exchange for something he had brought with him. The man Bobby had met had a huge feeling of relief for the moment since the meeting was finished, but he would have to see Bobby again.

Jan didn't have time to get the other man's name. The choice was clear. She had to follow Bobby to see where he went, but she would have to use the trailing techniques she had learned long ago in her many years of training as an operative and not a mind reader keeping her mind closed if she hoped to have any luck. If he caught her, he would and could overpower her mind and that might be the end of things in more ways than one.

Bobby straightened out his black leather jacket as he walked away from the restaurant. Inside the jacket was a small pocket just large enough to hold a CD, a floppy disk, or a jump drive. The meeting had gone well. He now had the information and the contact had his money. But his people wanted more. At first, his contact had been reluctant to give him what he wanted, but with a little pressure, mentally, physically, and morally, he had quickly changed his mind. Wives and families were always a liability, that's why he would never have either. It was only one reason why. Bobby paid little attention to anyone on the street; his mind was reading all their thoughts at a rapid rate. He smiled sickly as he dismissed all their problems, joys, and loves as petty and beneath him, and then he caught it. It was just a second, no more, but enough. He knew by no stretch of the imagination that another mind reader was present. His mind had encountered a darkness, or emptiness that could only be explained by someone who was blocking, deflecting his searching. Bobby never changed his pace, or his demeanor, but he now slowly and methodically started to search them out. If it was someone with the department he could easily dismiss them and be rid of the threat. The contact had not brought them with him so either he was being tailed or, and then the thought began to please Bobby, it was some one else, someone he had hoped to meet up with down here. As he probed each mind deeper he discovered it was also a mind he knew intimately. He started to check the cars on the street. He was looking for only one, a white Explorer. It was a couple of months ago, when he had made his first exchange of information that he had felt the pull of mind readers as he had crossed back over the border. He had known that Ward never would have been far away from Jan's assigned office, and that later she would have settled with him wherever he had been. This spot would make perfect sense. The only vehicle of Ward's that he knew of was a white Explorer. As far as he could tell, no Explorer was parked on the street, white or any other color.

Since he could see no vehicle that matched, he began to look at the people on the street. He thought back to the feeling that he had both times, now and back when he crossed the border. 'Yes,' he thought, 'there was something familiar in that mind he had sensed, something all too familiar.' He moved slightly to the left freeing up his right hand a bit more in the crowd of tourists. Ward wouldn't use a gun in such a crowded area, but he found nothing that would keep him from it if challenged. Finding that it might now be more of a battle between them he began to delight in the challenge. Indiscriminately he used others minds to look through their eyes to watch for a tail. If someone, anyone, was following him, they would have to use all they knew to avoid being detected while keeping their mind blocked, a very tiring process. He didn't know which he would like better; killing him right here on the street, or playing a few mind games with him first. Bobby's ego hadn't counted on the fact that it might not be Ward at all.

Jan had taken off down the street, careful to stay out of full view of Bobby, or any other mind he might be using. She could feel his cold and hard mind working away, and would drop back a little each time he got a little too close to her. It didn't surprise Jan that he was being careful. One couldn't be too careful when working on the other side of the law. She only needed to keep her mind tightly shut even if he could detect a reader near he wouldn't know who it was right away. If he saw into her mind, he could immediately pick her out, and keep track of her with it. Jan had seen some of the research on what he was able to do and it was scary. Ward had picked up on some of these skills and even Jan had been able to apply some, but neither one wanted to acquire the same type of power Bobby had. To them, it was more important to be able to defend against it.

With nothing more than a pair of sunglasses on her face, and a jacket tied around her waist she followed. Her backpack hung easily on her back. Nonchalantly she checked to make sure that her gun was easily accessible. Although it would not be her first choice to use it, it could be her only choice as she saw Bobby clearly move to the left to free up his gun hand. With her other hand she checked her knife. If he was on to her she would never discover if and where he was staying in town. Walking past many small curio shops and people trying to sell everything from gum to hair braiding she kept him in sight as he moved down the other side of the street. Jan chanced crossing the street only when the people started to thin and cover was hard to keep. Once on the other side she was only able to keep part of him in view as they walked past the noisy college bars and all the students hanging out in and around them. If he continued like this she would soon have to drop the tail. There were only a few more places in which he could go or be staying. If he got in a car, she would be lost. Her vehicle was not anywhere near, and she hadn't thought she would need a homing device on this outing so she didn't have one with her in her bag. There was one of course in the Monster, but the Monster was not here. Hugging the shadows she saw him turn toward the Rosarito Beach Hotel. She moved through the small cafe that sat on the opposite corner of the driveway into the hotel.

"Lo ciento scnor," was all she said as she moved through the cafe into the kitchen and out the backdoor. Jan was just in time to see him enter the hotel, and she smiled. Moving quickly she went toward the parking area and up to the top of the small ramp. The breeze from the ocean hit her face and the stress seemed to ease for a moment. Jan sat there for another thirty minutes just watching. He didn't go to the beach and he didn't come out the front. Whatever he was up to wasn't good. Bobby had been too careful, and too watchful, he could just be waiting the tail out. She sat contemplating her next move. Criminal activities and Bobby weren't anything new, but it was her job to discover what was going on and stop it. That unsettling feeling was back. It seeped down deep inside her and she knew that whatever was going on, ignoring Bobby would not make the problem go away. Jan knew that they were already involved; she could feel it in her bones. She half laughed at the thought. On some level or other, their lives had been tangled together with Bobby's since the beginning, and there was nothing she could do about it. He was in the hotel somewhere, and as she sat there she decided she was going to find out where and why.

Chapter 4

They had been walking continuously for the last six hours, and the sun was just beginning to set. For the last hour and a half the canopy of the rain forest, or jungle, had sufficiently blocked out the light making progress much slower. Ward had felt no one around for the last four of the six hours and that had allowed them to move without as many restrictions. This far into the jungle they now didn't have to worry about leaving a trail. Jack moved forward and he pushed the leaves aside to make a small path to travel along. They were staying within sight of the river and using it as a way to navigate. Jack stopped for a moment, sighed, and then he turned toward Ward.

"We need to find shelter before night is completely on us. We only have about thirty minutes of working light left and we won't be able to see what's after us once darkness hits," Ward gave him a quick nod of acceptance and Jack moved toward the river again hoping to find a small area in which to make camp. He was sore and stiff from their white water river trip earlier and ctopping not only sounded like a good idea, it had been what his body had been crying out for, for over the last hour. Jack had noticed that Ward's progress had slowed the later in the day it got. Although he had seen no external injuries on him, Ward must have also hit those rocks with some force, and he was likely bruised up pretty badly himself. He wondered if he should ask about it.

"If you set up camp, I'll take a look for something to eat," Ward turned and said. He hadn't expected Jack to say anything in answer. He also expected Jack not to comment on his physical condition. Jack could read him well enough to know that he was hurting. After all, Jack was naturally empathic, but it had turned out that the PED just hadn't been for him. His skills weren't strong enough. Both had had survival training so there would be no argument or rest yet. One of them needed to make a safe shelter for the night and someone needed to find food. Ward knew Jack wasn't in any condition to go hunting.

"There are emergency rations in the bag," Jack half smiled as he said this.

"Only supposed to be used in an emergency and I don't think we're there yet," Ward had never liked rations, but if they couldn't find food it would have to do. He was also well aware that it may take a little longer to get to a town as both of their injuries had started to slow them down. Ward was pretty sure by now that he had at least one cracked rib, and many other muscle pulls and strains. By morning they would be both stiff and sore and the going slower to begin with. He was amazed that Jack's wound hadn't reopened. It would be better to save the rations for a time when they were truly necessary; a time when they might be too tired to hunt for food.

"Plenty of snakes out here," Jack was now just baiting him.

"Bet they taste like chicken," and they both chuckled a bit. Ward had fixed rattlesnake once. It didn't taste like chicken, but it didn't taste all that bad either. If he could find snake it would provide good protein, what they needed.

"Just make sure you get them before they get you," and this time Jack was serious.

"You don't have to tell me twice," and they walked the rest of the way to the water in silence.

Jack busied himself making a small yet comfortable lean-to out of the surrounding leaves and branches. With the opening facing the rocky banks of the river he was fairly sure that it would be safe. He went about trying to find some dry branches and twigs. He came up with a precious few and with that he prepared an area in which they would try to build a fire when Ward returned. He had also found some healing plants and collected them. He didn't have any clue how long Ward's medicines would last and the knowledge he had of the jungle could provide what they needed in staving off infections and such until they got back to civilization.

Ward had moved carefully out from the site to look for food. The animals around here were not overly used to seeing people so their instincts were not always to run. He meticulously looked at every branch, every piece of ground and under and around the rocks. The knife he kept in his boot was now in his hand, ready to secure something eatable. He moved away from the camp in concentric circles, or semicircles really, looking for dinner. An odd thought crossed his mind that there were other animals out here looking for dinner as well, and he smiled. He could feel his right leg beginning to stiffen from the beating it had gotten and his ribs were tender as he breathed. By morning he would need a good amount of stretching just to be able to walk again. Jack was going to be in worse shape.

The brush was dense enough that it made it hard to see anything as the night started to settle in, fast. Ward looked at the impending darkness and realized that all too soon he would need to go back to camp and eat what ever was in the packs.

The noises of the forest began to increase and Ward slowly moved back toward the camp being careful where he stepped. With his right foot solidly planted on the ground he placed his left foot on a tree stump about two feet above the ground to get past a particularly muddy area. He was all but ready to step up when he felt, more than he saw, a movement around his right leg. Ward froze in place. The forest was full of snakes, venomous and constricting, depending on which it was he may have time, or be out of it. Slowly the snake began to wind itself around his leg. From the feel of it, the snake was at least three inches in diameter. He could feel it moving up his leg and as it moved, tightening its grip on him. Ward leaned back now sure that he was dealing with a constrictor, and readied his knife. He was also suddenly glad that he hadn't had both feet together. Taking aim, he had to be sure of the strike, or his hand might be caught in the snake's grip. If he dropped the knife it was sure to mean death for him. Focusing on the task at hand he prepared for, and then struck out at the snake. The first strike sliced the snake in two and gouged his boot as he let the thick leather on his boot took the force of his strike so as not to do the job halfway. As the snake began to involuntarily wriggle in the last moments of life, Ward sliced at him again releasing him from his leg and his death grip on Ward.

Jack looked up through the small opening in the canopy above the river and saw the first stars come out. Ward should have been back at camp. He had no illusions that he couldn't take care of himself, and he could surely use his mind as a guide back to camp in the dark if he needed, but the jungle was a living breathing being and they were only a small part of its existence right now.

On the first trip out to the rain forest jungle seven years ago, Jack had learned just how the jungle could swallow up the very heart and sole of those that chose to enter into it. He was on leave for a month from the CIA with his wife. They had only been married for a few months. Unknowingly his face hardened and he began to grimace as the bad memories began to surface voluntarily. It had been the last time they had shared together. The jungle had claimed his prize as its own. Now the only time he truly felt near her was when he was immersed in the jungle as he was now. Every time he had leave he spent it in this jungle, and had learned it like it was his own backyard with the help of some of the native peoples here. It was the only way he felt close to her now. He had also chosen to bury his mother here when she died. Jack hadn't followed all the traditions of his Native American background, partially because his mother hadn't followed them all either, but he had buried his two loved ones in the same place so that they could be together, so that he could be with them.

Slowly he made his way to the water and filled what containers he had with the fresh, fast flowing water. As long as the water was rushing over the rocks and moving at a swift speed, it was safe to drink; it was the jungle that was both dangerous as well as life saving. He had learned of many of the cures that lay here in the jungle. He had also learned more about himself over the years. He was less angry now, but still not healed.

Ward could feel Jack's thoughts as he approached the camp, but knew they were extremely personal and stayed away from reading them. It was a politeness, ethical concern really, that he had learned when first in the program. It was also the fact that he knew Jack trusted him to not intrude. He carried supper with him. He couldn't be sure of the kind of snake because it was too dark, but he was sure it was eatable, all snakes were. He sat on a rock near the pile of sticks and bark that was soon to be a campfire, and prepared the meat from the snake. Jack turned around to bring back the supply of fresh water he had collected and saw that he had company. He limped back toward the pile of kindling and took a seat on the opposite side. Taking a sip from the one container, he offered the other to Ward.

"Found something tasty," it was a statement from Jack as Ward held up the remnants of the snake he had caught.

"Once cooked, should taste better than what we were carrying, and has plenty of protein," Ward looked at the pile and knew that it would only burn for an hour if they were lucky.

"Got a lighter?" Jack looked toward Ward, "Lost the lot on the rocks."

"Here," Ward pulled out what was left of the cell phone and the battery. Pulling some of the wires loose he crossed the circuits and got a spark.   This he used to light the pile of sticks and dry moss.

"Good work," Jack's thought drifted off again and his gaze slowly took him to another time and place as he gently coaxed the fire to live. Neither said anything more as they watched the meat cook over the fire. They ate their fill and were picking at the leftovers before Jack said anything more.

"Sometimes I think that I should have never. . ."

"Don't."   Ward had known the directions of his thoughts without even reading them and stopped him. He knew that Jack had wished more than once that it had been him seven years ago, but even though both knew that the past could never be changed, at times like this it was hard for him not to live in it for a moment. It was that moment that could be dangerous though. Death sometimes was like a siren that called out to you in your despair enticing you to join it.

"In your department you were never allowed the freedom of finding someone that you loved more than life itself; wanting and needing to be with them more than eating and breathing. How could you know what it's like to. . ." and Jack stopped and stared into the blackness.

"Times have changed for me bro," Ward didn't want to get into details about the times he had almost lost Jan. He hadn't told his friend, his brother really, about Jan. There were many reasons why but the biggest was the fact that he had been there and watched how the death of Jack's wife had changed him, sucking the life from his soul. Ward was the reader that had kept them together until the last moments, and he knew with a certainty as one who had lived through it knew, that Jack still grieved over the loss of his wife.

"I take it there is someone waiting for you now," Jack kicked at the edges of the fire. He knew that Ward had left the PED, for what reasons he wasn't sure. He only knew that Ward was a wanted felon now and that couldn't be correct. Knowing Ward for as long as he had; going through what they had gone through together, there wasn't any way that Ward had betrayed his country or his job.

"We'd been secretly seeing each other before I left the department.   Got even more serious after I left," he didn't say anything more as he poked at the kindling. He didn't have to. Ward looked back at Jack and could tell that his mood had again begun to shift. Jack was both happy for him and sad, but most of all he was sheltering his thoughts from Ward.

The fire was slowly dying out and soon they would be sitting in the dark of the night. They sat and watched the last embers fade. They didn't talk, didn't share thoughts. Minutes after the last embers of the fire were gone they both moved back to the lean-to area and without speaking Ward took the first watch as Jack lay back quickly falling asleep.

Jack now had been on watch for the last three hours and he watched as dawn started painting the sky over the river rich colors of red and pink. The colors drifted through the leaves of the trees and cascaded to the ground putting his mind at ease. The most dangerous time in the jungle had ended. He moved to the edge of the water, sat down and started to chant in a low rhythmic way, a routine he had learned from his mother, and his mother had learned from her father. He never started the day without performing this Native American prayer ritual. His ancestors, and theirs before him had performed this ritual for centuries and it gave him comfort. He had been taught from a young age to say the ancient prayer to welcome the day asking for strength, protection, and guidance from his ancestors' spirits and those that had left this life for the next. Ward awoke with the soft chanting floating past his ears. They had become blood-brothers and in the past it had been a ritual they had shared together on many occasions. Ward could easily recall the words that now transported Jack back into the heart and soul of his people. Ward chose to be an onlooker this time, since Jack had begun without him, and he sat up slipping into his cycle of meditation as well.

As he settled into his own pattern he realized how long it had been since they had worked together. It was a friendship, a connection he had enjoyed and now realized that he had greatly missed. Jack had truly been the type of agent that understood the stress and the demands of Ward's skills, which had made him easy to work with.

Half an hour later, fighting against all the pain and without a word Jack and Ward packed up camp and began to move out early. They had taken apart the lean-to, and let the leaves drift down the river to help remove evidence of their presence. The ashes and the remains of last night's supper were dealt with in the same manor. When they left the area, it was hard to tell that they had even spent five minutes there to rest; no one would have suspected that they had spent the night. The river would take back the parts of the forest and distribute it in various places so that what they had used would be recycled and given back to feed the forest.

"So, how many more days until we reach the village?" Ward had walked behind Jack all the way. Their progress had definitely been slower, but neither one had mentioned it; they just pushed on. This had given Ward time to watch the trees and bushes not only for predators, but also for something that they could use as their next meal.

"I'm not heading for that village anymore. There's a local research station two, maybe three days from here. They have the ability to contact the outside world and a helicopter transport they can call in," Jack kept moving as he talked knowing that their progress was slow.

"Wait," Ward said as Jack let it go of the branch he was holding and it swung back nearly slapping Ward, "Someone gave you away back there, wanted you dead. When we get to the station we will contact my people first and see what the damage is so far."

"Fair enough," Jack's thoughts moved onto another subject. A more dangerous one for Ward, "Who is she?" The mud made a sucking sound as the two moved steadily forward.

"You don't know her," Ward moved with the same rhythm as Jack, his tone flat.

"Not part of the department huh," it was just a statement.

"Not any more," and after Ward said that Jack let out a low whistle. "Left almost a couple years after I did."

"So she knows the ropes then," and when Ward didn't say anything more he continued, "She a mind reader?" Jack wiped the sweat off his forehead.

"Nosy aren't we today," he sighed, "Yah," and Ward watched as Jack missed a step. Before he could tumble to the ground, Ward had caught his arm, "Time to rest for a bit. If we take a day or two more it won't matter," Ward saw him tense at that thought, his face tightening with anger at the idea that his injuries would cause them to slow down, "You're just too heavy to carry man," he paused, "I could also use the rest." Ward had noticed the swelling on his own thigh and although nothing was broken, the small and large tears to his muscle tissues were finally making themselves heard.

"Okay," and Jack sat down on the nearest curved branch of a tree. He knew that the wound hadn't reopened but it was hellishly sore. Ward hadn't asked to look at it again, he expected Jack to tell him if it needed treatment. "When we get to the research base we should be able to take a better look at the information on that hard drive and start to figure out what went wrong."

"I already have someone working on that," Ward spoke as he set his pack on the moist ground and gingerly sat down. Jack looked at him in amusement.

"I thought the phone was DOA," there was a small hint of skepticism in his eyes and his thoughts. Ward noticed that Jack was beginning to have a tougher time keeping his thoughts blocked. Being tired and injured often did that.

"I've been in contact with her since I got here. The other day I asked her to look up some names for me before you brought in the computer. I had been getting a strange feeling from you and there was nothing happening in the house we were watching," Ward stopped and looked at Jack. The expression on his face told Ward to continue, "We've worked together too many times for me not to be able to read your body language, as well as get around some of those blocks you put up. I could tell you were worried about something, and it wasn't the mission you had me working on."

"Leaks are not something you want to talk about in this business," Jack turned and looked deep into the forest as he leaned back against the tree, "I first suspected it when my partner was relatively a rookie to the area we are in. Not that it hadn't happened before, but he just doesn't seem to fit in around here. His assignments have been mostly in Europe and the Middle East," Jack paused to catch his breath, "Then there was the vagueness of this assignment. Things weren't adding up, and that feeling you get in the pit of your stomach that tells you something isn't right just kept growing."

"So you called me in. They would have no idea you were working with someone else and I would bend a few of the unbendable rules. Your ace in the hole," Ward smiled and Jack returned it.

"More like the only one I would trust right now to cover my back," Jack shook his head, "She won't start looking for us for days though."

"No," Ward said it with such self-assurance that Jack couldn't contain the surprise in his eyes, "I didn't call in last night. She will start checking the systems and she knows the names to connect with it all. By the time we get to the station we should have something tangible to work with."

"Like I said, the only one I would trust to cover my back," and with that Jack stood up and started on the long trek again.

Jan awoke to silence. There was hardly any sound from the ocean that lapped below, but the most disturbing part of the silence was there had been no call from Ward. It seemed silly, until now, that he had called nightly. It was still hard for her to get used to the changes their relationship was going through. Jan had become accustomed to the calls, and even enjoyed the stronger ties that were growing between them. She could almost call it normal. It would take time to rebuild what the department had taken so long to destroy, a sense of family, love and relationship. With Ward she had begun the journey, not willingly to begin with, but now the need to mend what was broken only strengthened what they had. It wasn't that the phone hadn't been on, or placed beside her on his pillow, and it wasn't as if they had never missed call times before, but that had been when she was still with the PED. That and the unsettling feeling that had steadily grown inside her since she saw Bobby yesterday set off alarms. Without wasting another moment Jan got up and went to the computer to search the reports that may have just been entered into the main computer at the agency in Peru. If something had happened it would be the first place to find something that would give her information.

Morning in Rosarito had brought its own problems though. Jan hadn't found anything on the computers that would signal a problem for Ward or Jack, but that lump in the pit of her stomach had grown to the size of a basketball. Turning off the computer she knew it was still too early for most people to be out and about. If she couldn't discover anything on the computer about them then there was another problem she needed to deal with. She would check the computer again later. If nothing showed up then, she would take the next step.

This time when she left the apartment she got the Monster out herself and was down the road before they had even started the day. Half an hour later she pulled into the small town of Rosarito and parked near the hotel. She checked her purse for her gun and tucked the knife she kept into the sheath strapped to the belt on her waist. Its looks were deceiving. The knife handle was six inches long, and once the blade was released it was also nearly six inches long. The best part of all the items she carried, except the gun, was that none were standard issue. Bobby would not know what he would find on her if she was caught. Not wanting to stay too close to Bobby she planned to put a locator on his car or somewhere in his luggage if she had a chance.

Walking into the lobby of the hotel, no one could have known that she was anything more than a tourist. With her hair French braided and in a pair of jeans and a white T-shirt over a bikini top with the ties hanging out the neckline of the shirt, she bounced into the hotel. She ambled over to the desk and waited to be served. Leaning casually on the counter she let her mind search the immediate area. If Bobby's energy was near she wanted to be able to retreat fast enough so he couldn't get a read on her. She relaxed only when she knew he wasn't anywhere near, and she allowed herself a bit more leeway in her reading. She had a few names that she was going to try on the clerk, but she would need to hit a name quickly or be under suspicion. She smiled at the clerk as he finished giving directions to the newlyweds, and then she climbed right into his thoughts.

She was looking for Bobby's face in all his thoughts, and was coming up with nothing. It was like he didn't exist, and then it dawned on her. Bobby was able to manipulate people's minds almost as easily as his own. If he chose for the clerk not to remember him then he would have no option in the matter.

"May I help you?" The clerk moved toward her. He was about her height and about twenty pounds over weight.

"Yes, thank you. I came down here to surprise my husband," she smiled coyly. "You see the conference ended early. Could you tell me which room he's in?" It was now time to pick a name, "R. Malone," and she hoped Bobby had seen no reason to hide his identity.

"I'm sorry ma'am there is no R. Malone registered here. Are you sure he is staying with us?" The clerk's mannerisms were very apologetic. Jan could see it in his face. She figured she had one more chance to give a name before she had to leave. She chose carefully.

"Oh, silly me, he told me he was going to check in under his pen name, it should be under B. Main," it was one he liked to use best, simple, not far off of his own name and easy to remember. The clerk typed the name into the computer and followed it with a smile. He had gotten a hit, and she was on her way.

"Ma'am his room number is 236. Those are the suites located down that hallway and out to the left," and he gave her a huge smile thinking that he was part of romantic liaison of some kind.

"Thank you so much," she turned on her sweetest smile and leaned onto the counter further as she whispered the next words, "Please don't tell him I'm here. I want it to be a surprise."

"Senora, I will not tell him. Enjoy your visit," and he moved on to the next customer. If it was only what he thought Jan mused. Jan turned and the smile faded. Her face became serious and her thoughts focused. She walked down the hallway in which she would get out to the rooms. As she got closer to the room she expected to feel his cold presence, but there was a strange emptiness that plagued her thoughts.

Jan slid the lock pick out of her purse and moved toward his door. The room was located below the pool area and within site of the beach. The large picture window would have looked out at the pier and the ocean. It was a nice place for a room except that all the outdoor parties were held only a matter of yards away and the noise could be deafening. But during the weekdays it would be a fairly quiet place to be. She could still not feel his presence, but she was also keeping her thoughts closely guarded. Not being able to open her mind could be keeping her from reading him, but that's not what had happened yesterday. Jan knew that she didn't need to read his thoughts to feel his presence, and right now she began to get just a little worried. She had spent all of yesterday watching the hotel, and he had never left. He had gone down to the beach late in the day and then returned later. It was eleven o'clock at night when Jan had finally called it a day thinking he would be in for the rest of the night. If he had already left then she wouldn't have much to go on.

As she approached the door she listened for any sound. Although it was eight in the morning, he may still be in the room. Hearing nothing she knocked and moved away from the door keeping the curtains in sight at all times. Nothing happened. Jan went back to the door and within seconds had it open and was quietly inside. Glancing quickly at the time she began to search the room.

There were only a few items dotted around the room. Across the bed lay a pair of pants and a couple pieces of paper. Jan looked at the papers and noticed that they were room service receipts dated for yesterday and today. Nothing special. She put the papers down and wasted no more time. She moved to the desk and noticed that not much was lying around. Opening drawers she let her fingers search every part of the draw quickly, including the top. In the second drawer she found what she thought she finally wanted. She undid the tape that held it to the inside of the drawer and pulled it out. It was a small jump drive. Jan pulled out the small Palm Pilot she had brought with her and hooked the jump drive into it. Downloading the information stored on it would help her discover what Bobby was up to. After the download finished she watched something totally unexpected happen. A program began to run and Jan just watched it.

A string of numbers and formulas flew past her eyes and then it all stopped and went dark. A simple animation began to play. It was a drawing of a bird catching a fish. Next came a pixilated shot from below and they both fell to earth. It was what had followed next that cemented the message he had obviously left for her. The scene went black and then all that the screen read was, "I'm watching you."

Chapter 5

Jan sat cross legged on the beach watching the sun go down. She had been there all day, watching for him to return to the room. She had moved throughout the day so that she wouldn't burn, wouldn't be noticed, and she wouldn't be an easy target. So far she had been propositioned by three college students, approached by six men selling jewelry, one from which she bought a small silver bangle.

By now she knew that Bobby had to have felt another mind reader nearby yesterday, and had somehow identified her. About the middle of the afternoon she had come to a realization that Bobby knew both of their minds too well. He also knew hers almost as well as Ward did. He had tried his new skills on the both of them, so there was nowhere to hide for either of them. Jan decided that it really didn't matter if Bobby knew whether it was her or Ward. The only realization was important was that he was on to them, and he had already left that message loud and clear.

Bobby had been nowhere to be found this morning, and Jan was not even sure that he was still in town. The items she had found were not really personal possessions, and may have been left as a decoy for her. The download into the Palm Pilot had destroyed the system after the message, and created a Palm paperweight. Jan figured it had been done to really drive the message home. If they kept after him then they would end up like the Palm Pilot, completely dead. Jan had left the room through the back window in case he was watching the front. She had gone down to the beach and waited, waited for that feeling to come back. It never had, and neither had Bobby so far. Jan was no closer to discovering what he was up to than before, but that wouldn't stop her. He was too close for comfort.

It had been an hour since she had used the phone to connect with the internet and she was thankful that she had brought it. It was time again to check up on CIA reports being filed at the end of the working day to see what was happening. As the sun went down Jan dialed the computer and connected aware that these two instances may or may not be related. While the machines talked Jan noticed that the sun painted the sky various shades of red and orange, which set the ocean on fire. Jan paid very little attention to any of that. The sound of the phone was turned off, but would have been overshadowed by the music of the ocean and dancing on the beach that was coming from the party places and bars. There were still some families out on the beach catching the last rays, building sand castles and flying kites. Not sure of what she was looking for and not sure of what she would find, Jan called up the reports on the mission in Peru and what she read didn't agree with what she knew. She read it one more time and then read the related reports that went with it.

The rest of the world melted away as the information she had been reading coalesced in her mind. She stood up and walked up the beach toward the hotel. Something was wrong and now it was her turn to step in. Whatever Bobby was doing would have to take a back seat to what Ward needed right now. Walking up the steps of the hotel and toward the pool, she felt a shiver go up her spine. Jan had kept her thoughts protected and she moved swiftly to the other side of the pool. Now was not the time she had wanted him to magically reappear. There were a bunch of college guys hanging around the spa with a group of girls. She moved to the back of the group and grabbed the nearest seat. The cold, inescapable feeling was getting closer and she knew that mind's signature; it was Bobby, and he had never left town. What was worse was he was getting closer, much closer to the person tracking him. Dropping her pack between her feet she unzipped the bag, getting ready for the worst, hoping for the best.

Jan felt him walk out of the hotel lobby and into the pool area. She kept her mind tightly under control, but she could feel his eyes scan the area. He had recognized her presence almost as easily as she had his. Worse yet, she felt his mind probing those around her, looking for her. Being near the group of college kids she tried to hide her mind in with theirs, mingling their thoughts into hers. Bobby's mind swept the area and stopped for a moment at the group by the spa. He didn't move for a moment, then only when he was satisfied did his mind and body move on. Without a reading of his thoughts Jan could not be positive that she had not been seen. Not wanting to risk what protection she might have had she relied solely on instinct, training, and a healthy amount of fear. She could be fairly certain that he would not have left her alone if his mind had found hers. He continued to walk toward his room. Jan had been careful to put back everything the way she had found it. It may give her a few days, or minutes before he knew someone had been in his room. The icy chill that had just filled the pool area moved off to the side and slowly faded away. Jan had followed many people in her time, but tracking a mind reader was taking all her skills to a new level. Sooner or later she would have to go face to face with him; she could just feel it, but now was not the time. Right now she had other things she needed to deal with, and she left the pool area and hotel as quickly as possible. If he was there to find them, she would deal with that later also. It wasn't a good thought. If he was here on other business then they may never get involved. She was almost out of the lobby when the hotel clerk she had talked to this morning called out to her from across the lobby.

“Senora! Senora, I sent down extra towels and pillows for you. I hope your surprise went well,” he was smiling, and genuinely trying to be helpful. Jan's pulse quickened by a couple of beats and her temper flared momentarily. Her face never let her emotions show though as she turned to look at the smiling gentleman. How could she be mad at someone who was only trying to be sweet?

“It was more of a surprise than you know. Just popping out to get something to eat,” and she smiled and left through the front door. Bobby was sure to know who to look for, and know that she had been to his room. She had taken no time to put a locator on anything when she left. He would be looking for that. Now it looked like she wouldn't need to, he would be looking for her. She walked over to the Monster and looked it over carefully before climbing in. Nothing had been touched. Every indicator had been left as she had left it. Climbing inside she started it and then made a snap decision. Instead of going straight back to the apartment, she decided she would make sure no one was following her. Bobby could easily have men working for him down here and she wouldn't find out until too late if she weren't careful. He could be completing his business down here as a sideline to finding them. Wouldn't that just suck. Checking her review mirrors she drove through town and at the last light she slipped on the five point harness taking off the seat belt and using that to secure her bag beside her. Up until now anyone in town could have been watching her from the street, a car, a window, or different stores. She intended to make sure if anyone were in a vehicle and trying to follow, that vehicle would have to rival the Monster itself.

The Monster had an engine that was new, and powerful. The body had been completely redone with compartments and camping equipment as well. If she was being followed she could get them lost out in the desert and then camp the night before she made her way back home. There were enough supplies hidden in this SUV to keep her out in the wilderness for at least a week. They had made sure that the vehicle could do anything it was asked to do, and the four wheel drive and lower center of gravity made it possible for the vehicle to go just about anywhere. Heading for the natives' part of town, she drove through the areas that had more dirt, grime and crime than should be in any town. Only once had she thought she saw a tail, but she still wasn't taking any chances. She pulled onto the dirt road headed south and through the desert and mountains just after the town ended.

She knew the back roads of the Baja well and it wasn't long before the Monster was doing what it did best, offroading. The trip home took her an extra hour, but it was worth the time to make sure that their home was protected. No one had followed her, and she had actually enjoyed the drive. Some of the roads she had been on had been questionable. It might have been better to call them cattle paths. When she drove into the housing development she saw Senor Garcia standing and waiting for her. Just how long he had been out there she was unsure and she wasn't going to read his mind to find out. Slowly he inspected the vehicle, noticing the amount of dirt and dust that covered it. The expression on his face was one of worry. She had seen it before. Jan slipped out of the harness and got out of the Monster. She could tell him nothing that would allay his fears, except that home was safe, so she decided to say nothing more than what she needed to. Looking at him she asked him to make sure the truck was washed and hidden. He took the keys and as he got into the truck he continued to shake his head.

Jan didn't wait; she went down to the apartment and let herself in. She could smell the warm, homey smell of enchiladas cooking in the oven. Mama G had been down to take care of her. The smell did nothing to tempt her. If she had to choose between food and a mission the food came in a distant second when a mission might be going sour. Looking at her watch it was now close to ten o'clock. She downloaded the information located in the phone to the computer and read through the notes she had made earlier carefully analyzing the two. By eleven o'clock she was ready to make a call. She needed a little help. Not much, but someone to run information for her so that she could do what she did best. And she needed someone with an in to find out who was doing all the information blocking. She could think of no one better for the job but an old and dear friend.

Picking up the phone she dialed a familiar number over her secure cell. Once the connection was made the sound of ringing came over the line. The only problem was that was all she was getting. He always had his cell phone with him. The only time he wouldn't answer the phone was if there were people around that would compromise him or her. Making a quick check on the database as to where he was and what he was currently working on Jan disconnected and redialed his home phone, an unsecured number. As long as she was on the line less than fifteen seconds, they would have no way to identify her or where the call came from if his calls were being monitored. The ringing began again, except this time there was an answer. The phone hit something before it reached his ear, and Jan guessed he was probably sleeping.

"State your emergency and then hang up the damn phone," Rob had never woken up in a good mood, and Jan smiled, "On second thought, you know what you can do with that . . ."

"Call me," was all she said in a low but firm voice and then she hung up.

Rob didn't move, didn't speak. The voice was enough to shock him into a heightened state of awareness shaking him from his deep sleep. He hadn't heard that voice for quite a while now. Something in her voice, even the few words she had said, told him that this was an emergency. Rob remembered that he had put his secure cell phone down in the kitchen and left it there last night when he went to bed. Quickly he threw off the covers and was out of bed making his way quickly out to the kitchen cursing all the way.

Rob had been Jan's partner long enough to know that 'call me' was not a request; it was a command. Rob leaned his five foot ten inch frame on the counter as he dialed the phone. He had been taken off field assignments about a year ago when Jan had left the department. For some reason they thought he might be the reason for her allegiance with Ward, but he had never let his physical training slack off because he wanted back, needed back, in the game. He looked as well toned today as when he had started with the FBI many years ago. He only wore sweat pants and there was no middle age spread to be found yet. It was something he was proud of. Something sent a chill down his spine. As the phone took time to connect Rob took a moment to ponder what may have caused the chill. He wasn't sure if it was the air conditioning in his apartment, or what might be happening with Jan. The waiting was awful but he managed to connect with her cell phone quickly.

"Getting a little slow," Jan answered the phone, "Took you five extra seconds to get back to me."

"Scare me half to death will ya'. Everything okay with you? Ward?" Although he tried he couldn't hide the worry in his voice, not with Jan, they knew each other too well. She was his family, the only family he had ever had, and he would protect her like a father would a daughter if need be. He had discovered that she had married Ward shortly before she left the department. It had amazed him that she had hid it that long from him. He had never approved of Ward as someone she should be romantically involved with. He seemed more like the use them and lose them type, but supposedly he had changed. It worried him now that something had gone wrong, dreadfully wrong, with their marriage.

"We're fine. He hasn't dumped me, cheated on me or gone gay," she tried to allay his fears knowing that he thought Ward had been a risk, "but I think you may have a problem up there that you want to look into to, and yes I know you are not currently on active duty but when has that mattered to us.

"Ward is helping Jack Golightly in Peru. Reports just in say that Golightly was killed in an attack on a surveillance post he had set up. Body was badly burned and mutilated. Said it was missing fingerprints and any identifying marks of any kind. To me that alone sounds fishy knowing all the ways we can identify a body if we really wanted to. Also, according to this file the body is currently being sent back to the states. DNA identification was requested and arranged but later, the report stated, no DNA identification will be done as per orders from Langley. It sounds a little strange to me. There were no names attached to the orders. In other words, no paper trail," Jan took a breath and let the information soak in.

"Ward set up the surveillance with him right?" Rob knew that it wasn't unheard of for agents to use outside people to help out. No one talked about it, and of course the people used were only the best around, but for Jack to call in Ward Rob knew that things had been a bit more serious. There was something he didn't want to share with his superiors. Golightly had been worried about something more than just the mission he was on.

"Right. He set up the post and was manning it with Golightly. Talked with Ward the day of the incident and Golightly was on his way back, Ward told me he was almost there. No one else was with Golightly, he was that close. They had no indication that the place they were watching was involved in any manor of illegal activity. Ward gave me a list of names of the people they were watching and who was working the case with Golightly," Jan took a breath.

"One body right," there was a pause, "Are you afraid the body was Ward or Jack?" Rob had to ask the question.

"No," Jan continued on very businesslike, "If you read the report someone took a lot of time to remove all types of easy identification on the body that was found. Why would they do that if they wanted to leave a message? Plus the fact that there was only one body and I am the only one who knows that two people were there sounds way too interesting. The body is three inches too tall to be Ward, but it is the same height as Jack. Remember, there were no fingerprints, no way to take dental records, the body was burned beyond recognition, and don't you think it's strange that they don't plan on trying for DNA identification at all?" It was quiet on the other end of the phone for a while. Jan let the information sink in.

"Point taken. So what do you need me to do?" Rob had already jumped to the next step as Jan had expected him to do. He was on board and ready to help.

"First I think you need to do a little investigating on your end as to why they are letting this one drop so easily. Who's in charge, and who's pulling the strings? Once you have that, I would like to know, just as a personal favor. And as always, I'll keep you informed from my end," Jan wasn't going to let everything slip, so she waited.

"I'll do my best," Rob knew that Jan had more she wanted, "Is there something you're not telling me? Most of this information you can get from Ward's highly intelligent machines."

"This is completely off topic, hopefully. I'll be sending you a picture now, and I need you to help me identify the person in it," Jan tapped a couple of keys on the computer and the picture was off.

"Have any prints or DNA?"

"If I had that I wouldn't need your computers, I'd just use my own," she smiled as she heard his muttered response on the other side of the phone. "I've got the computer busy doing other things so I would appreciate this."

"I didn't hear that," Rob blurted out the words as if it would erase what he had just heard. Jan could picture Rob's hand on his head, his fingers being pushed through his hair. She stifled a laugh.

"I suppose you didn't, but I would appreciate you getting back to me as soon as possible," Jan's tone became serious again.

"Anything else I should know about this guy that you just happen to have a picture of?" Rob's tone was serious. There was something else bothering Jan but he was pretty sure that she wasn't ready to share yet.

"No," she kept it short. As of yet, the warning Bobby had sent her had not panned out, and it was in fact, just a warning.

"Am I calling you back or you calling me?" Rob had thought that when she left it would be the last he would ever hear from her or Ward. He had worked with Ward over the years once he had left the department, but once Jan left he thought it might all be over. He never thought a relationship, professional or otherwise, would continue, with the both of them. Boy had he been surprised. They had both chosen to continue to challenge the cause.

"I'll call you. And by the way, thanks for your help, I knew I could count on you," Jan smiled even though Rob couldn't see it.

"Anytime for you," and Rob truly meant it. He disconnected the phone at the other end.

Jan sat looking at all the information she had compiled, and as she did a plan started to form. Soon she was searching the plane schedules.

Five Years Ago

He leaned against the outside of the building, under the eves to stay out of the rain. It was the only door out of the makeshift barracks that they had used to clean up in after the training operation. The session had finished about thirty minutes ago and it was now about five in the morning. He was tired. By all rights he should have crawled into the dorm and gone straight to sleep.

Instead he was standing outside waiting to drive back into town, hopefully with company. Ward had showered and changed in record time. He had left the locker room and had been standing in the rain for fifteen minutes waiting for her. Even if the dorm rooms were just fine for him, he had already checked and knew she had arranged to go back into town. He hoped he would find a better spot to sleep today.

Glancing at his watch he saw that it was still an hour before sunrise. They were ten miles out of town and deep in the woods. He watched the drops of water drip from the edges of the roof, and wondered just how much longer he would have to wait for her to come out. His skin began to tingle, the hair rising on his arms. For some odd reason, he couldn't read her mind, but he knew she was near. Ward could sense her breathing and her heartbeat, just not her thoughts. It was an odd, yet compelling feeling, and in some ways far more personal. He turned just in time to see her walk out of the door and out from under the cover of the roof into the rain. She turned to smile at him, and stopped. Her hair was still wet from the shower, and she had brushed it back off her face into a ponytail. Her face was free of make-up. Even without the conventional trappings she looked wonderful.

"That's how I did it," and he immediately knew what she was talking about. She had listened in on their conversation in the locker room without them knowing it. It wasn't fair but he should have expected it, she was that good. How much she had seen he began to wonder about, but not for too long. Ward had intrigued her as much as she intrigued him. She had felt that invisible pull the first time she had seen him. When the training mission had been assigned she had also done her work and known he had had a hand in setting it up and including her. From that moment on the game had begun.

"Interesting," may have only been one word but it covered the array of feelings and thoughts he was having. He hadn't moved from the side of the building. Jan took a step closer, intentionally increasing the heat between them. "Be interested in discussing it some more over breakfast?" Ward didn't move, just smiled. Yes she was his match in more ways than one.

"What do you have in mind?" Jan stood in the rain and Ward watched the rain dribble down the side of her face, all the while she ignored it. Ward was having a harder time ignoring it. He wanted to reach out and wipe it off of her cheek. She must have known because all she did was smile again as she looked him in the eye waiting for an answer.

"In about a half an hour a great little place in town will open up. It will serve just about anything you have in mind. We can catch the sunrise as we go in," Ward couldn't read anything in her mind. For that matter he wasn't allowing her to read anything from his mind either. At least he thought he wasn't. The word play was getting to him though, and for some odd reason she seemed to be enjoying the banter just as much as he was.

"How's the coffee?" Jan ran her hand through her hair, pushing the pieces that were beginning to wash back into her face behind her ears.

"Better than most, worse than others," Ward stood up and took the keys from his pocket. He wanted to pull her under the eves and out of the rain. Somehow she seemed to thrive standing in it, and she looked at home in it as well.

"Then shall we go before the rest of the genetic freaks get out here and they have to come along," she smiled and started to walk to the small parking area. With that one sentence she allowed him in on a secret as to whom she had been reading in the locker room.

"By the way. . ." was all he got out before she continued talking.

"If you get lucky I just may let you pay the bill," she had driven one of the department's cars and assumed Ward had done the same. To her surprise they climbed into a small nondescript, but adequate four door sedan. Most likely a department car, but of a different class altogether. As they drove off Bobby walked out of the small building that housed the locker rooms. Neither one of them saw him. He took a few minutes to watch Ward drive away with his prize, and a curious feeling he couldn't quite identify went through him.

Present Day

Watching the water drip off the top of the lean-to had let Ward's mind wander back to the time when he had fallen in love with Jan. Those were pleasant memories for Ward as he sat at the edge of water. He mused at the fact that this was the exact moment when he had fallen head over heals in love with her. Before that he had just been infatuated. Ward stirred the cold coals from the fire they had made last night. They had eaten well again, this time Jack had found some edible plants as well as fruits and nuts to go with the fish Ward had caught. Ward had given him another shot of antibiotics, and they had stopped earlier than planned. They had not seen or heard anyone during yesterday's travel. Ward had not sensed anybody even remotely near. Both were aching from their trek through the forest. They had planned to walk another three miles, but gave up the idea to gather a good meal for the evening and make a shelter from the wild animals, most of which they had avoided. If they were going to meet up with anyone it would be when they got to the research station.

Last night he had let Jack take the first watch and then woken up in the early hours of the morning to take over. He had been watching Jack's health, and was relatively sure that he was okay, but he needed rest to help heal the wound and fight off an infection. Ward would have volunteered to check out the wound again but knew, like all of them, that to show weakness of any sort would be taboo. He also knew that if Jack really needed treatment, he would ask. The shot of antibiotic would last another day or two, and then if they hadn't gotten to civilization he would have to give him another, the last one he had, or risk the jungle taking him as well. The sun was just beginning to peek through the trees and the rain had stopped about half an hour ago. Small patches of light filtered through and made a shadowy maze through the forest leaves and branches on the floor.

In the background he could mentally feel and hear Jack start to wake and move. Soon he would want to start his morning ritual. Ward started to get up and move away from the water. Although he had participated in this prayer session with Jack before, it had been a long time and wasn't sure he should. He wanted to give Jack his space. Some men would hate the forest for the pain it had caused. He on the other hand had found his peace with it.

Before Ward had gotten very far a hand came down on his shoulder and Ward turned to see Jack. His face was set, and Ward could tell that he was in pain from the beating his body had taken over the last few days. Ward understood it as well, he had been feeling the pain from all his injuries, but had said nothing. He had taken a few doses of Ibuprofen, about eight hundred milligrams at a time, but that was all.

"Join me brother," was all he needed to say; Ward knew it

was an honor, as like the other times before, to be asked. It implied that they were family, still family. This meant more to Ward than he had imagined it would. Ward nodded and they both moved to the water's edge. The sound of the running water served as a soothing background with the sun peeking through the clouds continuing to spot the floor of the jungle. Soon they began the age old chant in a language that was all but foreign to Ward, but the words brought on a deeper understanding of life, family, and even lulled him into a meditative state. For the next twenty minutes they sat facing the east chanting the words they hoped would please the spirits.

Chapter 6

It was four in the morning when the phone rang, again. This time he had placed his cell near the bed and answered it before the first ring had ended. It had been a long time since he had needed to keep the phone this near. Heck, it seemed like it had been a long time since he was even needed. He hadn't gotten much sleep that night; he was worried about what else was going on where Jan was. Over the years she had proven to be very capable, but back then she had the backing of the PED and the other departments they worked with. Now, in essence, she didn't even have Ward; he had hidden away somewhere. At least that's what Rob hoped had happened. He had just stopped worrying and drifted off to sleep when the ringing phone jarred him back into consciousness.

"Tell me," it was a command; one Rob was used to giving, even in his sleep.

"Want to take today off and give me a hand?" she sounded as if she had had a full nights sleep and was ready to tackle anything, oven though Rob was pretty sure that she had spent most of it planning for the mission ahead. Rob had trusted her with his life on more than one occasion, and even when they had had less sleep.

"I want to know more, in fact, I want to know all of it," Rob was now sitting up in bed and waiting for the answer. Looking at the window he noticed that the sun had just started to peek through.

"Are you sure? Because once you know there is no going back," and when she didn't get an answer she continued, "I have been doing my research, but I need to do some on site, one on one. Someone down there is not telling the truth, and the whole group might be in danger, yours and mine. I'd give it to you but you would have a hard time explaining where you got the information, justifying your presence, and Ward, so I'll go. I may also be of some assistance to them both."

"Sounds logical, but you don't really think that you'll be able to find them?" After he said it he could have slapped himself. Rob had no doubt that she could find them anywhere in the world, if that was her focus.

"You know better than. . ." was all Jan got out.

"Never mind, what was I thinking. If Ward calls me, I'll do what I can, but do you really think going there and finding them would be of the greatest help. From what you can tell me, no one knows where they are or even if they are alive," that hurt to say, "They also have no idea that Ward was there."

"I also have that same feeling. They may not be able to trust anyone else, so once they come out in the clear they will need some help. They may need you here. Their cover is broken and they will need a new face to do some digging. This time in the right areas," Jan finished and waited; she knew what the next question would be.

"So, why do you need me?" Rob waited, knowing that the answer would not be one he liked, or something simple. Worse yet, it was probably one he couldn't even imagine.

"Bobby is here. He met with the man you now have the picture of. I assumed they exchanged information. About what I don't know that's why I sent it your way, but things got complicated and I couldn't follow both. I chose Bobby, as he will be the most troublesome. The worst part," Rob heard her sigh a little as if just talking about him tired her out, "Bobby knows that Ward and I are somewhere around. No details, not necessary, but things could get fairly ugly for us if I let him think we are in this area for any other reason than to follow him. You need to help me convince him that we are running scared now that he has read us. Leaving to regroup," Jan waited and waited. It seemed like hours had passed before Rob spoke again.

Rob had looked over the last few years for their little hideaway, without luck. As he now understood it, Bobby was there on other business and just happened upon her, and that was a big maybe. She had been right though, once he knew there was no turning back. Just where it was he was sure she would never completely reveal. Now all he had to decide was how much to ask; how much would she tell him.

"Got a plan?" his voice was low and quiet, tired, not believing that he was letting himself get involved. One thing he was pretty sure of was that she would have to give him a general location right now for him to be able to help.

"Yes," Jan didn't wait to hear his sigh, "I'm going to let him get closer to me today and let him trail me for a change. Then you'll meet me in Tijuana, the Mexican side of the border, on the road to go back across. By nine in the morning it should be plenty backed up and that will make it easier to set the trap.

"When you see the Explorer you'll jump in. Keep your identity hidden and I'll keep the Explorer far enough away. He can't get too close or he knows I'll be able to feel him. He'll think I picked up Ward and then we'll head for Phoenix. You'll need to find someone who can take my place, play me, for a while once we get back in town. I'll leave for the airport as soon as it's safe. Then it will just be a matter of," Rob interrupted her.

"Keeping him off balance until we all get clear," Rob was already thinking about whom he would call to help him out. He had the perfect person in mind.

"That's right. If he thinks he lost us or we lost interest, then he may just forget about looking for us again for a while. One problem though, it will have to look like we have a base in town," Jan looked at the cup of cold coffee she had long since forgotten to drink.

"Not a problem," Rob's answer was quick and short and she thought she heard some guilt.

"It can't look like we just rented it," Jan pushed the chair back and stood up, "I'm sure if I can get those records it would be a piece of pie for him."

"Still not a problem," Rob didn't explain and this time she was sure she heard guilt.

"All right partner, your turn to spill it," Jan stood looking out the windows and into the ocean.

"You still have your apartment up here," Rob held the phone away from his ear just in case.

"What in the hell were you thinking!" Jan didn't mean to yell into the phone, but she did. It took her only a split second to regain composure.

"Forgive me honey. I didn't let the lease slip. I figured if something went wrong you might want to come back. I was about to let the lease go next month if that makes you feel any better," Rob waited. He could hear the rush of breath on the other end of the phone. Jan wanted to be mad, but that wasn't what she was feeling at all right now. After the initial shock she had this overwhelming feeling of being protected, of being loved, of being part of a family.

"It'll work then," was all she could say leaving everything else she could have said, unsaid, "anything more I'll explain in the car." Jan finished by giving Rob more details on where to meet her and when. He never asked just how she would get him to follow, or how she was sure Bobby would, but he knew Jan. She didn't like to fail, and this would be just another mission for her, the stakes a little higher than normal. He just had to hope that the cat and mouse game she planned wouldn't backfire.

About two hours later the white Explorer traveled into Rosarito. It was still early in the morning. Jan parked it in a hotel lot about halfway between the hotel Bobby was at and the restaurant she had seen him at the other day. Suddenly she had a strange feeling that this was the going to be the SUV's last mission. Letting her eyes roam about it, she remembered how reliable it had always been. She didn't like the idea that the Explorer might not be coming back from this trip. Jan had taken the time that morning to empty anything out of it of importance. Before she could leave Mexico, she had to make sure that Bobby would leave as well. Jan had to make sure that the Garcias would be safe. Ward and Jan could live anywhere, but the Garcias would have no idea what to do if something as evil as Bobby showed up. They could be used as pawns, and would be, if he thought it would bring them to him, and it would. That meant putting herself into a little more danger. Not something she wasn't used to, but this cat and mouse game was one she would have no choice but to win. Getting out of the vehicle she took extra time to secure it, and mark it. If he was going to tamper with it, she wanted to know about.

It was, as always, the simple things that she needed to do. First she brushed fresh dirt under the vehicle. If any lines were cut there would be one or two drops of fluid at least, and the dirt would be disturbed. She also swiped the tires of the car with chalk to make sure the vehicle hadn't been moved. At the bottom of each door she placed a small rock between the frame and door just big enough to stay in place until the door was opened. If the door was opened and closed the rock would fall, unnoticed hopefully, to the ground and leave her a clue that someone had been. The hood would be a bit touchier. If they were going to get under the hood, they would first check it out well. Jan rubbed her thumb in the dirt on the ground.

Her thumb came away black. Carefully she smudged the front of the hood where a hand would have to be placed to open the latch. It looked like every other smudge a mechanic would leave or just dirt gotten from driving on roads around here. Jan knew that she had left her thumbprint though. If that was gone there was no way she would start the vehicle without a complete inspection first.

Having completed her precautionary measures, Jan walked down the street and into the hotel where he was staying. This time she placed herself right by the pool, in nearly full view of everything. Her outfit was almost the same as yesterday's, a white tee-shirt with a bikini top under it. Instead of jeans, she wore jean shorts with tennis shoes, and she carried her bag over her left shoulder. She wanted it to be obvious, not blatant about her being there, to be seen. Taking off her tee-shirt she stretched out on a chaise lounge and put on sun glasses. It was now time to slowly and carefully open her mind little by little to lure him into her trap. She started to look for him at first close by and then little by little expanding out.

Even though the sun was warm on her skin and she was protected from the wind off the ocean, there was a bone chilling cold she could feel coming closer. She stopped opening her mind knowing full well what he could do to her if he got control of her thoughts, but not before she got the pattern of his heartbeat and breathing. She liked using this old trick. One she had never shared with anyone else but Ward. With that information she would be able to keep an eye on him, and him on her, and protect herself. Bobby walked toward the pool area. From what she was feeling she knew that he had spotted her. He was trying to get into her mind, and get control of it.

Jan rolled onto her stomach and placed her hand under the chaise. Instinctively she put her right hand in her purse on her gun, and let the other one position itself to flip her back over quickly if necessary. Jan was careful to keep her mind and body locked together, ready to move. The training missions they had done together would give both of them information on each other's skill levels, leaving a split second for failure on either of their parts. Once he got in the pool area she would have only a couple of minutes, and fear didn't need to be part of the equation.

Jan never looked his way, but she knew when he got there. He took on a casual air as he started to look around for her, but there was nothing casual about it. His eyes locked on her and it was then that the games began. Jan pulled her bag out and moved slowly off the chaise and over to the stairs. Bobby moved toward the doors that led into the hotel, all the time keeping an eye on her as she turned to follow him.

Jan knew that Bobby had spotted her. All the hair on the back of her neck was standing on end and it felt as if ice crystals were forming in her blood. She refused to look in his direction, but as he moved inside she could feel each step he took reverberate inside her head. If she locked eyes with him it might all be over.

Bobby had spotted her lying on the chaise. He would know that mind and body anywhere. He had once had the occasion to play around in her head, but he had gotten nothing except the satisfaction that he had nearly wiped out who she was from her memory. If it hadn't been for Ward's interference in her recovery, she never would have remembered. It soon would have driven her crazy. Somehow he had gotten to her, past the PED people, and helped her recover. This time he wasn't going to win though. He had thought the warning was clear enough, but then they really didn't know when to walk away, never had. If they continued to follow him, then it would spoil everything. His contact was jittery enough. It was now time to drive the point home. He was on his own right now, but with a phone call he could have about three more people down here. Walking into the hotel he turned and slid into the bar waiting for his shadow, Jan, to follow him. This time he would turn the tables and follow her.

He had wondered for years where Ward was hiding out, this could be just the break he needed. Once he finished this job it would be his pleasure to deal with them. If she thought she had lost him she might head home, and then the fun could begin. A few seconds later he saw exactly what he was hoping for. Jan walked into the hotel but didn't stop at the bar area. She continued on to the front desk area. Bobby closed his eyes and concentrated. He would enjoy using all his skills on her. Later he would benefit from it.

Jan felt flushed. She had never let go of his heartbeat and breathing, but now he was trying to gain access to her mind. It was an unwelcome intrusion, a violation that went far beyond the punishable by law kind. He had entered her mind before and done intense damage, this time she could tell he was just bent on leading her in the direction he wanted her to go. She felt as if she was slowly losing control of her thoughts, and with that observation she fought harder to keep the barriers up. He needed to have limited control so that the plan would work, but the strain was already beginning to pull on her.

Her mind clung to the training that Ward had given her after her recovery the last time. Being this close to evil and one that could enter your thoughts so easily was mentally and physically draining and painful. There were images, ones of the restaurant, the man, and the time in fifteen minutes from now. Without knowing it he was sending her all the signs she needed. He was trying to lead her back to the restaurant in hopes that she would see that she missed the meeting and then she would leave, or come back here. Bobby made it seem as if she were reading his mind, not that the thoughts she was getting were being forced upon her. He had left no part of his mind open to her though, and the only sure way Jan knew he was near was the constant beat of his heart and thoughts. His heartbeat pounding away in her head, beating against her brain had her struggling to diminish his effects.

Jan did as he was prodding her to do, walking quickly toward the restaurant. He wanted her to think she was too late to observe the meeting, so she hurried. His heart droned, near enough to feel, and his mind far enough to keep him from being detected. Jan put on her sunglasses, her bright green eyes showed the strain of the encounter and she didn't want to alert anyone. Her sunglasses hid the deepening lines as she walked past the lot in which she parked. She carefully looked in the general direction of the SUV. Jan was rewarded almost immediately with the confirmation that Bobby thought there was some importance to her glance. She knew because his heartbeat increased slightly for a second and then returned to the regular pace. Step one done.

Jan took up her position at the coffee shop to watch the restaurant. She ordered a mocha again, only this time she drank none of it. Bobby was careful not to come anywhere near the restaurant or the coffee shop. Jan only knew he was near by the constant drumming of his heart, but she wasn't sure just where. Half an hour later she started to get a bit nervous, for Bobby's benefit.

There was a sharp stab of pain in the back of her head, and she knew that he was again trying to force his way into her mind. When Ward came into her thoughts it was a gradual awareness she felt. It was almost his energy signature as well and that took her off guard for a second. It was close, but not close enough her mind knew who was there and the pain was a warning. Bobby had tried to invade Ward's mind as well at one time and knew both of their mental signatures. It wasn't possible to copy them completely but on face value, if she had accepted it, he could have gained access to her mind. When Ward knew he was not welcomed in he pulled back. Ward had learned the same techniques that Bobby had but never forced himself on anyone. With Bobby she felt his thoughts pushing into her mind, trying to take over all other thoughts, until she could only think what he wanted her to. Ward had taught her how to defend as much as possible against it, but he had never taught her how to open up just little portions of her mind for him to control. It was necessary if she wanted him to follow her and have him think it was his idea, but she knew she was playing with fire. Right now though she had only two choices; keep the flame close or get burned. Since getting burned wasn't a choice she had to fight back with all she had and that meant giving him just a bit of space in her head.

Images filled her mind. This time the images were ones of cars and leaving. They got more specific. Shaking her head she tried hard to remember that they were not her thoughts in the deepest part of her mind, the one he was never able to get at. If she believed those images he was sending her, she would believe that Bobby had already left for other places, but he gave her no clues to where. Images of the hotel room came to mind and it being empty. All the thoughts that he was placing in her head made her think that she had blown the surveillance, missed him.

Taking in a deep breath she concentrated again. His thoughts could have worked if she had actually had him under surveillance, and letting her mind be fully open to him. Taking his cues, she got up and walked out of the coffee shop and headed back to the Explorer. It was now time to make sure he had checked out of the hotel, or at least make it look that way and then head for the border. Jan looked at her watch. The timing would be just a little off if she didn't slow it down a bit. Jan started to watch the street a bit more carefully. His heartbeat was still in her ears pounding away at a constant and steady rhythm. At least she was still the cat in this dire game, she hoped as the sweat trickled down the side of her face even on this cool morning. There seemed to be nothing that was causing him stress. As for Jan, the stress was ever present as she pushed it off to the side.

Jan arrived at the entrance of the hotel. She now had a decision to make. If she went to the room, that would leave him an opening to get to her. There was also a chance that he hadn't left the room yet. If that was the case then it would blow his cover as well as force him to do something stupid, not listing the number of reasons why it would be stupid for her to go to his room, except for the obvious ones. She decided to go into the nearest shop and wait and watch, ignoring the thoughts she was getting. He wanted her to leave, to go home and regroup. The feeling was one of almost overwhelming panic on her part. She now realized what he had wanted from her today and was glad for the plan she had hatched up last night.

The one thing he had never been able to get from her or Ward's mind at anytime he had invaded their thoughts was the location of their hideaway. No one would ever get that out of them, not without a damn good reason. She made an effort to casually look at the items in the shop. Fifteen more minutes here, fifteen more minutes back to where she had parked, and few minutes in traffic should give her just the right amount of time. It was already nearing noon. Rob had assured her he would be ready at twelve thirty, and any other time would draw attention to him. Jan rubbed her temple unconsciously. She felt Bobby smile when he saw her do that. She was tiring and if she wasn't vigilant he would soon have her. Twelve thirty seemed like a lifetime away.

Jan moved out of the shop and into the hotel. Walking up to the counter she waited and then asked for the time. There was no need to ask anything else. If he was staying, he would have to come back over the border and by that time she would have him believing they lived in Phoenix. She walked back out and down the street. There was a pounding in her head that rivaled the beating of the loud music nearby, her mind was in turmoil being constantly assaulted by him, but she kept control. She had to keep her control. She wasn't going to lose to that piece of rubbish. Walking up to the entrance of the hotel she had parked in front of she went up to the desk. She could feel him prying at her mind like a crowbar at a rusty hinge, and she allowed him to think that she was checking out and leaving. She asked the attendant at the counter to tell her where the best pharmacy was. As he did, she rubbed at her temples again making it look to the entire world as if she had one world-class headache, which she did. She couldn't allow herself to think that she wouldn't be able to make it the next eight hours. For a moment she slipped and thought eight long hours against his mind. Pushing the thought away she left and went for the Explorer. Looking around the bottom of the car as she walked up to it, she made a half-hearted attempt to check for sabotage. He would expect her to do this. It was normal behavior at least for them. Bobby pushed into her head again, forcing her to feel the need to go home more urgently, to find Ward. Jan pushed the thought to the side of her brain she had given up to him, and climbed in the vehicle.

Quickly his mind left hers. A wave of relief washed over her and she took a deep breath. He had released her mind just long enough to get his car. Placing her head on the headrest she allowed herself just one minute to rest, it would be all she got and all she needed. Bobby had to know how tired she was, and this would give him time to get his car and be ready to play follow the leader.

Jan lifted her head, started the car, and drove out of the lot. She waited for the force of his thoughts at hers again, and was not disappointed when only two minutes later she felt them steamrolling into her head. The slam of the headache returned with them. She drove at a normal pace and soon spotted his car. It was a silver Z350. The car never got too close, yet never got more than fifteen car lengths away. As she got closer to Tijuana the car got closer too. Watching traffic she tried to access just how much Bobby was able to read and see into her mind. His view was minimally obstructed, but not by much. As for his thoughts, she was still having him believe she was headed home. It wasn't that far off track either. She was heading back to an apartment she had lived in for a long time. The traffic began to become oppressive and they both had to rely less on their thoughts concentrating on the traffic and more on the training they had received to play the chase game. It was pretty clear by now that he was on his own. She had not seen another tail and he had never let her get too far away from him. Not a good way to handle things but it would work in her favor. As she pulled into the line to get back across the border she eyed the bridge.

"Where was he?" the words echoed in the SUV. Just as suddenly she noticed some Hispanic gentlemen standing and selling blankets, icons, chairs, hammocks, and other items on the bridge to get the last few pesos out of the tourists that they could, like they always did. Jan waited in traffic as they inched forward. Now that they were moving like snails Bobby had started to probe her mind once more. God help her but she wanted to smack Bobby, hard. As she got closer to the bridge the man selling blankets started to move through the traffic showing off his wares. His clothes were old and ragged, but they sufficiently covered him from head to toe. His head and face were shaded by the hat and scarf he had on.

He sold two of the ones he carried and moved over another lane. He was watching the traffic so carefully that he had noticed both the Explorer and the Z350 traveling in the same lane at times, and always staying a suitable distance away each other. The Z350 varied the distance between them ever so slightly so as to draw no suspicion from the person in the Explorer. As he sold his third blanket, he looked at the driver of the Explorer and his heart ached. She looked tired already, and every few minutes she would rub her temple. She had on sunglasses, which was not a good sign. Three more cars, he couldn't look anxious, that would give him away. It also wouldn't help her. Clamping down on any stray thoughts he looked for another car to move toward. Another sale, and as he took the money the Explorer moved into position.

"Gracias Senor," he handed the blankets and the money to the man in the car, "a special today. You may have all the blankets I have," and he threw the last two blankets into his car and moved on to the next lane where the Explorer sat. He opened the driver's door and pushed his way in.

"Get over," and Jan moved over with pleasure.

"Nice outfit," and then she leaned over grabbing the front of his shirt and pulling him to her as she kissed him like she had been thirsting for it all day and night long.

"That's one hell of a way to say 'Hello'. I take it, it was for Bobby's benefit and not just because I am so handsome in this outfit," he smiled outside, but inside he worried. Jan already looked painfully tired and they still had a long drive ahead of them.

"He didn't believe it until I kissed you. He is pretty sure you're Ward now," Jan leaned back in the passenger seat and closed her eyes.

"A little strange, but all in a days work. How long can you keep this up?" Rob watched the road and drove closer to the crossing, the driver of the Z350 was keeping them in sight.

"As long as I need to, and longer since you are driving now," she attempted a smile, "And by the way he won't see you at all. I'm blocking you as well," Rob didn't ask how, figured she had learned a few tricks from Ward. He knew that as a professional she would keep going until she dropped out of sheer exhaustion, which she wasn't close to yet, "Stop worrying, I'll sleep on the plane." He did stop then; it was a useless emotion anyway. He concentrated on the drive after crossing the border until Jan was ready to talk again.

"I have a friend who is ready to cover for you if necessary, and as it looks it may be. She is waiting at the apartment. I think you might know her, name's Maria," Jan smiled, the first complete one Rob had seen since climbing in the car.

"She doing well?"

"Hired her myself. Good find, well educated, very smart," the road continued on out of the San Diego area and up into the hills, the Z350 in sight for some of the time, and changing positions on the road, "She's a good asset."

"So, what do you want to know?" and Jan emphasized the do.

"Only what I need to, otherwise I may compromise you or the mission," before she could say another word he continued, "Yes, I said mission. From what I can pick up there could be a bunch of dirty agents down there and we need to do a complete flush and catch them all.

"You and Ward have been contacted and signed on as deep cover whether or not you like it or know it. So yes, you're on a mission to capture moles. Without hard facts it won't happen. So far they have covered themselves fairly well, and are ready to kill to keep it a secret. What they are dealing in we don't know yet, but hopefully you'll discover it and let me in on the secret. There are two options for the spawn of the devil behind us. One, he is either involved and that's scary, or he just happened to complicate things. Do I have it about right?" Rob smiled as he chanced a glance at Jan before returning his eyes to the road.

"Are you sure I'm the mind reader here?" Jan rubbed at one temple again, "We will go in the apartment, and out through the back, by the time he realizes that we have slipped out, he won't know where to look. I'll leave the Explorer at the apartment and the keys with you. You will need to move it a couple of times, but be careful. What I didn't tell you is that he left me a message. He plans to kill us this time round if we get in his way," the news didn't even shock Rob. Bobby had nearly killed all three of them on many occasions. He would have been dead already if it hadn't been for Jan and Ward and their sheer determination to do what was right.

"We need to let him see us in the apartment to make it convincing, and when he lets his guard down we get out. I will head off in one direction and you and Maria in another. Then you need to make sure to get Maria out of danger for me," they traveled in silence for a while. Rob said nothing more for a while. When he couldn't take it anymore he finally asked.

"Are you happy with him? With the life you've chosen?" He had to know for sure.

"He makes me happy, Dad," she had added a little sarcasm. "More happy than I have ever been in my entire life," and they drove the rest of the way in silence.

Chapter 7

As the wheels of the plane left the ground she could feel the familiar pull on her body while the plane climbed higher in the sky, and she smiled. It had worked. Bobby had followed them all the way to her apartment. It had been odd going back after all this time. She had walked back in time to a life she no longer lived or wanted. Rob had emptied the place out of most things, although there had never been anything really personal in it. The department long ago had consumed anything that had been personal and she had become the job. Over the years as she had worked with the PED she had never imagined it any other way.

Jan thought back to when she first went back into the apartment. Maria was waiting for them to show up. When she first saw Jan she stood up and impulsively hugged her.

"See, I told you I was headed for a better life," Jan hugged her back and was pleased to see that it had worked out for her. Jan couldn't help but wonder just how many it hadn't worked out for though. She couldn't linger on the souls they had lost, or they would risk losing even more now.

"You're being careful of this man. He will work you to death," Jan spoke to Maria in perfect Spanish as she teased her about Rob.

"Don't forget, I'm also fluent," Rob filled Maria in on what had happened and what they were going to do next. Jan was surprised at how well she took in the information and processed it. She was ready. Jan could see it in her mind. Rob had made sure she had gotten some training since she had last seen her.

Jan walked over to the window and looked out from behind the blind. One of Bobby's men took over the surveillance for Bobby. He got closer than Bobby had ever been, and Jan took that as a good sign. It told her what she needed to know without doing a reading on him. Her mind was already tired enough, and the fact that Bobby was about to leave would give her a break. There was no way this manifestation of evil was going to get the better of them.

Ward and Jan had never been sure if Bobby had started to train others on the techniques of mind reading. It was not a skill that many could master, so they held on to the belief that he hadn't. What Jan had just seen proved it though. No mind reader would have ever risked getting that close for fear of being picked out way too easily. The energy signature would have given him away. Bobby was feeling comfortable, too comfortable with this situation. He wanted her to know they were being watched.

"We've got company at three o'clock," Jan voice was all business. "The good kind. Not a reader. Seen him only once before, and that is a long forgotten memory," she referred back to the time when Bobby had tried to wipe her mind, and nearly succeeded. That man had been there.

"Got him," Rob had walked to the other side of the window. Jan moved away, and as she did she could feel Bobby's presence leave her mind. She also felt comfortable letting his life signs fade that she had so stubbornly hung onto all this time. Rob immediately picked up on her body language, something he had never forgotten how to do, and continued. The relief she felt was almost contagious.

"Now that he's gone, you need to get out of here. You may not have much time, and we will need to leave as well," looking at his watch, "about fifteen minutes after you do." Jan walked over to Rob, and gave him a hug. It was a gesture she had rarely done in the past, but now it just seemed the right thing to do. He was risking a lot for them.

"Thanks for the help," and with that she moved to the back of the apartment and out through the sliding doors and down the side of the building undetected behind the climbing vine. She had done this a million times before. Some things never changed. She had originally chosen this place because of that.

Once in the airport she felt a bit safer even though she never allowed her guard to drop. She was out in the open and could be picked up by anyone, including department personnel. They had only looked at her funny for a moment when she checked in with no baggage, and only a purse that served as a carry all. Jan simply stated that her husband had gone on ahead on business yesterday and taken the luggage. When the associate stated how nice that was, Jan only replied that her husband was simply one of the best men out there.

When she got on the plane the initial checks of the minds aboard led her to believe that she would be able to finally get a little rest before she began the next part of her adventure. If someone had occupied the seat next to her they would not have been able to tell, but Jan's breathing slowed, and her pulse rate dropped. She entered into a deep meditative state that would last for a couple of hours. This would allow her to be better rested than if she had just slept. Power sleeping had been a survival skill Ward and Jan had refined with their skills. With just two hours of meditation, it would seem to her body that she had been asleep for a solid eight. She would wake before the change of planes and have the next flight to review the information she had learned. Maybe even pick up some more over the Internet during the layover.

As planned she woke just before they landed in Mexico, and changed planes. There were more people on this plane, but she managed to convince them to keep the seat empty beside her. She had time to download any information that Rob had put up for her and a few other things from other sites before they announced electronics off. Jan looked over the information again reading and rereading it until she could come to no other conclusion. One or more of the officers, or agents, were bad. There were no clues as to the type of information that was being passed on. It happened, people got greedy and the drug lords and military dictators paid double agents very well. She would find who had recently gotten a lot of money. Gaining access to bank accounts was a little trickier. These people knew how to hide things like that. Somehow though, Golightly must have gotten too close to the truth and they needed to get rid of him. The last report of the killing she had accessed over the net had not been any different than the first. That was suspicious. Usually on closer examination there were more details, data, and pieces of evidence entered. Trivial things had been changed, but nothing that would imply a deeper investigation. All the reports matched too well. No one was going to make a stink over this one, and that was exactly what someone wanted.

Jan began to make mental notes as to what she would need to acquire when she got into Lima. That would be quite the shopping list and she would have to rely on those that liked to deal with things that would not be found on a grocery shelf. As for what she would tackle first, she would start at the main office. It would require a couple days surveillance to see when the best time to enter the building would be, and just how to do it without being caught on tape. A cleaning woman was always a good cover, and a great way to get some of the equipment she would need. She would need to know when and how the cleaning people entered and left. She looked out the window as the pilot announced their approach into Lima. It was busy, dirty, and congested; big cities were all the same as you looked down at them from the air.

Immigration and Customs had not been a hassle at all. Jan had learned long ago how to handle them, but once she left the relative safety of the passengers she had traveled with she was again on guard. She was all business as she left the processing area. She glanced around the waiting area quickly accessing each of the minds. As she was about to finish her sweep of the area she noticed a man with a baseball cap, Arizona Diamondbacks, sitting with his back to the wall and watching the people coming through the little door out of the customs area. As her eyes got to him he let a smile spread across his lips and he tipped his hat. Upon seeing him Jan gave a half smile but never really looked right at him. Jan continued to walk and soon he fell into step beside her.

"Excuse me," was all he said as he bumped into her and dropped his bags as well as a handful of papers. Bill was a friend of Ward's, ex-agent. He had helped him out on many of Ward's missions before but it was a surprise to see him here. He had left this game long ago, but it seemed that for them he would always bend the rules just a bit. His mind was open to her and she allowed herself to read it as he had planned. Jan bent over and helped to pick up the papers and realized that the bag he was carrying was for her. She picked it up and casually placed it over her shoulder as she handed back the pile of papers and other assorted items to Bill.

"A layover?" Jan half smiled. She knew that the layover was nowhere near the route he had planned to get back to Phoenix. Hadn't even known that Bill had left Phoenix, but Rob had known who to call for help.

"He thought you should have some standard items, and I was on my way home from a trip. Used it as an excuse to have me bring a bag out," their voices were low and quiet.

"Didn't mean to get you involved," they turned and started to walk through the airport and over to the security post by the gates Bill needed to be at.

"I'm not. I'm leaving in two hours and what happens after that is not my concern. I'm just the messenger. Heard anything?" She knew that Bill was concerned about Ward and the others; even if he didn't know them by name they were all still part of the same family.

"Not yet," saying anything else Jan realized would just be trying to placate the notion that what they were about to do would not be dangerous. And how would she tell him that the agency couldn't be trusted; if not them, then who. That is where people like Jan and Ward came in she guessed, cosmic cleaners at your service.

"Thought you stopped working for these guys?" It was a half question, half accusation and Jan just smiled at him. This time it was a full smile.

"Most of them yes, but some of them I just can't say no to," and he winked. Jan shook his hand and turned to leave. She caught Bill's final thought and it kept the smile on her face. It was true, neither one worked for the government anymore, but none of them, even Ward, could quite get it completely out of their blood especially if the mission they took on was the right thing to do. They parted ways, and she didn't watch him head for the gates as she left the small airport and hailed a cab just outside the doors.

There was a hum outside the airport that only third world countries could produce. It was a mixture of the first world sights and sounds of planes and vehicles with the mixture of the sounds of the hawkers and sellers. One could see the poverty of the area, people begging on the sidewalk, and those who were selling whatever they could just to make a living of some kind. There were fumes of diesel and pollution that hung over the city and halfway up the surrounding mountains like a large noxious cloud. It wasn't overwhelming, but it was noticeable. Jan got in the cab throwing her bags on the seat and asked the driver to take her to city center. She had a plan and time on her hands since some of her shopping had been done for her. It would take most of the afternoon to gather the information she would need, but it put her a day ahead of schedule.

Rob looked at his watch, took a deep breath and released it with a sigh. It was close to six in the evening. If everything was working right, then Jan would have the bag, and Bill would be on his way back. No one would have to be the wiser to what he had done. In the bag he had put all the essentials that they would normally be allowed, and a few that only Jan would want. He didn't agree with or like what was going on, but someone would have to investigate it. If he started an internal investigation now it might scare off those involved. If that happened they may never find the problem, and there was a problem. Rob had reviewed the reports himself and came to the same conclusion as Jan. Someone had wanted Golightly out of the way and they would kill, had killed, to do it. This meant that all of them were in danger, but from what Rob could tell it didn't seem to matter where they were, danger just hung over them like a natural aura. Wiping his forehead and refocusing on the computer screen Rob clicked the mouse and watched the faces on the screen change. The only thing he could do was to do what he had promised Jan and find out who the man Bobby met with was. A whole new array of twenty faces appeared on the screen. The facial scan was good but it still took a person on the other end to put all the facts together and that meant time to identify a true match. No match yet to the picture that Jan had given him. He had been through many databases already; each photo ever taken for a security identity card was loaded in a database for that particular agency with a link to their personnel file. Each company that had ever contracted with the government at any time also had a complete file. These were checks that had been given to employees for security clearances as well as other things. Rob clicked on the next button again. As he clicked through the pictures one by one he thought back on what had really happened.

It was seven in the evening and he had chosen to stay at the office and bed down in one of the efficiency apartments that night. He had also made Maria stay at a friend's place. Knowing what Bobby was capable of made it easy for him to not allow Maria to stay at the apartment. If he didn't take the right precautions then the whole facade would be for nothing. It had been hard for Jan to call him. She had to admit to a general area of where they were living. Rob wondered how Ward would feel about that. He clicked onto the next database and began another search through photos. He had wanted to get back to the apartment and move the Explorer at least once before the night was finished, but as he looked through the photos he knew it may be late into the night, or not at all. If he asked why he was going through the photo bases he would just simply say research. With any luck they would believe him, and he may find who this was in the next six hours.

Having done her research on the area, and pulling up what blueprints she could get on such short notice, Jan knew that the building the agency used was near the old town area, across from a small park. It was the best area for surveillance, but it was also a bad area to get caught at it as well. Not too much cover. She walked through the hotel lobby and out the other side without thinking twice about going back to the room. She was headed for a small group of apartments located just off the old town area.

As she approached the apartments, Jan was not surprised to see that these were just a step up from slum. A one-story adobe dwelling that housed about twelve private apartments circled a small and unkempt center courtyard. The apartments were now the homes of those that were on the edge of the low level criminal society as well as economic one. The courtyard was filled with trash and what could be human refuse. At one time these homes had been those of the upper society. It had been a shame that they had now been dragged down into disrepair and the seamy side of life. Jan had picked this place as a safe house for her and hopefully Ward and Jack when she found them or they her. She had tried not to give it much thought as she focused in on her work, but every now and then she wondered just where they might be. On any mission distraction wasn't a good thing and this one was no exception. If they were going to get through this they would need a safe house to hide out and work in.

After going through the process of renting one of the apartments for a month, a time period that it seemed was a long period of time here, she started to stow everything away. Jan pulled out the locked box she carried on a mission. Inside this box she had identity documents that could get her in and out of any country with a variety of names. She took a couple of moments to assess where the best place was to leave this box. Walking over to the sink she opened the cabinet under the sink. Something small and gray scurried back behind the wallboard. Trying not to think about that, and the fact that there were many more, she pulled the board away just far enough to push the box back behind the pipes and the nest of chewed paper and other items better left unmentioned. It wasn't that she hadn't ever been in situations like this before it just helped not to think about it. Quickly she moved back across the room and left, securing the door and marking it.

Walking around the area she pulled her camera out of her purse and began to look more like a tourist. The old colonial Spanish buildings mixed with the modern trappings of the city, cars, pollution, and people. The people of Peru had preserved the buildings well and the integrity of the old town still existed amongst the new. Jan wandered in and out of many stores and shops picking up items she would need to keep her cover before she sat watching the agency employees. A regular type of surveillance would take weeks, and may still turn up nothing. Jan, and the skills that she and people like her possessed, made the work a bit quicker, not easier, just quicker. That is what made them so valuable on any mission. It had been the reason they were so highly trained in all the covert fields and with all branches. At any time they could be and had been called to serve with all of the armed forces, departments and secretive government agencies even if they had originally been a CIA creation or experiment. Jan made her way to the park bench in front of the agency building with a newspaper and a small supper, sufficient to keep her sitting there for at least an hour without being obvious.

Jan sat on the park bench across the street from the storefront that housed the agency. On the plane Jan had studied the faces, names, and files of all the people housed here. She had researched their history for the past ten years as well. As she picked at the lettuce in her salad there had been three people who had left the building. Jan had read each of their minds as they walked either toward or away from her. Nothing she saw there would have made anyone think twice, especially not Jan. These people had left for their homes or bars to meet other people. They were specialists, hired only to make the necessary documents and items needed in clandestine jobs. They were the people that would and could make or break an operation. Jan had had some training in this area and over the years had come to highly respect their skills and their time commitments to the job. Their thoughts had been firstly on their jobs, then on their families and friends. A few were still grieving over the death of Golightly, thinking that it had somehow been their fault that his cover was broken. Little did they know that she suspected he was still alive. She was fairly sure. Finding nothing that would make her want to follow up on any of them she had continued to sit, and wait, for those that may yet come and go from the office. The one remaining case officer stationed here and the two junior agents, as well as the director, had yet to make an appearance. Jan tried to reach into the building with her mind and had found at least two more minds inside, but she was not close enough to read either properly yet or to see any more, so she waited. She picked at her salad and opened the paper.

Over an hour later she was reading the last bits of the newspaper and finishing the small meal she had brought with her when she noticed another person come out of the office. From the look on her face none of the people near her would have known that she had taken any notice of the man who had just left the building. He was walking her way, and she was intently going through his mind. Jan had recognized him as the director of operations down here. There was a lot in his mind and Jan was finding it hard to sort through all of it as he quickly strode past. The issues involving Golightly were still at the top of his thoughts, and she was thankful for that. He hated to lose a good man. He had placed all the reports in the correct files and sent them to the official departments, but he didn't understand why there had been no further forensics ordered. To Jan, that was a good thought, it meant that he was not directly involved in the assassination attempt. There were a couple of problems with all of this for Jan. First, if he wasn't involved then he may become a target, and even though he had filed all the reports, why hadn't he seen the discrepancies in the descriptions that she could see in his mind? As he walked past her Jan continued to look as if she was finishing the section of paper she had already read. She continued through his thoughts about what had possibly gone wrong, and he knew there was something wrong. As he moved farther away from her he became harder to read clearly.

After only a few moments he turned and looked straight at her, half pretending that he had turned to watch the sunset. Instead of stopping, and letting him know that he had made her, Jan continued to walk past him right over to the trash can and dropped the paper in it. She then turned around and walked back to the park bench and sat back down. That seemed to allay his fears a bit about being followed for now, and Jan had picked up another piece of useful information. The director had no idea that the reports that had been recorded were now falsified. Jan sat and again waited for the next person. Whoever was dirty, it wasn't him. Only one person was left in the office and he didn't seem to want to leave any time soon. Jan stayed on the bench until the director was out of sight.

Standing and picking up her bag, Jan moved across the street and near the door to the storefront. Because she had studied the files, she was able to identify the only mind left in the building. It was Golightly's partner and he was nowhere near finishing for the night. He was focused on the files of the case. It had been the third time he had studied them and still he couldn't find what he was looking for. Jan looked deeper into his mind. She felt his despair. He felt responsible for what had happened and was trying to find the piece to the puzzle that would allow him to put Jack's memory to rest. Jan knew that because she had read the same files herself many times looking for that key. As she eavesdropped on his thoughts she could feel his anger build. It soon reached a point he could no longer control and he shoved himself back from the desk with force. Jan could tell that he was getting ready to leave and it was time to make her move. She got ready.

Toby grabbed his jacket and walked toward the door. He had spent most of the afternoon looking over the reports on file. He had requested the files that had been sent into the agency as well, but had gotten no response yet. Toby carefully tucked his gun in its holster and zipped his jacket halfway up covering up any notion that he had a weapon. He flipped the light on his desk off and walked toward the door. The last meal he had eaten was breakfast and now he was starved. Tomorrow he would be pulled off this case and reassigned. Something he didn't want to talk about, didn't want to think about and really didn't want to happen. As far as the agency was concerned Golightly's death was a closed case and a new case officer would be assigned to the area. As only a junior, he could be kept on or relieved and sent off somewhere else. Toby pulled the inner door closed and set the security programs. Walking out of the dark building and into the fading sunset he suddenly bumped into a tourist. She was average height, good looking, and had shoulder length light brown hair. The contents of her purse were also now all over the sidewalk.

"Oh damn," Jan said.

"I'm sorry, it's my fault," Toby hadn't seen her coming, but he had felt the impact. He bent to help her pick up her stuff.

"I'm so sorry. I was looking at the architecture of all the buildings in the contrasting sunlight and must have just gotten carried away," Jan was busy picking up items that she had purposely dumped all over the sidewalk, and keeping his mind open to hers. Although he was being careful, he had no idea that she was a reader, not many people in the world actually knew they existed, and that gave her the advantage here.

"So I take it you're interested in architecture?" He was only making small talk as he helped her out. Jan needed to make sure that their contact would last longer.

"You're speaking English. You're American?" She said very convincingly in disbelief and relief.

"Yes, I work here," he gave no more information, which was standard procedure.

"Wow! That's so fascinating. It must be wonderful to be among these old buildings all the time. You see I was an architect student for six years, and then became an associate professor for the University of California, Bakersfield. I've just gotten a new job as a professor there. Now don't say it," they stood and looked at each other as she placed the last couple of items back in her purse that he handed her.

"Say what?" He was trying to be nice, and Jan could tell that he was mildly interested in the conversation. What he was doing was slowly becoming more interested in what she was wearing and what she looked like.

"The obvious, that there can't be much of a need for a professor of architecture in Bakersfield," Jan let some of the items slip back out of her hands on purpose sighing as she bent over again to pick them up, and recklessly dropping more items. She needed this encounter to last as long as she could. She had to get him to believe her story, her legend, before she could relax a bit and begin to sift through his mind.

"Let me get that," he bent again to pick up the items she had dropped with a small smile on his face, as well as some annoyance.

"This was so stupid," Jan said, more to herself than to him, as she shook her head. Again she had pulled him back into her web.

"What?" Toby was confused, but oddly drawn to her helpless soul. She seemed totally out of her element and lost. It was that helpless female act she had hoped to snag him with.

"I just got in today and I couldn't wait to get out and see everything," Jan leaned against the building letting her shoulders drop and her head tilt downwards, "I knew I should have stayed at the hotel today and gotten some rest before I tried to walk around the city, but obviously the air flights have caught up with me," and she stopped. It was a very calculated pause. Changing the topic all together and giving a wave of her hand she went on, "You probably have somewhere else to be and listening to a foolish woman ramble on is probably not too high on your list." Jan started to look up and down the street as if she was looking for a landmark, or something familiar. She began to furrow her brow, "Thanks so much for helping me pick up all this junk," this time she was careful to make the furrow a bit deeper and not make any eye contact until the last part of the question as she sounded just a bit distracted, "If it wouldn't be too much trouble could you point me in the direction of the Hotel de Lima?"

"It's just," and he paused. Toby let a smile stretch across his face. When he had picked up her items for a second time he had checked her ring finger for any signs of a commitment and found nothing. Jan of course knew what he was thinking and she knew she had captured her prey, "Have you had supper?"

"What?"   Now it was her turn to feign disbelief, "I really couldn't, I've taken up too much of your time already," and he didn't let her finish. Jan knew that he would be careful not to mention what he did, and that he himself would follow all policies including staying in character. But that didn't matter to Jan, she would see right through him anyway.

"You have to eat. You're lost, and I don't have anything planned for tonight. I haven't had any lunch and I'm starved. Let me take you back to the hotel and we will grab a quick bite to eat at a good place near there. Then you can go back to your room, and I can go home knowing that I didn't leave you down here wandering the streets alone," he was honest, and caring. Jan knew from all that she had picked out so far that he had not been involved in the alleged attempted murder on Golightly. If she got more of his thoughts she might just be able to weave all of this together. She had an established cover now and would be able to pick up on all his conversations. His memory training would come in handy as she looked through his thoughts without his knowledge. The best mind to read was one that was well trained for remembering facts.

"Only on one condition," and Jan smiled, "you let me pay. It's the least I can do for all your help."

"Deal," together they started to walk the familiar route back to the hotel where Jan had registered under her alias, "By the way, name's Toby."

"Elizabeth, Liz for short."

Chapter 8

They talked architecture the entire way back to the hotel. Toby was impressed by her knowledge of the subject and love for it. He was lured into her trap by the topic as she easily talked of the Spanish influence and local details of the buildings he had known for the last two years. She seemed thoroughly consumed by the subject as she spoke and walked aimlessly allowing him to take the lead with his hand on her arm.

Jan on the other hand had spent the time giving facts that she had read in the books and on the web as she had traveled down here to help build a reality to her persona. It had been easy to do this, as she chatted mindlessly on it allowed her to have more access to his thoughts on the way. Jan had sensed his feelings of despair and remorse over an operation gone wrong. It had been another case officer that had been sent up to the Amazon Basin to check on what had gone totally bottoms up and not him. Although he had to acquiesce to his bosses and agree that it was risky to go in after a mission failed. He had tried hard to get included, but the request was rejected all three times. He had spent most of his free time the last couple of days going over the pictures and reports that Jack had sent in to the office. Jan's readings were interrupted as Toby stopped walking.

"Here we are," Toby pointed to the hotel entrance, "Why don't you drop your things off and I'll wait down here." Toby turned and leaned up against the lamppost, trying his best at being gallant.

"Be right back," and Jan slipped into the hotel. She got up the stairs and into her room quickly and changed into the simple sundress she had brought along. The browns and copper tones highlighted her hair and enhanced her sun-drenched skin. She wanted him focused on one thing, and one thing alone. She headed back down the stairs ten minutes later. When she walked out of the entrance she noticed that he had been studying one of the older buildings that she had spent time talking about at length.

"Beautiful isn't it," and as Jan saw him turn to look at her she didn't have to read his thoughts to know that the dress had its desired effects. "I hope you don't mind that I changed from my traveling clothes?"

"Glad you did. Shall we go?" With one hand Toby pointed the way and with the other he took her arm as they walked along in the crowds of people who were ambling their way home. As they walked Jan continued to discuss the architecture as well as pick at his mind. She had gotten precious little information by the end of the evening, except that he couldn't find any reason for the agency to be following the men, they had no records, and the evidence against them was pretty sketchy. Jan would have liked more, but time being what it was she knew that it may take a few days to collect all the information from him that she could. The phone that she had placed in her bra had stayed quiet all day long and into the evening. As they walked back to the hotel again Toby chanced putting his arm around her. She fell into a comfortable pace beside him. They were silent until they reached the hotel.

"I haven't learned so much in a long time," he sighed as Jan smiled when he turned to face her.

"Sorry if I ranted on too much, but," and he cut her off again.

"No, I've been here nearly two years and never even once gave the building designs a second thought as to why they were the way they were or the history involved with it," he moved her a bit closer and Jan did nothing to discourage it. "How long are you going to be in town?"

"Two weeks," Jan knew full well she planned on finding both Ward and Jack faster than that.

"Well Liz, I would love to be able to see you again. My schedule the next couple of days is still up in the air, but if I get a chance," he paused and smiled innocently, "may I call on you?" It was quaint the way he asked, and Jan replied with very inviting smile and let her finger trace his arm.

"I think I'd like that," and as he drew closer to her for a kiss she lifted her face to meet his. Just before his lips reached hers though, she turned her face trying hard to stifle a yawn. "I'm so sorry, I guess that the traveling has made me really tired," she gave him a quick peck on the cheek. "I'll be looking forward to your call," and she went inside the hotel leaving a crooked smile on his face and his head full of thoughts.

When she got back to the hotel room there were no signs on her face or in her mannerisms that she had ever been tired. Pulling out the PDA and the phone she began to check the databases again for any new information that might have become available and found nothing. Frustrated, she took a bit more time on the web to learn a few more interesting facts on the local architecture and then closed up the system. It looked like she would need to spend some more time with Toby. Looking at the phone she wished it would ring. It had been a while since that worried feeling had surfaced and she quickly pushed it down. Where ever he, they, were she was almost sure they were safe. Problem was she wanted to know where they were. Standing up she made plans to go over the topographical maps of their last known location before crawling in for a couple of hours of sleep.

Stretching, she moved to her bag and changed into something more to her liking for night, a black tank top and a pair of black yoga pants. She started into her tai chi routine slowly and patiently as she let the motion take over her thoughts and her actions. Her muscles and mind melding together until the two seemed like one. An hour later she was sitting on the bed and deep in meditation. Thoughts came and went as she sat perfectly still, and then there was nothing. Slowly she opened her eyes and allowed herself to lie down to sleep for a couple of hours, keeping the phone near her.

The sun had just barely come up when Jan finished dressing like a local. She wasted no time and went down to the street. She had dressed that way to disappear into the background. Planning ahead, she had purchased these items yesterday when she had walked toward the agency offices. The bus was pulling up to the stop as she stepped up to the curb. Getting on the city bus, she headed for the residential area where the director lived. Sitting down in the back of the bus she mentally checked off the items in her bag that she would need. She had set the phone to vibrate and strapped it to her thigh. Rob had sent her some listening devices, bugs, via Bill in the bag and a local identity card for her. Jan didn't even want to know how that had happened. It didn't matter how she looked at it, he had illegally made her forged documents, if he had been caught that would have been the end for him. Watching as the bus wound its way through the city and then out into the housing areas she noted the stops and the street signs.

On the plane she had memorized all the addresses of the operatives in the area, knowing that a visit to their houses might prove to be the fastest way to uncover anything. She had all but ruled Toby out by what she had been able to read in his thoughts last night. He would prove to be a good source but Jan was sure he wasn't involved. If she had to search his place she would save it for last. The most obvious place to start was with the director. His service record was good, in fact admirable for most people. He had spent a great amount of time in Central America dealing with Nicaragua and helping to organize and train factions there. Over the last few years he had finally been promoted to director and accepted the spot in Peru because of the political unrest that had plagued the area. He had been instrumental, with the help of Golightly, in decreasing the production of plants that fed the other surrounding countries with the raw materials they needed to make drugs; the drugs that would make their way to the States. It had been because of these actions that Golightly had suffered a great loss. Supposedly they were winning the drug war. Jan only knew the basics of what had happened with Golightly, and Ward didn't share much more of his experiences with it. Jack's new wife had been murdered by one of the factions involved in the cartel, and gun trafficking. Ward's orders had been changed in the middle of a job so that he could be brought to the scene to help out, but it had been too late. They had reached her, but only in time for them to be there as she died.

Jan had read the report on the airplane. It had been a slow and painful death. Ward had to have been in her mind for them to communicate. The weight of what she had learned, and what they must have gone through was still with her. It had given her two bits of very important information. One, it explained what had forged Jack and Ward's friendship. It had also started a string of disagreements between the current director stationed in Lima and Jack. Jan had to do something to rule out the director before she could feel comfortable with Ward and Jack coming back into Lima. That was if they were still alive. She wanted to slap herself for that negative thought. The jungle was unforgiving at best, and even the best-trained and healthiest agents could find themselves in trouble. Jan could not assume that they were unharmed, or that they had ever made it out of the jungle. Jack knew the jungle almost as well as any of the natives and Ward had enough medical knowledge. All she could assume now was that if it was possible for them to survive, they would.

Jan stood up and got off the bus two stops early. She began to walk down the little side street toward the neighborhood in which she would find the director's house. This was an old established area with large colonial houses, midrange in price, but well kept. On an American salary they would easily be able to afford living here. Looking at every detail she continued walking nonchalantly down the roads until she got nearer his street. If she was lucky, there would be no one at home and it would be easy. If the director's wife was home, Jan would have to wait, or if necessary, chance entering his study with her in the house. Not the choice she would want. Noticing that there was a broom leaning against the house four doors down from his she walked over to grab it. Walking past the director's residence she searched for any signs of thoughts, security, and easy access points. As she had expected the wife was still at home. Jan walked on past the house and four doors down. She started to sweep the sidewalk patiently. As she slowly moved closer to the house once more she got the layout of the house from the wife's mind. The alarm was located just off the kitchen area and it was in the back of a broom closet. It was a good hiding place and it would take time to get to for anyone just breaking in. The den was located on the first floor and toward the back of the house, near the kitchen. The wife was about to go run errands, so Jan continued to sweep up and down the sidewalk waiting patiently reading her every thought, including the security code, until she saw the car pull out of the driveway.

Knowing that the house was empty now she moved up to the front door. Knocking, she waited to see if there was an answering bark, and then quickly pulled on a pair of surgical gloves and pulled out her lock pick, opening the door herself. It wasn't the trickiest of locks but it was designed to keep out the casual burglar. It was easy for Jan; she had a talent for getting into places that were designed to keep most people out. To anyone just glancing they would have assumed that someone had opened the door to let her in. The foyer was a small hall with doorways that opened off of both sides of it. It was decorated in the traditional Spanish style to stay with the trappings of the house. Wrapping the black scarf she carried around her head and face as she entered, Jan moved past both of these doors and toward the end of the small hall where the alarm was located. It was standard Government Issue she noticed. As the warning beeps continued to count down the time she had left to disarm it, Jan counted as well as she removed a couple of items from her bag. She then entered the code and the alarm ceased.

The first item she had from the bag was one of the little toys that Bill had brought to her. Pulling the alarm panel she saw the port to plug in the download device. Jan popped the small card device into the port and she was then able to get the layout of the alarm and security systems. The card would bypass all the connected and secondary security systems connected to this unit and report no interruptions in the circuits, as well as turn off any cameras that may be on the premises. This would take the whole system off-line for the time she was here. Unless he was a very cautious man his den would be on the same system.

Walking into the den she visually checked the area for surveillance devices. She also pulled out the small electronic box that had also been stowed in the bag. Later on today she would send Rob a thank you note. As she turned it on she waited to see if the flashing lights would indicate any listening devices in the room. When the green light gave her the all clear, she moved farther into the room sure that she was safe from cameras and recorders. One hand flipped on the computer as the other started to open the desk drawers and looked through them. She could sweep a room and put it back together in about fifteen minutes. Time was essential. Staying too long in a house would put an agent at risk; sometimes it could mean their lives

His room was very unimaginative in style, although it was different from the rest of the house. She guessed that he had done all his own decorating. The desk was standard issue with two drawers on each side and a center pull that had a small and useless lock. He really should have replaced it, but he probably didn't keep anything in the drawer worth locking up. Jan noticed that the room, like the desk, had little to no personality. Little knick knacks from previous locations he had been assigned to had been put around the room. She confirmed what she had read, that he had been stationed in at least six different countries, and visited many more by the looks of the pieces he had collected. The more items associated with a particular country or region signaled Jan that he had once been assigned there. There was only one small window in the room and it was covered with a simple piece of gauze. On the far wall there was a map of the world. Her focus was back on the desk again. None of the drawers were locked. Pulling out what looked to be the only address book she opened the cover and began photographing each page with the small digital camera. Later she would take the time to check out each name and number.

Besides general correspondence in the drawers, there seemed to be nothing more in it that she could use. Looking at the computer screen she discovered exactly what she expected, a password entry. She had only brought Ward's items that she knew how to use, and the encryption device was one of her favorites. Plugging it into the USB port on the machine she set it to run as she looked though the trash can. Moving on to the body of the desk itself she ran her fingers along the frame and the undersides of the drawers. She then ran her fingers on the underside and back of the shelves in the room. Ten minutes later she had the code and had sufficiently swept the room for any documents or evidence that might come in handy. As of yet she hadn't found anything that would be unusual in his office. Pulling out the encryption device she attached a small portable hard drive. At a rate even a computer geek would be envious of she set about copying the contents of the hard drive. When fifteen minutes was up she was ready to leave, and the room looked just as neat as when she had entered it. Closing the door there was no way anyone would be able to tell that she had been there.

After seeing his system, Jan knew that there was no reason to leave out the front door; she glanced out the back window. It was a stupid security risk not to have a camera on that area. She noticed that the fence around the perimeter of the backyard was lower in one area. The entire yard backed up to a park. There wasn't a door in the wall; that at least had been a smart move. Another quick look at the wall and Jan knew it was quite manageable to get over as long as no one was watching from the other side. Jan packed up her items and checked the secured black scarf she had around her head and face once more to make sure it hadn't slipped. Moving silently and effortlessly through the small red kitchen she could still smell the remnants of breakfast, eggs and bacon. Jan removed the blocking device from the alarm box and heard the warning beep begin. Before she counted to ten she was out the backdoor. It took her only another two minutes to get to the wall and vault over it and be on her way.

Once in the park she walked about six yards and undid her scarf and packed it back in the bag. She pulled out a tote bag and placed her black go bag inside of it. Taking out the camera she again looked more like a tourist than who she really was as she walked clear of the bushes. This time she cut through the park and made her way to a bus stop just outside the entrance. Then she sat and waited. Jan had gained access to many places before, some far more prestigious than the director's house. There was not a moment when her heartbeat had raced, or when she had been nervous. Nerves had never once entered into the equation as she calmly climbed on to the arriving bus with the information safely tucked away.

Back in the downtown area Jan grabbed herself a bite to eat and headed back to the hotel room to check just in case someone was trying to get a hold of the professor of architecture. Later, once she had gotten back to the safe house, she would study the information she had gotten. As she entered the hotel she picked up her messages at the desk and was happy to see that there had been one from Toby. It simply read, "Supper tonight. See you at seven if you can make it. I'll wait in the lobby." Jan walked back out of the hotel and carefully made her way to the safe house she had set up. Glancing at her watch she made a mental note of exactly how much time she had. Varying her route and doubling back on herself she would be sure that when she arrived no one had followed her there.

There were many people in the cafes and on the sidewalks in the older part of town. Jan didn't even notice the old colonial style buildings with their symmetrical shapes, colorful tiles and colonial structure. She walked to the center of the court area and over toward the corner apartment she had leased for the month. She let herself in and before she unpacked the bag she checked the place for bugs of any kind. Removing the hidden items in the room she hooked up the handheld and the keyboard that went with it. Soon she was immersed in the files she had downloaded. It was safe to assume that no one would suspect her here and that she could devote all of her effort to deciphering the information. Time passed without her realizing what was going on around her.

She was deep in thought unsure of just how long she had been at work when the phone rang. Grabbing at it she was unsure of whom to expect on the other end. Looking at the display before answering it, she noticed that it was a number she didn't recognize, a local number. It took a split second, and only a split second, for hope to well up inside her and then she got back to the business of taking care of things.

"Hello," she was cautious at first.

"Is Ms. Marple there?" Ward's voice was clear, strong, and warm in her ear. Jan also knew by the code, one they had set up long ago, that the line was not secure. She knew it didn't matter, as she released a breath, he was safe. She smiled and continued, keeping with the code.

"No she's not, may I take a message?" This let Ward know that she was able to talk on her side, and she was safe.

"I'm sorry I missed her. If I call back tomorrow afternoon at twelve, seven, or five would that help?" Ward was letting her know that he was going to be back in Lima in about twenty-four hours when she added up the numbers.

"I think she would be more than happy to get that call," Jan wanted to let Ward know that she was already in town, "She even has an appointment open around that time if you need to make one."

"Really?" It was half question and half surprise. Although Ward wasn't too surprised, he was beginning to wonder what she had been up to. "Did she leave any messages for me? I've been on the road for a while." He knew that he would have to wait to hear everything, but he couldn't help but fish for information anyway.

"Yes, just one," with that said, Jan knew that he would be coming in by bus, "She has redecorated the office and would love to have your opinion."

"That is so nice of her; I hope my friend is welcome?" Hearing her voice had done more to restore his health than the hot meal and good company of the scientists at the research station. He was beginning to feel that there wasn't anything they couldn't tackle.

"She would love to have him come to the office as soon as possible," Jan smiled as she said this knowing that they were both still alive and in decent shape. Ward picked up on her clues and knew that Jack's life was still in danger.

"It was good to talk with you and I hope to be speaking with Ms. Marple soon," Ward was leaning back now and smiling as well. Even though the distance didn't allow mind reading they knew each other well enough, and the sound of her voice plus the knowledge that she was already on the case made him both relax and smile. He didn't know if she had found out much, but he knew that some things would be dealt with by the time they got to Lima and they would be safe when they got back to town. He hung up the radiophone still smiling like a kid, unaware of Jack's gaze. Golightly watched him closely as he made the call, and didn't say anything. Even though Jack knew and trusted the scientists here well enough, he also recognized the fact that Ward had just been in the middle of an elaborate code with his contact. A contact that made him smile like a teenager. Most likely it had been set up years ago as smooth as it was.

"Let me show you some of the experiments they are working on here," he nudged Ward, then turned and in perfect Spanish let the others know where they were going. Ward knew this was to get them some time in order to compare notes about what he may have learned. They walked out of the office area that served both as lab and domestic quarters then toward some of the makeshift greenhouses off to the side. The jungle had hid them for the last few days, and they had been lucky it hadn't killed them. The sights and sounds were now no longer a thing to be wary of, but ones to enjoy as they walked along in silence.

"So?" Jack had been as patient as he could. He had a small limp as they walked along and Ward knew that there was some pain from the injury he had received, but he hadn't complained. Ward would check how well it was healing later when the others were asleep. Jack had already silently pointed out where the medical supplies were kept and his mind let Ward know that if some disappeared no one would say anything about it.

"She's in Lima and has a safe house set up for us. She will meet us at the bus station tomorrow although I couldn't tell her when we will be getting in exactly, but that won't be a problem for her," Ward took a breath as he looked at the exotic plants in the greenhouse. It was amazing the different varieties that existed in here that he had never seen, or imagined, before. One plant was flowering. The bud looked very similar to an orchid, but the smell instead of being sweet was way past rancid.

"The pollen has local medicinal purposes for migraines, the sap has other qualities. Too much and it could cause paralysis and even death," Jack filling in the answers to Ward's unasked questions.

"I can only guess, but I believe she has been in town to do a little investigating for our benefit. She hasn't cleared the Lima office yet," Ward fingered another plant that seemed to shimmer. "You're still dead to them and need to remain that way so she has set up a safe house for us."

"A genetically engineered hybrid of the last plant, more potent and this time deadly," he waited a moment, "I'm looking forward to meeting her." Ward turned and smiled back at Jack, knowing the loss he had felt in the last couple days would make it harder for him when he met Jan. Ward had suspected it, but the last few days had confirmed it; Jack had truly never gotten over losing his Susan.

The bare bulb of the desk lamp was the only thing that lit the room. Rob's head was propped precariously on his arm as he had fallen asleep at the computer terminal. It had been a long night. The stark nearly empty room had never inspired individuality. It didn't matter that he had fallen asleep at the computer terminal. Even if he had made it to the hard, small bed in the makeshift quarters he wouldn't have gotten any better sleep. The ringing of the phone beside the machine woke him. Glancing at his watch he saw that he would have to be back in his office in about an hour. He had found no matches for the picture yet and wished he could put it on the data base search instead of paging through the files himself. Without an official investigation, that wouldn't happen. The phone rang for a second time and Rob picked it up as he glanced at the small but serviceable kitchen area and empty coffee maker. He wished it were the kind of pot that had a timer in it to automatically turn on thinking that a cup of coffee would just hit the spot.

"Yes." It was the interdepartmental phone and anyone using this line would have to know who they were calling.

"I think you better get in here, we had a situation develop overnight," it was Gregg's voice on the other end. Although he had little respect for the current director he was still responsible to him. By Gregg's gravely harsh tone Rob was sure that he had spent as much time as he was going to be able to on Jan's problem for now. Hanging up the phone he switched off the computer, and thought a few choice words himself.

"Sorry Jan," he said to no one as he got up and slipped on his jacket giving one more wistful look towards the coffee maker before going out into the bullpen and to the director's office.

Chapter 9

Jan stretched and glanced at the time on the phone. She had known that it was getting close to time for her to pack up if she planned on meeting with Toby that night; she just hadn't known how close. Her mind didn't stop reviewing the information she had read so far as she packed up the items. Then she carefully removed the piece of wallboard that would hide everything. She had studied the director's address file over and over and had come up with no one she knew. All these contacts would have to be followed up on and checked out. It would be helpful to have two more sets of hands to help out, but she would have to make do right now with what she had. Once she found out the medical condition Jack and Ward were in she would know just how much help she could rely on. In his address file were a list of numbers under no names at all, and that wasn't too unusual. It would be a bit harder to track down the numbers and some he may have coded making it nearly impossible. Jan was frustrated that she hadn't gotten farther than this. In truth she hadn't expected to, she was dealing with professionals that had been in the job of covering up different aspects of their lives in many ways for many years. If she had found a blatant bit of information, she wouldn't have believed it anyway. What she had found was the normal clutter of an operative's life. What she hoped was that somewhere in that clutter she would be able to filter out a clue. She closed and locked the door to the apartment and turned to leave.

If Toby was hiding something it would be like many other jobs she had worked. He had worked his way up the ranks in the agency for one reason; he was good. He wouldn't keep important information like that at the office, and it was a possibility that it was only in his head, but unlikely. Running through different scenarios she decided on the one most likely to get her a few more answers.

By that time she was back at the hotel and in her room. Opening the small bag of clothes she had brought, she pulled out a black sleeveless dress with a mock turtleneck. Putting it on Jan tied a colorful scarf she had bought earlier in the day around her waist. Looking in the mirror she carefully reapplied the small amount of make-up she wore and pulled her hair up into a loose French knot with small tendrils falling and curling around her face and neck to soften the look.

Carefully she pulled up the edge of the skirt and attached the sheath for the knife she would normally carry when a gun was much too bulky. She didn't plan on letting him get close enough to discover the knife so she didn't worry too much about having it on. She would be worried if she didn't have her knife with her; she always carried her knife. Jan took one last look in the mirror. Her bodylines were soft, smooth, and the curves were just revealing enough to keep him staring. She decided that it was just the look she was going for. Carefully she locked up her room and made sure that the 'Do Not Disturb' sign got caught in the door. She could barely see the corner of it, but it would be enough to let her know if anyone was checking up on her and had her room searched. She had left nothing in the hotel room except the fact that she hadn't brought a lot of luggage with her.

Toby walked into the hotel lobby. Surrounded by the highly polished dark wood, antique red velvet chairs, and frosted glass fixtures he wondered what he was doing here. Was it really only yesterday that he had met Liz? He wasn't usually so easily drawn in by a woman, but she had seemed to be so helpless yet very knowledgeable. Maybe that was what had attracted him, that and he wasn't ashamed to say that he didn't mind looking at that body of hers. Right now he was so frustrated with the mission he was on, and today had been even worse. He thought about the day as he took a seat in a nearby chair to wait and see if Liz would show up. His fingers played absentmindedly with the paper lying on the small side table beside the chair as he thought.

Golightly's case had been closed for lack of evidence. All that time wasted and an agent, a friend, dead. Nathan Moore had called the office to say that he had wrapped up the investigation, found nothing, and was headed back to the Lima office. The office in Iquitos was generally manned most of the time with one case officer or a couple tactical people. Occasionally Toby had been stationed there to watch the rebel groups or drug traffickers. Golightly was the agent generally assigned to go up there when needed. No one knew the area like he did. That's how Toby had gotten to know him. Jack had had a special way, a connection, with the locals up there as well as with the jungle. Some would say that Golightly spent so much of his free time in the jungle that he was a part of it, or it was a part of him. Toby had heard about how Golightly's wife had died up there. He regretted now that he had never asked Jack about it. The thought of losing one so dear and then to continually return to the same location sent shivers up Toby's spine. If he ever found the right woman and then lost her tragically, the spot of her death would be the last place he would want to be. The way he had it figured though, was at least if Golightly had to die in his job, it was in the same place as his wife. It seemed to fit with the way of the world.

Something still felt wrong. The details and pictures he had seen of Jack's remains were close, but not accurate enough for Toby. He was a detail man and not all the details seemed to match. Then there was the fact that he hadn't been able to identify any of the pictures of the people Golightly had given him with already known crime rings or groups, they just weren't wanted by anyone big. Lastly there was no type of identity found in or around Golightly. Toby knew it was a silly feeling but a lot of times there was no place else to look for clues and gut instinct was the only way to solve a case.

His gut said there was something definitely wrong with this case even if the director had closed the files and told him to move on. It wasn't as if there weren't enough things to work on, but Toby had always hated leaving a 't' uncrossed. When Moore went back to work in the morning he would have to discuss his suspicions with him, he may have another take on it, something he had missed. He looked toward the stairs and saw Liz standing patiently near the check in desk watching him. He smiled. She looked wonderful and if he had any doubt about how he felt about hanging around her after the kiss last night, there was none now. Toby wondered how long she had been standing there, but it was only for a moment.

"Nice," was all Toby said as he stood up and walked toward her. Jan returned the smile. She had been standing there long enough to pick up on most of his thoughts about Golightly's mission. Having seen all the same information as he had she knew she still had one more piece to this puzzle; she knew he was still alive. "How long have you been standing there?"

"Not long. You looked like you were in deep thought and I didn't want to interrupt," Jan gave a little swish of the skirt and twirled it a bit, "I hope this is okay? The airlines lost my luggage and I had to make do with what I had and a few things I picked up today."

"You look great," and Toby again felt a bit unsure as to how she might feel about going out with him. At first, from her looks he would have guessed that she was trying for a bit of a fling. He had checked and it seemed like her story checked out; she had checked in with no luggage except a carry on yesterday. The airline losing her luggage did not fit the flirtatious scenario, it could be that was the only thing she had to wear, but glancing at her again he decided that she might just be in for a fling, and he was definitely up for that. He hated dating. He could track down, train and eliminate terrorists. He was good at divulging the secrets contained in any document. Suddenly ridding the world of gunrunners, drug dealers, and a multitude of other unseemly characters seemed easy compared to what he had to face now. He had to figure out what was in a woman's mind, and this continued to baffle him and could become his most dangerous assignment. "Shall we go?"

"I'd love to," said Jan. Toby held out his arm, just a bit, and Jan, or Liz as he knew her, looped her arm casually into his. She smiled knowing that Toby had never had a steady girlfriend and regarded dating as desirable as playing with a live grenade. She just needed to keep him on a string long enough to get the information she needed, and with a little tender loving care she would be able to do that. On the weekend there would be a reception for the new American Ambassador. It was an obligation to attend for all government workers, including and especially the official and unofficial CIA. She was going to convince him that he would want to take a date to make the evening nicer, and she was going to be that date.

"I've had such a good time today just looking around and doing a little shopping that I'm ready for anything," she let her words drop into the silence between them. The folk music that drifted in from the streets filled the empty space in the conversation. She felt Toby's mental pause and knew that the timing had been perfect, "It must be wonderful to work for a company that lets you live in such an historic and beautiful place," Jan knew it was The Company, as so many who worked for it called it, but he never caught her pun.

"It has its up and downs," being careful not to talk about what he actually did. Toby had planned to take her for a night of dinner and dancing, in that order, and then to see how the date progressed. Earlier that day, he had run a simple background check to see if a Liz Roland, or an Elizabeth, worked for the University of California in Berkley. It was an occupational hazard, being paranoid. She had checked out, so he hadn't bothered to dig any farther. Had he taken the time he might have discovered it was a fake file, planted in the system just recently, but most likely he never would have spent enough time on it to discover that. Jan had covered hers and other's trails like that for years, and although it was easier with a team to do it, one person was capable of planting the information properly especially for a newly appointed professor. Unless Toby made direct contact with the university, he'd never know, and he had no reason to call the university.

With Jan knowing that Ward was still alive, as well as Golightly, she let that mood lifter slip into the character she played. This made the night wonderful, having one less thing to worry about just for the evening, later would be another story. Tomorrow she would check the bus routes and times for the most logical arrival of the two. She had learned no more from Toby except that he couldn't find any logical reason either for Golightly, and Ward, to have been watching or following those men. Since she knew that Toby was going to discuss the matter with Moore, the only one she hadn't had a chance to do a read on or visit with, she would have to keep the affair going with Toby long enough to get her close to him. Flirting just enough, whenever possible, to keep him interested and dangling on her hook. More importantly, if there was a mole Toby was still in danger. The last thing she needed was another dead agent added to the list.

At the end of the evening Toby and Jan walked back toward the hotel. About a block or two before they got there Toby boldly took hold of her hand and Jan let him. He wasn't really falling for her, but he did like the way she looked in the dress. Jan had also discovered that he was more interested in coming up to her room than she hoped. This would truly go against all rules and regulations followed by most undercover agents, not only the agency's but also Jan's own rules. He wasn't planning on being in love, only lust. She had done her job well. Just before they got to the hotel, he stopped and leaned in to kiss her. Jan figuratively bit her tongue and allowed him the kiss, hoping that he didn't try to go too far with it. It was a job, an important job, and to do it right she might have to allow a few kisses, but no more. Both Jan and Ward adhered to that policy to keep them both sane, but she would have expected Ward to allow the same if the tables were turned.

"I'd invite you up, but there is no coffee or anything and it just might sound a little too," and Jan hesitated. It was all in how you played your part she thought to herself as she let her mind read his. Too forward and he might think something is up, and too standoffish and he might just fall off her hook.

"Not a problem," his mind betrayed him as his voice brushed her cheek. He was mentally berating himself for moving a bit too fast for her, "I understand. I won't push for anything more, but maybe you would honor me by meeting me for coffee tomorrow. No pressure," and she saw him grimace, just slightly, "Sorry, tomorrow's not good for me, I'm going to have a couple of projects due and I'll most likely be working late, too busy for coffee or pleasure," and he let his finger trace the curve of her cheek. He thought for a moment longer pulling back to look into her eyes, and he could see the saddened look on her face. Jan wasn't worried, as she had already seen what was in his mind. The sad look was easy to put on; she was worried about his safety in all this especially since she couldn't tell him about it. The projects he had to accomplish were to start creating new identities for most of the CIA agents in the area in case there had been any leaks. This was an emergency procedure that would probably not be needed. This would take a good couple of days at least, and would only be a stopgap procedure at most if they had been compromised. What it would accomplish would be to get the agents out of the country and harms way. Toby didn't have to do all the work, but he was still going to have to double check through all the papers to make sure that there weren't any mistakes. There was a fear that it might have been something simple that had cost Golightly his life.

"That's okay," she said with a touch of sadness, "I enjoyed seeing you again."

"I want to make it up to you," he was seeing his upper hand disappear and like a true power junkie he went after it again, "In a couple of days, if you're still here and would like to meet up again, there is this stuffy dinner to welcome the new American Ambassador to Peru. I have to attend this, and it will be the only free time I have between now and then.   It would be wonderful to have you accompany me if you think it could be something you could stomach?"

"Wow," Jan sounded impressed. She had already seen this event on the director's calendar and was playing Toby tonight so he would invite her to it. Her instincts had paid off, "I'm here for another three weeks on vacation and research. It sound's like an honor to be invited to this event; I would love to go with you. Will this be okay to wear?" Jan skipped what was in Toby's thoughts, as he looked her over. Some thoughts were just not for public or even semi-private display, "Maybe I should get something a little nicer."

"Well, don't get your hopes too high. There is lots of talk and polite party conversation, but it really could bore the socks off most people," like me was the only thing he omitted. Jan had been to events like this before. They went both ways, but a mind reader could usually find a way to entertain themselves during one of these functions. Most of what they learned was unmentionable, fun, but it did break up the monotony of the evening. This time though Jan would be looking for more than just brain clutter to interest her. "What you're wearing will be fine; it is semi-formal so black will work well, and I can't imagine you could look better in anything else," he left off another bit, and Jan ignored it.

"What time should I be ready?" Jan looked into Toby's eyes. Someday, maybe she would tell him that all this deception had all been necessary. After all he was basically a nice guy.

"Saturday at four. That will leave you the next two days on your own," making a sad face Toby started to think about leaning in for another kiss again and Jan quickly added to the conversation,

"That works out just perfectly," she clapped her hands together excitely, "I had planned to take a trip up to the ruins around Caracas and study the building styles of the Incas and this will give me time to do it without feeling like I'm being rude, you've been so nice," Toby smiled as Jan's compliment stroked his ego and her finger stroked his shoulder.

"Thank ya' ma'am," and they laughed as she walked him toward the door of the hotel. There was another goodnight kiss, this time a bit more insistent but Jan was soon up the stairs and out of Toby's sight. She had other things planned for the night.

It took her only seconds in the room to change into a completely black outfit, lightweight and soundless when she moved.

She had carefully chosen this room in the hotel for the location it was in. Silently she climbed out the window and down the vine that crawled up the wall. The whole process reminded her of old times at her apartment and times not so old. In the shadows she was invisible, and as she gracefully made her way down to the bottom she was also preparing her mind for the night ahead of her. It took only ten minutes to get to the safe house. Everything was as she left it. Letting herself in she quickly went to work. As she didn't expect to meet up with anyone she chose to take only the knife, and strapped on another one for a spare. She picked up the pack that she had readied for the evening expedition, and she was out the door. It took her only forty-five minutes to get to her first target.

Golightly lived in a two-story apartment building that was fairly new. It had a touch of the old world colonial style, but since it was located out in the suburbs it was made up mostly of concrete. His address had been on his files and Jan figured that if she were going to check out the department, she would need to check them all out, including him. Ward may know Jack and trust him, that should be good enough for her, but everything was in the details, and people changed. They had experienced all too much of that in their years of service. Jack's place was on the second floor and on the end. She had suspected that the department had already been through it. Jan tied the black scarf around her head and face making her very hard to be seen at all or be described later.

When Jan opened the door, she was right. She flashed the penlight around the room and caught glimpses of furniture, picture frames, and other personal items. Jan went straight for the corner desk where all his work sat. Quickly she paged through it and discovered what she had expected to find, nothing. She carefully put everything back and was scanning the rest of the desk quickly when the light caught the picture on the corner. It was a picture of him and a lovely lady, they looked so happy. The two in the picture were totally focused on each other and looked so in love. It reminded her of a picture that she had sitting on her dresser at home. Jan's heart felt very heavy as she remembered the rest of Golightly's file, and the fact that his wife had died because of what he did for a living. What really made her depressed was that what had happened to Jack could happen to Ward or her at any time. The only difference would be that they both understood what they had signed on for. It wouldn't, couldn't make the hurt any less.

Taking a few more minutes she searched the rest of the apartment for anything unusual. Finding nothing, Jan went to the bedroom and opened the closet. The least she could do was to get a couple changes of clothes for him. As she went to the door she stopped. By the front door there stood a small picture frame and Jan couldn't take her eyes off of it. It was a fascinating picture of his wife, and something in the eyes spoke to her. Under the picture was a half burnt piece of incense and Jan instinctively picked both up carefully wrapping it in a nearby cloth and placing it in a bag. Closing the door she made sure it was locked, and was on her way to the next place.

Moore's home was only twenty minutes away. He lived, by contrast, in a small but adequate home. From the information that Jan had found, the house had been built about sixty years ago. It was in a well-established neighborhood, and it was the smallest one on the block, nothing out of the ordinary. Jan looked at it, and as she hoped, it was completely dark. She again fastened her scarf on to keep others from seeing her. This time she went up to the house by the backdoor. She checked out the doors and windows. Up until now she hadn't found one person whom she would expect to sell out the department. She really hoped that she wouldn't find that here either. He was a sixteen year veteran at the job, brought in many bad guys and had helped to collect information that had been essential to the country. She didn't want it to be him, but she wasn't going to rule him out just because of his record. He had security, good security. It took her a couple minutes to shut it down. It wasn't standard issue. In general this would not cause suspicion, many agents set up their own systems, and he was just one of the many right now.

One hour later Jan locked the place back up and made sure that all the items were back in place, exactly where he had left them. She had found nothing, and she meant nothing. There was nothing personal in his place, no letters, notes, bills, or even scraps where he had jotted down stray thoughts or dentist appointments. She had been very thorough. This set off a couple of alarm bells, and even under her scarf, her face was furrowed. Jan went down the street committing every item to memory. It was the only place she had felt on edge, like her life may be in danger if she wasn't careful. Details, sometimes it was all that kept some people alive. She didn't relax until she got into the safe house. In the side room she carefully set up Jack's things making sure that the picture and stick were placed with respect. She then tacked up the extra piece of cloth she had purchased yesterday for the room divider. The apartment would easily sleep four but the privacy was pretty poor as there were no doors to speak of outside of the main entrance into the apartment.

Storing her pack she made her way back to the hotel and went again to the back of the hotel. Her eyes checked out the area carefully as she stood still. Even her breathing seemed nonexistent. She needed to make an appearance at staying here until tomorrow morning and when the coast was clear she climbed back up the trellis and into her room. There didn't seem to be any messages for her left at the door, and no one had been in the room. Toby didn't know it but he had left her the perfect opening. When he said he couldn't see her for a couple days she took the opportunity to suggest that she may be out of town on a ruins trip. This way he wouldn't look for her at the hotel and she could stay at the safe house with them. Jan stripped off her outfit and got in a warm shower letting the warm water wash over her and relax each tired muscle.

Slipping on a tee shirt and shorts she went through her tai chi routine and then crawled into bed for a good rest. In the morning she would again go through the tai chi routine to make sure she was ready for anything that may come up. Too many leads were slipping away, and she knew that soon they would find the one they needed if they kept trying, if they were fast enough. In her head she made a list of things that needed to be done in the morning. Topping the list was to book Liz on a two-day trip to the Inca cities. The details needed to be attended to or it would all fall apart. With all these thoughts pouring through her head, it was the last thought though, as she fell asleep, that brought the smile to her face. With any luck, tomorrow night she would not be sleeping alone.

Chapter 10

"Damn. Damn. Damn," was all Rob could say as he pushed his hand through his hair. He watched the tow truck pull the beaten and battered remains of the Explorer into the lab area in the basement where the PED was housed. Earlier that day he had had no clue as to why the director called him into his office. It wasn't until Gregg slid the file across the desk that Rob had felt the cold chill that raised every hair on the back of his neck. He had had plenty of time now to go through it in his mind while he waited for the garage doors to open, only this time replaying the whole conversation in his head.

"Do you know anything about this?" and the file came flying at him from across the desk. When he looked down the name on the top of the file was unmistakable, Janice Tara. Rob knew now that Gregg had more information at this point than he did. Rob decided to play it safe. He didn't know where the attack was going to come from. He had blocked his thoughts and he had a reasonable excuse for being off task last night. He had worked three weeks straight and it was time he took some comp time for it. It had been almost too easy to get the day off so he could help her. Now it might prove to be a problem.

"She was my partner, and a friend. Haven't heard from her in a while, not since she saved my ass when the department was ready to let it rot in that old deserted mine" Rob spoke defiantly as he looked Gregg right in the eyes. "What's up now?"

"Seems that we got a call about a white Explorer, or what was left of one, that was found in the parking lot of Jan's old apartment; or current one. The Explorer has been trashed. The pictures are inside if you want to see them. When the cops did a preliminary print search hers came up. Blew all the whistles here," Jan had cleaned the vehicle before hand but with Bobby and his men watching there was no way to wipe it down when they got to the apartment. Rob wondered if Jan had suspected that Bobby would trash the Explorer. Somehow he didn't put it past Bobby to make his point violently. Guess she had just assumed that the vehicle wouldn't be left in any condition to get a print from.

"And this is our or my problem how?" Rob opened the folder and looked at the pictures. By the looks of things the only place they may have been able to take a print at all was from the hood, the rest of the vehicle was mutilated and nearly unrecognizable. Ward was going to kill him; he loved that car.

"I still want them," was all he said at first. "They are also still wanted by this department among others. If they are in town they are now without transportation for a bit and it should be easier to track them down," he said sternly to clarify the department's position on the matter.

"I thought I would be the last one you would trust with this?" Rob was looking at him but couldn't tell what he had planned.

"You'd think, but you were burned by both of them and I just thought you might like to bring her in yourself," he waited for the reaction on Rob's face. There was no reason for Gregg to believe that Rob had heard from either one of them since that time in the mine. Rob couldn't lie, he'd love to be able to turn the clock back to where they had been years before, but that could never happen he had discovered that the other day. Gregg's face began to smile as he saw the understanding on Rob's face, "I need you to pose as a Fed and go down and collect it from the police. Take Pat along with you for support."

"For who, you or me?" Rob waited only a second before he continued, "On my way sir," and as Rob stood up he knew that Pat was there to make sure he kept the department first, and his feelings last. Pat had never asked any questions of him the last year, and she seemed to have stayed to herself. Something had changed over the year and as much as he hated to admit it, she was comforting to have around sometimes.

Now he stood in the PED garage. All had gone smooth, almost too smooth, but Rob was used to that part of it. He had presented the ID card and filled out some paper work and the car was transferred to them. The lab boys would pick apart what was left of the vehicle, and they would find nothing. Jan had assured him that she had removed anything and everything before she had left.

Pat had gone back up to start on the paperwork and Rob was watching them pull it in. As a piece of the bumper fell off Rob got an idea. He had placed the picture of Bobby's contact in the pocket of his jacket. He walked over to the bumper and carefully wiped the prints from the picture. Taking out a hanky he picked up the bumper and placed the picture inside the metal. When they walked around to him Rob handed them the bumper and gave them a wave as he walked to the stairs. If he was going to hunt down Jan, then he guessed the department could help them out a bit and hunt down who she was looking for.

Jan had been up since the crack of dawn and had gotten all the arrangements made for the trip and had even packed a small bag leaving only what she could afford to lose in the room. Taking the next few minutes she centered herself and stood motionless readying herself for the tai chi routine. Twenty minutes later she ended the routine the same way she began it, standing still and calm.

At nine thirty Jan grabbed her bag and was out the door. The trip left promptly at ten, or ten fifteen from the bus station. She walked over to the station carefully watching for a tail, but not really expecting one. She spotted none when she stopped to pick up a paper, and then a snack. Once at the station she asked in perfect Spanish about the arrival times for buses this afternoon. The first one to arrive from the north was only in at two, and then at three, three thirty, four fifteen and four thirty. A couple arrived right around five and again at five thirty. Jan thanked the man and slipped into the crowd. The rush time crowd covered her making her nearly invisible to anyone who might be watching. Jan pulled the colorful scarf from her bag and knotted it around her head in normal fashion allowing her to blend in just a bit more. As she moved through and around more of the people she took off the jacket she had on and placed it in the bag revealing a short-sleeved dress. Wrapping the skirt around her legs she quickly slipped the pant legs under the hemline. Letting her shoulders slump made her look a couple inches shorter as she took out the locally made tote bag and transferred everything else inside of it. When she was sure of her transformation and relatively sure that no one was watching she headed back to the safe house to do some research before her company arrived.

Promptly at one thirty she arrived back at the station looking more like a mountain native ready to sell their baskets to anyone who would buy them. She had bought about a half dozen of them before she had left the station this morning making sure she paid them a good price for each basket. Lots of locals from the mountains came into the city to try and make a living, some did and some didn't, but it was a good cover. She made herself comfortable in a small corner by another woman and waited. She sold one of her baskets to a gentleman from England and haggled with at least three others while she waited patiently for Ward's arrival. With her mind wide open she continued to watch the areas around her. Ward had arranged for them to meet here in the afternoon, but he may not arrive by bus at all, it was just a bet. It was four thirty when she felt that familiar warm feeling drift into her head. Her eyes began to scan the area until she found the bus where it was coming from. Before they could even lock eyes, their minds were wrapped around each other enjoying what they had missed for days. They weren't exchanging information or catching up on the job, they were just enjoying the feel of each other for a moment before they would have to enter into reality again.

Ward and Jack had sat in different places on the bus. As it pulled into the station Ward started to look for Jan's mind. He had patiently waited as they traveled from the science station into Lima. They had ridden out in the helicopter with the other scientists and caught a small flight into a neighboring city. Then they took the bus into Lima. It seemed a very round about way to get here, but when someone was trying to kill them, they had to try to do their best to stay out of the way and keep their heads down. Her mind seeped into his and it felt good to be connected again and he couldn't help but smile a little. Wherever he was physically it didn't matter, he was now home.

Jan got up and gave the rest of her baskets to the lady beside her. She gave Jan a puzzled look and Jan just smiled and walked away before she could say anything. Watching the people get off the bus she let her eyes settle on the man she called husband. Her reflex thought was, *He looks so good*, and she quickly got a response to her thought.

You're looking pretty good too, and that was the end of the small talk. Jan quickly gave Ward the layout of the town and the location of the safe house. It took only seconds and as she finished giving Ward the information she saw Jack get off the bus and turn to wait beside Ward for the luggage that was being unloaded from the bus. She knew that neither one had luggage but it was a way for her to give the location of the safe house to Jack. Making her way into the crowd of passengers she moved toward Jack. Ward stuck out his foot, on purpose and on cue. Jan moved toward it and tripped falling into Jack and momentarily touching him. Pardoning herself in Spanish she again made her way out of the crowd and then disappeared from his sight, but not quite from Ward's mind. She left him with an explicit parting thought that made him grin before she left the area.

"Get anything?" Jack didn't look at Ward as he talked. He was moving slowly to the back of the crowd following Ward's lead. Jack felt like a target out in the open and was hoping that Jan was here somewhere. With Ward's skill he should be able to pick her right out of the crowd.

"Check your pocket, and I'll see you there," with that said Ward was gone. He planned on taking the route she had showed him in her mind. All the pain and bruises seemed to vanish when he thought that he would see her soon, and he moved with a speed and agility he didn't know was still in him.

Jack put his hand in his back pockets and found nothing. Strange for Ward to tell him something that wasn't true. He put his hand in his front pocket and found a small folded piece of paper. Opening it up he found an address and a set of directions to what he could only assume was the safe house. "Holy cow," he let the words slip out and even though they weren't loud enough for anyone to hear them he still checked to see if anyone had. He moved in the opposite direction that Ward had and with a small smile he started to make his way to the apartment complex he knew and had passed by a couple of times when he was in need of a long walk in the center of the city. Pulling the cap farther down on his head he recalled the location of the place and he was pleased. He knew it well and it wouldn't be a place they, or anyone else, would be looked for. It housed mostly older folks that couldn't afford to live anywhere else, a couple druggies that weren't worth the police's attention, and it even housed some homeless under the eves and in the courtyard.

Jan had made it back to the safe house about ten minutes before everyone else. She heard the lock on the door turn. Having only enough time to take off the clothes she was wearing as a disguise she was standing in her black bike shorts and sports bra. Jan thought about putting on a tee shirt quickly and got the returning thoughts from the man at the door just as the lock clicked free.

Don't you dare. She waited and watched Ward walk through the door. His face covered with five days of beard growth and his hair looking a little wild. His eyes held hers and the depths of them seemed to swallow her up. Closing and locking the door quickly behind him he said nothing as he dropped his bag and walked up to her. They let their bodies slam together intensely like their minds had already entangled. It was a while before he stopped kissing and touching her and her him. Slowly they released each other and he let his eyes travel up and down her body and pulling her close he whispered in her ear.

"Babs you smell wonderful," and his lips brushed over her ear as his arms pulled her even closer to him.

"Hi Trouble," was all she could muster. Time seemed to stand still and all the troubles vanished. Jan knew that Ward had been injured; she had read that in his mind at the bus station. Later she would take inventory of all his wounds and check them out personally. She smiled at the thought of this and knew that all the injuries were healing. She felt his question and answered it before he asked it, "About five more minutes before he gets here," she answered breathlessly.

"Not enough time," and he kissed her passionately and then let her go. Jan slipped into a shirt just in time to hear the lock on the door being undone again. Ward and Jan exchanged looks and moved away from the door's line of sight. The door slowly opened again and Jack slipped in silently. Jan noticed that he and Ward were about of the same build. She guessed that in some ways they all had the same general characteristics. Both men were in good physical and mental shape, and made it a point to stay that way. There was a look in the eyes she thought, something that outsiders would never understand. It had to do with all they had seen, done, and knew. Jack was definitely a few inches taller than Ward and he was partly Native American. His file had said all this, but now she was able to finally put all the information she had read to a face and a man. His eyes were deep and dark brown and she could see by his thoughts how passionate a man he was. He was zealous about everything he did and believed in. It was no wonder Ward hadn't questioned his reasons and rushed off to help him when he had called.

"Welcome to the Ritz," Ward stated first, and smiled

lopsidedly as he stepped back into Jack's line of sight.   Jan had gathered that Jack knew more about their relationship than most and it was confirmed with Ward's next words, "I'd like you to meet the Missus. Jan this is Jack, Jack Jan," this time it was Jan's turn to step back out into the line of sight.   Jack extended his hand and Jan shook it.   Jack held up the piece of paper and looked at the both of them in turn with one eyebrow raised.

Jack's first impression of Jan was favorable.   She was above average height, and a very nice weight and shape.   It looked as if she took her physical fitness as serious as Ward did.   Her hair was brown, simply brown, and she would easily blend in anywhere she would choose to, which was how he had missed her.   Her grip was strong enough, and her eyes were clear and deep.   A solid character and one he knew was well suited to Ward just by the look on her face.   He also got another hunch as he glanced at the two of them.   He had come in the middle of something, and the thought that he should have taken a bit longer passed through his mind.

"Glad you're here safe and not still wandering around out there," Jan had picked up on the last thought and wanted to take the uneasy feeling out of the air.   They were on a mission and she would have plenty of time with Ward later.   It wouldn't be good to have him out of their sight just yet.   With his mind at ease and the introductions over, Jack got straight to business.

"Just how did you get this in my pocket?" his voice held just a touch of anger at himself and one of amazement for her.

"I told you she was good," Ward paused before he continued, "just not how good," and Ward smiled.   Years ago Jan may have blushed at that comment and the implications of it, but instead she just flashed Ward a mischievous smiled.

"I had a little help," and she shrugged looking back at Jack, "I couldn't take a chance on the back pockets getting picked and you losing the address so I chose the front pocket, and if you know what you're doing it's easy," and in her head she thought, *also, if you have enough practice.*   The last comment was for Ward's benefit and she saw him cough to cover up an involuntary laugh.

"So, do you still work for us, or are you independent like Ward?"   Jack really wanted to know just what Jan's talents were.   Ward had hinted, but never let on.   Basics were good to know but he was putting his life in their hands.   Jack could sense that they were continually in contact with their minds, exhausting for some, but right now it looked as if it were both healing and re-energizing. He had tried out for the PED's at one time and wasn't a good candidate for completing the mind reader training. He was talented at reading people's emotions, empathic, but they had been unable to develop anything else in him. He chose to stay with the CIA at that point instead of signing on to be a handling agent with them. The rules were a bit strict he had thought if all he was going to be was a handler. It appeared though as if Jan had worked for the PED in some capacity. Somehow they had gotten past that hurdle and if they were going to be working together then he wanted a bit more information.

"Quick bio, I'm retired PED. Yes I read minds, and my status with the PED is about the same as Ward's," Jack turned back to Ward. She walked over and pulled out the equipment she had stored in the place, "I've trained with most of the special forces in some way or other," and she paused, "and excelled."

"You certainly know how to pick them," and Jack sat down on the old threadbare couch.

"Told you she knew her stuff," Ward followed suit as well. Jan set the technical equipment on the small and wobbly table in the center of the room, and then sat down. It was time to get down to business.

"What happened?" Jan leaned back and waited for one of them to start.

"You have read all the reports and we were able to read them when we got to the science station," and Jan nodded an affirmative, "After the attack we made our way through the jungle to a research station that Jack knows. I discovered some interesting information and it's on the hard drive that I brought with me. Phone's a goner, and so I will need a new one. I think I can find one here that will do and I'll program it when we get it," Ward's eyes stayed on Jan. He was seeing something in her mind, but she wasn't quite letting him near it. It was something that didn't have to do with what they were talking about.

"They tracked us into the jungle for a while and then decided that nature would take care of us. We avoided the nearest towns as we have both come to the conclusion that there is a mole loose somewhere," Jack confirmed her suspicions.

"I've come to the same conclusion; I'm just having trouble finding him. So far I have checked out the director and downloaded his home files on the portable. Been through about half and need to start checking the phone numbers and addresses of the people he had listed. Made a trip to the office," she felt Ward's mind tighten, "Don't worry, I sat outside and read them as they came out. Not a soul there I would consider a risk, even the director seems to be proving clean. Made contact with Toby and am currently dating him so that I can get closer to the last one I need to read, Nathan Moore. He's the one that was sent up to Iquitos, and the one that is the most likely suspect right now," Jack shot a look at Ward and saw nothing there but his complete trust. They had moved out of the lover's role and back into work mode. They made a good team. Jack's admiration for both increased as a smile teased at the corners of his lips, "On Saturday I have been invited to the Ambassador's welcoming party by Toby and that should allow me to read Nathan Moore and anyone I haven't had a chance to.

"When I went into Moore's house I got the impression that no one lived there," she continued, "All the dishes in place and matching with a thin layer of dust. Nothing in the desk, including things that should be there, as in any other house."

"You're dating Toby?" Jack was half amazed and half bewildered.

"Yes," Jan directed his gaze at him.

"He doesn't date," Jack looked back at Jan and then at Ward, "He. . ."

"I know," was all she had to say.

"You're right, you didn't tell me how good," and his voice was more serious.

"How did you get into the director's house?" Ward knew about the security systems that were installed in the director's homes and even for some of the operatives at times. He had seen how easy it had been in her mind and he was a bit worried, for other reasons, at how she had gotten in.

"Bill brought me a bag on his way through Lima, courtesy of Rob," Jan turned and looked straight at Ward and she saw the hint of anger in his eyes and the set of his jaw line. "Don't worry, it's over. He knows I'm not going back to the PED. He just didn't want me to go empty handed," and with that Jan looked back at the table and started to hook items together including the security download device. If Jack had not been watching he would have missed the slight clues that had been passed between the two. Even if they had thought that it wasn't perceivable, Jack knew that a sore point had just surfaced. Jan's phone lay on the table beside all the equipment. When it beeped to signal a text message Ward looked at her. Without saying a word Jan picked up the phone and tossed it to Ward. She had an idea who the message was from, but not what it said. The sheer act of letting him retrieve it eased the tension and went a long way to rebuilding the trust.

"So you're still in touch with the department?" Jack let Ward read the message, and directed his question to Jan.

"Not any more than Ward is. We both have our contacts, some the same. His network is more developed than mine. He has been doing this longer than I have, and they are trustworthy," Jan felt Ward tense and it didn't dissipate this time. Jack saw the slight change of Jan's expression and they both turned to look at Ward. His face was hard, his brow knitted in anger and his jaw set. He looked at Jan and ignored the fact that Jack was even in the room.

"When in hell were you going to tell me?" His tone was restrained, but his voice was low, deep and dangerous. Jan knew he was speaking only to her, and with a glimpse in his mind she knew about what.

"I thought the situation was under control for the moment. Until we went back it seemed to be a waste of time to deal with it. What's happened?" Jan had been able to see that the message on the phone was from Bobby, but not what was in it. Ward pitched the phone back at her. Jan picked it up and began to read the message.

"Hey Doll, did you get my message? Next time instead of the Explorer it will be one of you," Jan felt cold inside, "Stay out of my business or die trying to find out. This time I won't miss." That was the end of the message, but it was enough. She realized that she had guessed wrong at the identity of the caller.

"Start explaining Babs," Ward's arms rested on his knees, but he was in a fighting mood. His anger was misplaced. Jan knew he was mad at her, but that wasn't all he was mad at. He was mad at the years he felt he had been taken in by Bobby, by the loss of trust. Ward had only let very few people in his life. Bobby was the one person that Ward had felt connected to as family, and Bobby was the one that could and would come after them just for the sport of it. Even though Ward had built new friendships, and connections it still bothered him to no end. Jack started to get up and without looking both Ward and Jan issued a command they expected to be followed.

"Sit," without any sound, Jack sat back down on the couch and tried his best to mold himself into the furniture.

"Short story, he was in Rosarito," when Jack heard that he filed the information away. "We accidentally read each other. He was purchasing information from an unknown source. Rob is checking on that for me now as I got a picture of the man with him. I needed him to believe I was, or we were following him," Jan met Ward's gaze with steely force. Continuing the thought in her head, Ward leaned back and ran his fingers through his hair. Jan's tone softened. "Rob agreed to play you at the border so that the illusion would work. The last time I saw the Explorer it was safely in the parking lot of my old place," Jan saw Ward burrow his gaze back into her, "Don't go there, I'm not pleased with that either."

Even though they were talking in half sentences at times Jack caught most of the story. There were other players in this now, most likely the department contact from the tension he felt at the beginning, and someone else. He sat still, so still that they almost forgot he was in the room with them. Ward let his head drop back against the frayed cushion, and looked at the ceiling letting out a long sigh. He was impressed that Jan had carried it off. The last time she had come up against Bobby she had come out on the worse side, he had almost lost her then. It had been fear that had sparked his anger. From the look of the message, Bobby believed her story. At this point he needed to step back emotionally from the situation and learn a bit more. A new concern entered his mind.

"I really liked that car," he paused, "What about Rob?" Ward was more businesslike, the emotions beginning to drain away.

"Haven't heard from him, but from the tone of the message Rob wasn't anywhere near the vehicle. As I figure it, we will have to deal with him only if we choose to. I was worried about the information he was buying, but with Rob on it that may be settled without us, if he's not already sweating bullets about the Explorer. What we have to do now is worry about who tried to kill Jack, and to smoke out the mole," Ward knew she was right, and even had admiration for her ability to adjust and then refocus on the goal. She had done her job well, and therefore their place, their home, was still safe, as were the Garcias. As the thought of the Garcias entered into his mind she allayed his fears and he released the air in his lungs, "I told Manuel to keep an eye out. Nothing more. Business as usual."

"Okay, back to the business at hand," Ward moved over to the handheld hook up on the table. As his fingers touched the keypad that was connected to it he began to refocus. Jack got up and went over to the bag to retrieve the hard drive. Jan saw him slightly favor one side as he handed the drive to Ward.

"You all right?" She pointed to the spot that Ward had glued closed.

"It's nothing. The new dressing is a bit tight," and he moved away. He was amazed at how easily she had picked up the location of the wound. Since Ward left the department, Jack hadn't requested to work with the PED, and had forgotten just how easily a reader could pick up on different items, even if you were blocking, and he was.

"It's a knack she has," Ward stated the obvious without looking up from the small screen.

"I set up a space for you behind the curtain over there. Got you a couple changes of clothes as well," Jan could see in his mind that it didn't surprise him that she had checked out his place as well. Jack would have been worried if she hadn't. Right now it was their job to suspect everyone until proven otherwise. He was just glad that he had checked out in her mind. "You saw something, heard something, or were somewhere you shouldn't be. And as you know, that made you a target."

"I have been racking my brain to figure that out," he paused. "By the way, how many places have you let yourself into?" Jack looked at her as he sat down beside Ward to see what was coming up on the screens.

"Only three and Moore's place was the most interesting," they both stopped and looked at her, "Like I said, Moore's place was clean as a whistle, nothing that would cause one iota of suspicion. It was as if it he had purposely set every thing in place. No papers lying about, nothing that was personal. It was cold, no emotion, no wrinkles. Way too clean," Jan smiled deviously, "I'm looking forward to meeting him on Saturday."

The rest of the evening they worked on deciphering, decoding, and comparing notes. All discussions were confined to business, all concentration devoted to the mission. Ward's instincts matched what Jan had pulled off of the data bases she was on before she came down. None of the information that they had though matched the information on the download of the director's drive in essence clearing him of any suspicions so far. She had made a trip out to get food, nothing fancy but it kept them going. They had each been through about four cokes apiece. It was late when they all decided to call it a night. Jack stood up and even if he showed no discomfort Jan could feel it in her mind. She glanced at Ward and he gave a slight wave of his hand, and she let it drop.

"Night," was all he said as he went over to the place she had carved out for him. It had been half dining room and half kitchen area. Now it was the only place he had to recuperate. He pushed the curtain aside and saw a small but adequate bed turned down and ready for him. His clothes had been neatly stacked up beside his bed and on the other side sat the picture and smudge stick. He stopped for a moment, and turned to look back at Jan. His face looked confused, and there was a bit of sadness in his eyes. It was a look that she had seen on too many faces over the years. "How?" was all he said and then he turned back toward his area and disappeared behind the curtain not waiting for an answer. Dealing with one reader had been hard enough at times, but two was proving to be a very complicated mixture. He had never known that readers were so different in their skills as well as their training. It shocked Jack for a second how naive it would be to assume that they were all the same. Ward looked at Jan and smiled. The word 'thanks' wasn't enough and he knew it. He got up, gave Jan a peck on the top of her head and walked to the small bedroom she had kept for them. Jan gave him a few minutes head start closing up her computer links and stowing the gear.

When she walked into the bedroom, Ward was stretched out on the bed still dressed. She let the curtain that closed off the doorframe drop behind her, and leaned up against the frame. It would have been tempting to use her mind to communicate but then it was much more tempting to tease with it as she spoke.

"I thought you were going to check me out to make sure I was okay?" Ward's hands were behind his head, his body exposed, and his smile stretching from ear to ear. The things she was thinking only added to his smile.

"I was thinking you might need a little exercise as well," Jan started to move slowly to the bed.

"Humm," and he rolled his eyes back to think, "Might not hurt to do a few push-ups."

As she started to unbutton his shirt and expose his chest, she started to see all the new bruises and scratches. Even though the scratches had started to heal and the bruises were large yellowing blobs that covered one whole side of his chest, she quickly put those thoughts out of her mind and moved on to something a lot more fun.

Chapter 11

What he had just read wasn't good. There was no way to spin it to even make it sound good. He sat at his desk and reread the file that had just come in. All Rob could do was shake his head. He had planted the evidence and now they were in deeper than even he had planned. If what he read was correct, then their skills were needed more than the department would ever want to accept. It was good that they were outsiders on this one, playing by any rules in this game could only get you dead. He didn't know who he would rather face, Gregg, Jan, or Ward. Rob picked up his cell and typed in the text message. It was simple and short. Nothing more than what needed to be said and he hit send.

Getting up from his chair he went toward the elevator. Looking at his watch it was just past seven in the morning, and he had been working since four. It was time for breakfast and coffee, lots of coffee. Tony was manning the entrance when he walked out and Rob gave him a wave as he pushed the elevator button. When the elevator doors opened he could see Pat standing just inside the elevator. When Rob got on Pat stayed on and rode the elevator down again. Rob was careful to guard his thoughts this time. One slip up with her and you could lose your shirt as they said in poker.

"You need to tell them they are in too deep on this one," Pat looked straight ahead. "They aren't working with us anymore and they don't have any protection, or back up." Rob said nothing. As far as he could tell she hadn't been in his thoughts, but who really knew. "I know they are out there working on something, but no one is going to back up what they do. They can serve time, lots of time." Rob continued to watch the floors count down. "Rob?"

"I heard you. But I think you may have a few facts wrong," the doors opened and he stepped out just clear of the doors. He wasn't out far enough to allow Pat to follow, and she graciously allowed the doors to close and go back up. Rob walked out of the parking garage and onto the street. He smiled as the sun hit his face. Whatever information Pat got from him, if any, had been pretty accurate, but it didn't seem like she was going to pass it on to anybody. At least not yet and that may be something worth remembering.

She woke to the smell of coffee and a warm body next to her. Jan could tell he had been awake for the last ten minutes and had just been staring at her. She let her finger trace the edge of the rather large bruise on his chest. They stayed that way for another five minutes, just enjoying the warmth of each other. On a mission these moments were rare, and precious.

"I think he's beat us to the coffee. Should we get moving?" Jan turned her face upwards to look into Ward's eyes. Ward bent toward her and kissed her. It was filled with desire as his lips brushed hers, and then just as quick he was up. There was too much to do for them to allow themselves to be caught up in each other again. They both knew that.

"The coffee's for us, he never touches the stuff," Ward slipped into a tee shirt and black jeans. Jan lay quietly on the bed and watched. Seconds later Ward tossed her some clothes. "Come on sleepy. We have work to do."

Once out in the grimy little room that housed all the equipment, Ward saw that Jack was about to begin his sunrise ritual. He sat down beside him. In this trip he had realized that not all the departments were like the one he had been connected to, and not all the people outside his inner circle harbored the potential to go bad. Jan had helped him grow a long way, and to heal. He had begun to realize that over the years he had automatically distrusted anybody in the business. As the meditation and chanting soothed his mind and body he began to see, and to let go of the past permanently. By the time Jan emerged from the doorway of the small bedroom both of the men were centered and in the middle of the meditative chant. Jan could feel the calm and the strength it brought to both of them and was very careful not to disturb them. Although it didn't surprise her that he held to some of his native customs, it did surprise her to feel the changes happening in Ward. She sipped at her coffee and then found a small corner in which to meditate herself. She didn't want to be the only one not centered today. For the next three quarters of an hour the three went silently through their morning routines of meditation, prayer, and rigorous exercise. By the time they were finished they were ready for breakfast, and another more deadly ritual. It was time to prepare the equipment and clean the weapons.

Ward looked in the small refrigerator. It smelled like it had been used to store rotting meat in it. Nothing but cool drinks were safe in the refrigerator because of this. Jan walked into the alcove and pulled open the cupboard door. All that was in there were meager rations, that was for sure, and Ward frowned. There were a couple boxes of cereal, cans of soup and various canned meats, dried fruits, and nuts. Ward knew that this was good enough to sustain them, but he couldn't resist the thought that a good steak would be nice.

"In your dreams Trouble," she had called him Trouble early on in their relationship for various reasons, and the name fit. Jan had easily picked up on his thoughts and commented on them. Jack watched them work together, both speaking and reading each other to the point that there was no way to follow a conversation between them at all. "Make due till we get a chance."

"Good thing I never married you because of your cooking ability," and Ward continued the thought of why he did marry her in his head. Fifteen minutes later after they each grabbed something to eat, they were all back at the computers and paging through numbers and contacts. Jack was working on the files downloaded from the director's computer. If Jack were to look through those files it might be a way for him to trigger a memory that could explain the reason he was a perceived threat. An hour and a half later they were all rubbing their heads and finding nothing. When the phone signaled another text message Jan scooped it up and opened the file. Ward didn't move but she could feel him in her thoughts, waiting to see just what the new message would say. Both were surprised to discover that the message was not from Bobby but from Rob.

"Want to clue me in?" Jack interrupted their thoughts, knowing that he had been left out of the loop.

"It's from our department contact. It says, 'Hope you found what you're looking for. I found out something as well. You're not going to like it, so call me. R' and I don't think he means the Explorer," Jan had switched the message off and started to dial the number. No one said anything in the room. They all sat and waited to hear what was happening. It took a little time for the connection to go through and in that time Jan stared at the wall noticing that the paint had started to peel. The paint used in these places probably contained lead. The wall paper that only half existed on some walls must have been put up at the time of the building's construction and over the years had worn off. The ceiling had water marks on it in many places, some very suspect of what the marks may be. Suddenly the phone came to life in her ear and she could hear the ringing on the other side. Jan was sure that the phone was not really ringing on the other side, but vibrating. Rob was too smart to get caught in direct communication with her.

"Yes," was all he said.

"'Lo Old Man," Jan tried to keep the mood light. "Where are you?"

"I'm at a coffee shop so it's safe to talk. Been waiting on your call," Rob paused for only a second, "I've got a couple of pieces of news for you and I'm hoping you have some good news for me."

"Affirmative on the second. Got the packages sitting right here. All in one piece, mostly, but I have heard that the Explorer is not anymore," Jan paused, and Rob suspected that she had heard from Bobby.

"That's the second piece of news I have for you. The first is that we have found the information that you were looking for," nothing got past Jan and she latched on to the 'we' in the sentence.

"What do you mean 'we'?" The words came out harsher than she had planned and Ward was now locked solidly in her head. She put up a few barriers, but to try and keep him out would only anger him more than he was already at this point.

"Hold on. I planted the pic in what was left of the Explorer. He did a nice job on it by the way, but the police were still able to pull a print off of it somewhere, and it rang bells here. If you can believe it, I was put on the case to find the owners. He's got the crazy idea that I might enjoy getting even," as Rob took a breath, Ward started to smile. That would be Gregg's way of thinking. Somewhere deep down Rob understood why he had left to begin with. After Bobby had used Rob and left him for dead, he was sure that Rob understood. "I wasn't getting anywhere with the pic and I saw an opportunity to use the photo recognition software instead of the time consuming search I was doing. I just took it," there was a sigh, "Let the man know if he isn't climbing through your head right now that I'm sorry about the

Explorer."

"He knows. So, what's the worst?" Jan sat looking at no one. Knowing there had to be more. She had picked up a pencil and was waiting to scribble down anything of interest.

"The pic is of a scientist who works for a company routinely contracted by the government, MedLab Tech. They are specialists in the biotech field. All around a bad situation," Rob waited for a second. He let the information soak in with the both of them. He knew that Ward was in the room and if he was in the room he was listening in on their conversation through Jan. The implications of someone selling their modified genes to the highest bidder in the terrorist world were scary. He wasn't quite sure how to phrase the next part, "Problem is you two are now implicated, funny huh?" Rob continued after the uneasy pause in the conversation, "By the way, Pat says you need to turn it over and stay out of it." He rubbed his head as he waited for a response from Jan, knowing that this wouldn't be good. He wished he could see either of them to try and gage their reaction.

"Pat said what?" Jan said it in an almost controlled voice; Ward thought it at the same time. Jack got up, stretched, and walked back into his little area. He could feel the tension mounting and knew that the problem they faced right now was something they had to deal with. He had no idea who the contact was, but he figured it wasn't good news they were getting from the furrows on both of their faces.

"I'm pretty sure she hasn't gotten much info from me, but whatever she's got, she's not passing it on to Gregg for whatever reason. Right now you're safe but I'm not sure of the intentions and I'm more worried about how this is going to play out right now. And tell him to relax cause he's giving me an ulcer," Jan looked at Ward and saw the half smile on his face. "I'm going to take it that you don't have time for this one right now so I'll keep the heat off. I'll also see what I can dig up on this guy that will get the department's attention. If Bobby thinks you're up here that should keep you clear till you get back."

Jan should have felt good about this, but she didn't. Ward was looking at Jan his face more serious than before. They both hated the fact that Bobby walked around completely free selling his skills to anyone that had enough money to buy them. The idea that he was dealing with biotech materials now was very scary. She could see the muscle tense on the side of Ward's face and unconsciously he rubbed the small scar on his eyebrow as he thought about what was happening. Jan was tense as well. She wanted to bring Bobby in as much as Ward did. He had once tried to remove her memories and replace them with an all-consuming emptiness. He had left her to die or something worse than that, and she had nearly succumbed to it.

"We can't let him get away with it," Jan made the statement for all of them in a low voice.

"He won't. I'll say I'm looking for you two, but I will be doing the follow-up on this and on him," his voice held that old tone.

"We'll get back to help as soon as possible," Jan made the decision for both of them.

"Take care of things there first, we need that solved almost as much as this one. Keep in touch," Rob ended the call before Jan could state the obvious, to be careful. Each time they encountered Bobby he seemed to be more tainted than the time before. They didn't need to worry about what Bobby was up to now. Rob was right, what they were working on was just as important. If there was a problem in that office, or with the people Jack had under surveillance, they were the best that could be put on the job.

Rob finished his last bite of bagel and sip of coffee. He got up and walked out of the coffee shop and went back to the office. It was going to be a long day. He toyed with a new idea. One that either would get him hung, killed, or solve everything. He wondered if Pat would like to join him back in the field for this one.

Jan, Ward and Jack put in three more hours of intense work before they spoke again or moved from their seats. Jack wondered for a while, but saw nothing but professionals working on the job at hand. Whatever had happened was not going to interfere with the present mission. It was Ward who broke the silence first.

"Damn, can't find a thing. They have their tracks covered well," Ward still hadn't shaved and he combed his fingers through his hair, an expression of frustration on his face only added to the wild look he had right now.

"I think we have done about as much as we can do here for now," Jack's voice was low, but plainly stated what they were all feeling.

"Shall we get ready," Jan smiled that familiar smile that was a mixture of enjoyment and the thrill of the job. They spent the rest of the day in and out never leaving together and never meeting up on the outside. With Jack's growth of beard, dark glasses, and a hat he was not likely to be spotted. Ward didn't have to worry about being spotted, but the change in the way he looked made sure that no one could identify him later.

By nightfall they were organizing a different set of gear, ready for the next day's activity. The plans were set, and she was the bait. Jack lay in bed and thought about the two of them. Even though they may not have a tomorrow they seemed to enjoy the day for what it was, taking each step as it came. He may not be able to read their minds but he sure could feel their happiness. He had dated only a couple of times since Susan's death, but her death had left a huge gaping hole in his heart. All of the women he dated he measured up to her, and sooner or later the ghost won out. But this time the ghost seemed to be telling him something different. It was finally time to move on. He really did want what they had, but wasn't sure if he would ever, could ever find it again. Finding it once had been amazing, but like lightning, could it strike in the same place twice? Not being one to dwell on things that he couldn't change, he turned off his thoughts and rested for the mission to come.

Jan watched as Ward undressed and then crawled in the bed beside her. The room was barely large enough for a twin bed, but somehow they had managed to squeeze a small double in the room. Instead of making love right away they just laid together silently, skin touching skin. They both knew what the other was thinking. It wasn't hard to figure it out. The mission was either coming to a head or a dead end. They weren't scared of the problems or dangers that they had to face; it was a dead end they were afraid of. Fear was a catalyst if used correctly. If all the leads fell away the trail would grow cold, with no where to look. Right now they had only one good lead, Moore. There was a possibility of discovering another lead at the party tomorrow night, but it was a long shot. Jan chose to speak first.

"What do we do if we don't find the mole?" Jack wouldn't be safe until they did. Ward had carefully avoided the topic when the three of them had been together, and Jan had respected that even though they both knew Jack had thought the same thing. But now they were alone.

"What we have to. We may have a house guest, do you mind?" Jan lay silently for a few minutes looking through Ward's thoughts. His mind was completely open to hers and she noticed that there had been changes. They were good changes; he had allowed some of the apparitions of the past that he had been carrying around to dissolve. She was visibly impressed and Ward noticed. "What, I'm not allowed to change, evolve?"

"I'm just amazed what effect, this, he has had on you," she carefully concealed the rest of the thought to herself.

"Since Bobby reared his ugly mug again you mean," he rose up on his arm to be able to look into her eyes.

"Yes, I can see the change in your thinking and it is more like the Ward I first met and fell in love with. If Jack needs a place to hide, we have the perfect one," and that was the last thing she had time to say before Ward brought his face down close to hers, starting to kiss her gently to begin with. Jan's mind didn't stop thinking though. She thought of the picture of Jack and Susan that was so similar to hers and Ward's. Remembering the large bruise on Ward's chest and the numerous scares they both had from previous missions she wondered just how long it would be before one of them would be missing from their photo. Ward let his mouth skim past her ear. Gently kissing it as he whispered to her.

"No more thinking," and his lips continued their torment, "We promised each other only our todays and we can't change who we are and what we do." His hands started to caress her, "Nor would we want to," and the time for thinking was over.

When morning came they were again locked into their roles, in the mission. No longer were they lovers, but they were team members on assignment. They sat preparing their equipment and readying the weapons. What they didn't have one of them went out and got. Each time they left the apartment they looked a bit different. It wasn't so much for the people in the apartments around them; these people were used to not seeing anything. They changed their appearances so that when they entered back into the civilized world they would not be recognized, remembered, or connected to the items they were collecting. When mid-day came Jan excused herself and left to get a few supplies she needed for the party this evening. Ward and Jack took off to make a reconnaissance on both the banquet hall in which the party would be held and the hotel she was booked into. No one would have noticed them, or been able to identify them later that evening as having already been there. Since this was an official gathering any radio equipment would be out, it would be detected by periodic sweeps. They would have to rely on

Jan and Ward's ability to communicate. Jack and Ward would use the cell phones they now had, and they would stay as close to Jan as possible.

The building was old world colonial architecture style from what he could see on the front. It was well kept and looked elegant. The building was made of both brick and plaster. It had been one of the first buildings to be redone in the large renovation period that Lima went through. It drew the attention of most dignitaries stationed in Lima and was used by the many different countries for the many different and formal functions. Ward was able to pick out a spot in which he could stay behind the trash bins and be close enough to be able to read Jan in the building without too much strain. With as many people as was going to be in attendance tonight he would need to be near or touching the building itself. Naturally, he would choose the role of bum tonight to stay inconspicuous, and with any luck they wouldn't try to clear all the indigents from the area. Jack would work a stand, that was about two to three hundred feet from the front entrance, and sell street food for the night to the local foot traffic. If they didn't clear him away, and there was no reason they would, he would have a great view of the entrance in the front. There were 'ifs' and the only way they could be sure of what was going to happen was to look back on it tomorrow when this was all over with. Jack and Ward though had been to enough of these parties that they were pretty sure where and what they had chosen wouldn't be caught by the agency's watchful eye. Jack would have to have one good disguise though. With Ward in the back and Jack in the front, they would have the building well covered for being four men shy of a complete team. Feeling like they had a handle on the building they split up and went back to the safe house as it was time to drag their gear to the hotel. Yesterday Ward had checked into the same hotel under a different name. His room was located on the same floor as Jan's but on the other end of the hall, and that had taken some work. Not great positioning, but all they needed was a reason to be in the hotel itself.

It was now three hours till game time, and Jack knew that if he had assembled a team to find the mole he couldn't have gotten any better people.

Chapter 12

Jack sat on the bed in the hotel room as Ward leaned up against the wall next to the window. Although Jack's appearance had changed, he still wasn't completely in disguise. He had added extensions to his hair and it had been traditionally styled into a long loose braid down the back. Something he never did. At the temples he had added some gray. Jack never brought attention to his Native American heritage, but this time it would come in handy as it had many other times before down here. His clothes were bulky to hide his frame and size, and they had yet to add the facial touches that would completely alter who he looked like. His naturally green eyes would become a deep rich brown with the colored contacts, and the self tan makeup would darken his complexion even more to make it look as if he had lived most of his life outside. In his bag he had a traditional Peruvian hat from one of the local indigenous groups. Large plastic frame glasses with a small tint to them would round out his face and give the finishing touches. He would look like most of the street vendors, dirty apron and all, except he would have a 9mm handy under the apron in case something went wrong.

Ward had carefully sewn two jackets together for himself. The bulk of it hid his frame well. The outside jacket, which he wore now, was brown, light-weight, modest and well kept. Once he got out onto the streets he would turn the jacket inside out and he would then be wearing a jacket that was thread-bare, dirty, and torn. In the hidden pockets he had a tube of grease for his hair and beard, and some graying paste, which would make him look older than he was. He wasn't concerned about being recognized by someone he knew, what did concern him was being picked out as a fake, or recognized later. In the small of his back Ward carried his 9mm, hoping not to have to use it. Both men had attached a back up weapon on their calves as well. Unless something went wrong, no one would ever know that the weapons existed. This night should just be about gathering information, but as they had all experienced so many times these situations could go bad quickly. If there was a mole in there and the mole caught a whiff of them, then all the scenarios would change.

"It really is different working with two readers and not just one," Jack placed his arms behind him and leaned back on the bed. Ward smiled a rare smile. Once into the heart of a mission, Ward rarely smiled, and then it was usually only for Jan, but that was where his mind was right now, and how good she looked in that dress in the bathroom. He had been eavesdropping on her mind and looking through her eyes watching her dress, and she hadn't stopped him. "The agency should pair readers together more often, it's safer."

"They did at one time, and still do I hear depending on the job at hand. But it becomes too risky and the losses could be too high. They put a lot of training and money into us," now the smile was truly sarcastic. "It's hard enough to lose one expensive weapon, but how could they justify two. That's why readers are given so much defensive and combat training. Helps keep us alive."

"I just have been admiring how," was all he had time to say before the bathroom door opened and Jan walked out into the small but well kept hotel room. She was in the same black dress with the mock turtle neck and what Jack could only guess was a push up bra. Her hair was elegantly pulled up in a bun with brown tendrils framing her face perfectly. She had put sun highlights in it to make it look as if she had been outside a lot the last two days instead of inside pinned to a computer screen. Colored contacts changed the look of her eyes. Jack noticed that the dress clung to her frame hiding nothing, and showing off her beautiful figure. Jan had bought a simple gold chain earlier today and with it wrapped and fastened loosely around her waist leaving the ends to dangle gracefully across the one hip. She was wearing make-up, more than he had seen her wear before, but not enough to look over done. The thought that she really didn't need it crossed his mind quickly until he noticed that it changed her look slightly, making her look a little more exotic. The amount of leg she showed looked long and well defined.

"Whoa!" Jack gasped, and Jan smiled in appreciation. Jack looked back at Ward afraid he had offended him, "Sorry, I didn't mean. . ."

"No problem, she looks great," it was Ward's turn now to look her up and down, but he looked longer and with more knowledge than he knew Jack would ever have. He had never felt the need to be possessive of Jan. She had always made it quite clear to him that she was his. There had only been one time he ever worried about it, and it was the time she had lost her memory long ago. Somehow though, she had recognized her connection with him even then. Jack's appreciation of her looks just reminded him of how lucky he was. "Very nice," his voice was an octave deeper as he spoke to her.

"If you dressed like that with Toby I can understand what reeled him in," Jack looked again at Jan this time for something more specific. His gaze was more intense, but it wasn't admiring her figure, or the material. He was looking for something. There was no place he looked that she could have it hiding, and he began to worry. No one went in unprepared on this one, "Okay, where you hiding the weapon?"

"Really want to know?" She was toying with him now. Ward knew exactly where it was and what she had. It was one of her favorites. A thought went through his mind, and Ward knew exactly what she wanted him to do. A split second later he came after her, throwing a blow from the right and then quickly switching to the left. Her motion was fluid and faster than Jack could see. It was a routine they had practiced and trained with many times. Each time Jan would pull the knife only in a self-defensive mode allowing Ward to block it. When Ward had blocked the blow, then Jack saw the knife.

It was a six inch retractable blade, black, and very professional looking. It wasn't standard issue but he knew the training she had received to get a weapon of that caliber, especially one that wouldn't show up on any scan. It wasn't training normally open to women, or just any man, and the training itself usually left its own scars. He started to wonder where the scars were. Ward cleared his throat, and Jack changed his thoughts quickly. In close quarters there was no better weapon, or training, than what she had. The knife was undetectable by any detector made, and the way her dress fit, no one would even consider that she had it on her. She would be easily cleared as she entered the reception. As she lifted her skirt to replace the knife securely in its sheath, fastened to her thigh Jack just shook his head in disbelief.

"Remind me not to surprise you any time soon. Any other hidden talents I should know about?" After the words left his mouth, he regretted saying it and shook his head. Both Jan and Ward broke out in laughter.

"Need to know basis only brother," was all Ward said. Jan had seen the trust he was willing to give to others not just Jack, and was looking forward to the prospects it presented for them. Jan held out her hands to Ward and he complied by covering the tips of her fingers with the gel that would keep her identity a secret from all at the reception.

"Nice touch," Jack didn't ask where it had come from, it was probably in the bag she had gotten from their contact, or, and he didn't want to go there. As a precaution they all painted their fingerprints away. No one would be able to easily get a bead on any of them. Out of habit they all wiped the room down for prints.

"Time to get this show on the road," Jan had looked at her watch and the time was about ten minutes later than Toby had told her he would pick her up. She had called and left a message with the desk to tell him that she was on her way down, but that was fifteen minutes ago. They still had plenty of time to get there; Jan had made sure of that. It was all in the details, what woman would be ready on time? Ward grabbed Jan around the waist and kissed her deeply. Jan returned the kiss just as fiercely. It was a ritual they kept, to remember that they really only had the present. Jack turned his head to give them a bit of privacy.

"Go get 'em Babs," and he let her go. Just as easily they returned to their roles. Jan grabbed her shawl and walked out, not saying good-bye or looking back. She knew she would be back, they all would be.

Toby had been waiting in the lobby for the last fifteen minutes. He had checked his watch for the fifth time. It really didn't surprise him that she was late. What he did know about women was that not a one of them were ever on time when it came to getting dressed up for a formal affair. The last two days he had been hard at work. He had been reassigned and been busy working on new documentation for all staffers, as well as Moore's new identity. It really galled Toby that when Moore had reported in last night, he wasn't able to shed any light on the reasons to why Golightly had been killed. Moore had left his report and headed home. His report stated that the complex was in ruins and that there were no good leads; case closed. Toby knew that until the group under surveillance resurfaced there was little to no hope to figure out what had really happened. He hadn't talked to Moore figuring that he was pretty tired from the journey and the ordeal. It wasn't an easy life to begin with but when one of your own was lost it made the game much harder. He was hoping that he would get a chance to speak with Moore tonight. Toby planned on setting up a time they could get together tonight to compare notes. There had to be something they were all missing. He wasn't ready to just let Golightly go. Suddenly his thoughts were interrupted by a voice.

"You look very nice," and he did, she mused as she let her eyes take him in. Toby was dressed in a nicely cut tuxedo that hid his service weapon well. He would be carrying it with him tonight as part of regulations. Most likely he wouldn't need it they usually didn't at events like this, but just like them, an agent never went anywhere without their weapons. He looked fresh, a little young, but his eyes held the story of what he had just been thinking about. She had read his sadness, dismay, and even distress over what had happened as she came down. She gave herself a moment to ponder just what he would think if Jack came down the stairs right now. She guessed she wouldn't find out. Making sure Jack stayed dead to the Company would give them the upper hand, and right now it seemed that was the only advantage they had.

"My, my," the look in his eyes changed quickly. His eyes trailed up and then down her body, slowly soaking in every bit, "You're going to turn some heads tonight."

"Thank you, but I only wanted to turn one head," she said playfully, not bothering to tell him it wasn't his. He offered his arm and she gracefully took it as they walked out of the lobby. Toby didn't notice that they were being watched. He had no reason to suspect they were going to be followed so he didn't bother to double check the area as well as he would have when they left the hotel. Ward entered the lobby just as they walked out. He didn't need to stay too close right now as he had a lock on Jan's mind. Ward took a moment to read Toby, and Ward had to agree with Jan. There was no way Toby could be the mole, he was still too obsessed with Jack's death. Moles didn't kill people off and then regret it.

"Did you enjoy your trip?" Toby tried to keep the conversation light to begin with. The cool breeze of the night played with the ends of the shawl as they walked down the street.

"It was spectacular. I spent a lot of time just walking the ruins. It's amazing the type of building techniques they used and architectural styles," Jan had done her homework and let the information she needed to convince him of the trip come pouring out of her in a rush. He wasn't interested in architecture at all which was to her benefit. She let her mind look for Ward and found him. He had gotten ahead of them and was making his way towards the reception faster. He wanted to be in position early so that he could practice reading her, and picking her out of the crowd. As they got closer to the center of town the amount of people increased. The nightlife in Lima revolved around the outdoor cafes and music that filled the old town at night. Ward had to close the distance between them.

"Sounds wonderful," It was only six blocks to the building. Toby was paying more attention to the road they were on and enjoying the envious looks of the males around him as he walked with what he thought was his prize. Toby hadn't told her they were going to walk there; she had just assumed it because her hotel was so close to the hall. To stay in character she thought she should ask though because as Liz she had never asked where the reception was.

"Are we walking all the way?" she looked toward his face as they waited to cross the road. He was only a bit taller than she was.

"Yes," all of a sudden it hit Toby; he had never asked if she would rather catch a ride to the reception. He looked at her feet and shoes, "I'm so sorry, I didn't even ask. Are you okay to walk? It's only a few more blocks. Should I call a cab?"

"No, no I'll be fine. I just wondered how far it was," she lied.

"Not much farther. If you look just over there you will see the building," he pointed to the beautifully redone building in the center of the old town, and they continued on in silence for a while with his arm around her waist. His mind was not quiet though. Jan could tell that he was focusing on the situation now. He was beginning to come to the same conclusions they were. Toby was watching for someone that had the reception under surveillance. Occasionally he would look toward her and wonder. It crossed his mind that all his checking up on her may not have been enough, but it left just as quickly.

Jan was glad of that. She only needed his services for one last night. After that, who cared what he thought. The closer they got the more he scanned the area. Standard procedure. If she hadn't been a trained operative she never would have recognized what he was doing. If he had been watching her, he might have seen her doing the same things. Nearer the hall there were more people and traffic. He leaned over and looked down into her face, getting lost in her eyes, "There's hardly any parking around and the hotel was so close that I thought walking would be better."

"I love to walk so this was perfect," she noticed the dignitaries in their gowns and tuxedos entering the hall. Toby was still looking at her, and the questions about her were back. She had to alleviate his fears, "You have been so nice to me. I just can't believe all this is happening. I feel more like Cinderella if that doesn't sound too strange," and she quickly gave him a peck on the check, ousting all his fears, "Thank you for making my vacation so special."

She was now able to get back to business as she saw him smile at her and return his attention to their surroundings. Outside the hall, in traditional spots, were the security teams. Being careful not to linger too long on any one person she counted them, and memorized their faces. It was a combination of both American security and Peruvian national security teams in place, a joint effort and a show of good faith. There were only ten people positioned outside, two more were on the roofs. Those were the ones to watch out for, they were military, American, and they were sharp shooters. She tried to relay the information to Ward, and after a couple of minutes she found his mind.

Ward had stumbled down the alley and behind the trashcans looking for all intents and purposes like he had passed out drunk. There were only five people in the back of the hall on the outside; Ward assumed there were more in the kitchen area. No one seemed to take notice, or even cared. One of the guards had even thought he had gone out the other side of the alley. He'd let Golightly know about that one. Security could so easily be compromised if one man didn't do his job right. The alley was dark and the service doors were still a hundred yards away. Ward was pretty safe where he was. He got Jan's message and returned the favor letting her know how many were in the back. He'd check the kitchen area in a moment to see just how many more were around. Nestling in behind the cans he put the ear bud from the phone in his ear. It was set to connect to Jack's at the slightest nudge of the phone which was safely positioned in-between the two coats just under his left elbow. The alley itself smelled of rotting food and decaying matter of all sorts. All big cities, no matter where, had the same problems. Except for the occasional cockroach or rat Ward felt no one around him that was taking the slightest bit of interest in what he was doing.

"I'll take onions on that," was all he said into the mike on the phone and sounding like a crazy man on his end.

"Got your order to go sir, just putting the onions in right now," was all he heard Jack say. Both men were in position and ready to work. Ward knew he would be able to talk freer than Jack, so they had set up a basic code that afternoon. Ward had asked about the onions, code for Jan, and Jack told him that Jan was now in the building.

"Have you seen the guest we're looking for yet?" Ward wanted Jan to meet up with Moore as soon as possible. The plan was that as soon as she got a good reading from him and anyone else she thought she might need to read, she would feign tiredness, or illness, and have Toby take her back to the hotel.

"Sir, I didn't use rotting tomatoes. I made sure they were fresh today," Jack was serving up food to the tourists and locals around him. There were some reporters standing around waiting to be served. They had been trying to get pictures and interviews with some of the people who went into the reception, but they hadn't had any luck. Some people turned and looked at him funny after his comment, but Jack casually looked toward another customer with his eyes, indicating that they were the ones that had made a comment about his food that had required his answer. Everyone always thought spy work was glamorous and exciting, but most of the time it was downright boring.

Ward maintained silence from that point on. Gently he bumped the phone to disconnect. Too much communication and they could accidentally be picked up. He locked on to Jan's thoughts, and started to glance through the others there as well. If they both worked the room, then later they would compare notes, and if necessary he could let her know if there was a person she needed to make contact with in the party itself before she left. Jack had been right. Two readers working together had its benefits, and they all knew what they were. They also knew what the problems could be as well. A cool wind blew across his face bringing the smells of the alley with it, and he could hear the scamper of the rats around him. So much for the glamorous life he thought he would lead when he joined years ago. He had spent so many nights, and days, in places like this over the years. If he thought about it, the alley was better than a lot of places he had been put in his life.

The hall was exquisitely decorated for the evening, with glass chandeliers and incandescent light to hide any flaws, or guest that may not want publicity. The band was better than average, and the music had been classical for the first forty-five minutes to allow the guests to enter and settle in before the dancing began. An hour and a half into the night Jan was feeling frustrated. Even though Toby wanted to talk with Moore, he refused to go near him with Jan near. Jan had spotted him twice and made sure that Ward had a good description and a look through her eyes at him. He was going to need that for later. Moore's thoughts were also just as frustrating to her. He wore a tuxedo that was the same style as Toby's to hide the fact that he was also carrying. The fact that Moore was people watching, with very few thoughts about his job, or what had happened, made it harder for Jan to get deeper into his thoughts this far away. Jan noticed that she didn't sense the same regret in him as she had in the others in the room about Jack's death. This was both good and bad news. She tried to dig deeper, but she needed to be closer. With all these people in the room there was just too much static. She would need more of his thoughts brought to the surface and that required her to be closer.

"Most, if not all, of the American community is here as well as many Peruvian officials. Some of the other diplomatic embassy staffers from other countries are here as well. Over there you will see the Mexican officials, and there," he pointed in the opposite directions, "are the Chileans." It wasn't the fact that Toby had been neglecting his duties; he had introduced her to many of the American Embassy staff. The conversation always lingered on how nice it was to have new people come to these functions; the American community in Lima was too small. They talked about where she came from, and what she was doing in Lima. Everyone had a story to tell her either about the building they were in, about California, the best things about Peru, and the worst. Also, anyone that knew Toby had been just a little bit shocked to discover that he had brought a date, even if they didn't say anything to his face. It was fairly amusing to Jan as she read all their thoughts, and really found out how totally out of character this was for Toby. He was definitely more of a player and never ever hooked up with one woman for more than a couple of dates, and they were already on their third.

The conversation drifted off to the weather. Noticing her lack of interest Toby finally asked her to dance. Jan accepted willingly. He had mistaken her look for boredom and not what it really was, frustration. She had met with just about everyone that she had needed to read. She had even met with the assistant to the new ambassador as well. She had read each one and filed away the information for later, even though none of it seemed to make any difference. Taking her gently by the arm Toby led her out onto the dance floor amongst all the others. He danced well although he wasn't used to doing it she could tell. He was a little bit stiff. He did hold her close enough to whisper in her ear.

"Didn't I tell you it would be boring?" he smiled as he said it, the words gently flowing past her ear. His hold on her demanded nothing, for now.

"I'm not sure I could have taken much more small talk. Dancing was a marvelous idea," Jan let him lead her around the floor and weave through the people. He began to pull her closer, their bodies beginning to touch. As he approached the small tables set up on the sides of the dance floor she got an idea. Deliberately she stumbled, and brushed her head with one hand, "I think I need to sit down for moment," and she stumbled slightly again. It wasn't enough to throw them off balance, but it was enough that concern tugged at his face.

"You okay?" he asked as he glided her toward a table his hand and arm now supporting her around the waist as she allowed him to hold her closer as he physically almost carried her.

"Fine, I just think with all the walking I have been doing the last couple of days, the altitude change, and it is a bit warm in here, that I just need to sit down for a moment," Jan knew what was coming next as Toby pulled the chair out for her.

"I'll get us something cool to drink," he did a quick medical assessment, "I'll be right back," Toby straightened up, letting his hand brush down the side of her face to reassure her that she was really alright.

"Don't hurry, I'll be fine," and she flashed him a smile as she let her hand trail down the arm of his tuxedo. "I'm feeling better already," she needed to flirt just a little to let him know that she was interested in him, on a more personal level tonight. Toby smiled as he let her hand gently brush past his fingers. As he walked away he wondered if she wasn't signaling for something more and wanted to leave with him. He again cursed his inexperience with women that had more to them than come on up and see me. They were a strange oddity to him. Jan could see his confusion and knew that was what she needed. He saw Moore on his way over to the bar. Toby knew if Jan did want to leave, he better go over and talk with Moore now before they left.

Jan watched him closely from the table, much as one would if they were infatuated with the other person. If he turned back and looked at her, all he would get was more flirting. All the signals she had given him had hit their mark. She was pretty sure that he was going to ask her to leave after having the drink. Looking into his mind one more time Jan read the fact that he was going to approach Moore before they left, and before he returned to her. After all, Company business always came first. Her dramatic production had worked in her favor.

Toby picked two glasses of ginger ale. He wasn't sure if he should bring her something stronger or not. Deciding that he didn't want her to feel pressured into anything, he had chosen a fizzy drink without alcohol. He could always pick up something later. He decided he needed to get out more with high-quality women, as this was too embarrassing. Turning, he smiled at her, and she returned his smile, a small seductive one. Toby was torn at that point and almost decided to go straight back to the table. He couldn't change the past could he; couldn't bring Golightly back? And then he saw her attention drawn away from him by a couple he had introduced her to earlier from the embassy. With her busy he looked for Moore and returned to Company business. Moore was standing near the bar and talking with some of the other agency people from the office. He was half a head taller than Toby, and he was broader in the shoulders. He wore his hair short and looked a bit like a movie star the way he carried himself right now. He could also disappear from sight faster than most. Toby also knew that their training had made him deadly. He had seen him use those skills before when it was necessary. Toby didn't notice Jan break away from her conversation and move into the crowd slowly. She didn't want to get too close too fast or Toby wouldn't have a chance to bring Moore's memories to the surface. Once on the surface it would make her job much easier.

From her position both Jan and Ward were able to hear and see the conversation. Ward locked on to Jan's thoughts, Jan welcomed the closer contact. Jan looked through the surrounding people's thoughts quickly, and returned to her target, focusing in on what was being said.

"Hey Nathan," as Toby walked up to Nathan the others

seemed to back off, and disappear.

"Toby," the man was interested in conversation, "Heard you brought a date, is that right?"

"Yah, she's over there," and Toby tipped his head in the general direction, "News travels fast."

"Small community," Nathan Moore shrugged and continued to scan the rest of the room, "Not bad looking either."

"Glad to see you back," Toby only paused for a second, "We need to go over your report in the next day or two. I want to try and figure out what happened."

"The report says it all. I didn't find anything, and the station chief has closed the case. His enclosure had been discovered," Nathan looked coolly at Toby. Jan was getting a reading from Nathan but something was wrong, definitely wrong. The coolness went much deeper. He was hiding his thoughts even though he didn't know a mind reader was near. As she went toward Toby and Nathan she got a message from Ward.

"Careful, I've got a bad feeling about this one."

Chapter 13

Careful was right. As Jan walked closer to the pair at the bar she began to get a cold feeling. It was similar to the one she had in Rosarito, but not as strong. Evil had its own feeling and she needed to locate who it was coming from, she had a sick feeling she knew who it was coming from. As she picked her way through the sea of people she started to collect more of Moore's thoughts. The room was filled with many people standing and talking and as she made her way past the gowns that were far more exquisite than hers and some that were not much more than what she had on. She could also hear a variety of languages being spoken, most of which she could understand. Small clicks of people had begun to form as the evening had progressed. Although Jan was fluent in a few languages, capable of speaking many more, she didn't stop to read any of the people nearby, or listen in on their conversations. She nodded and acknowledged those that she had met earlier but never once stopped to talk. Making sure she was always in a tangle of people she was able to keep both Toby and Moore from seeing her approach. With Moore's thoughts guarded she would need to be closer than she wanted to try and get a better read, if she could.

Since the Company, had created the mind reading program years ago they had also intentionally prepared most of their people to keep readers out without actually telling them that there were people out there that could read their minds. It was the understanding that you couldn't be sure who could be around watching your every move. Some of the agents had come to know that mind readers did exist, or something in that area had existed for a while. The PED department was used by all agencies, but not all the agencies were told about their unique abilities. That was why readers had a regular partner assigned to handle them. The department was advertised as the best of the best and when hard cases came along any of the other agencies could ask for their assistance. Some jobs were accepted, some were not. Sometimes it just had to deal with the resources that were available at the time. Jack had learned the secret by being recruited to join. He had been one of the few who had been given a choice on what to do once he left the training. He was the exception to most agents in the field.

As Jan got closer she could read the flow of the conversation and see the workings behind the words. Toby had started in talking about Golightly but Nathan had refused. Not in the usual way, but passed it off to the side like it didn't matter. It was true that the case had been closed, based on his reports, but there was something more to it, something he wasn't saying.

"Who's contacting the family?" Toby was curious. He was watching Moore intently. He had picked up the dismissal, or something in Moore's facial features that had triggered his natural instincts to be wary. Jan picked up the doubt in Toby's mind. If he wasn't careful, and Moore was the mole, then he would be the next one fitted for a box. She decided now would be the best time to appear and change the tension, drawing it away from Toby.

"My opinion, no one is in danger of being discovered, so no need to change identities. As I said the set up was probably . . .," and Moore stopped as she approached. He looked her up and down, slowly, and the cold feeling returned creeping into the very core of her being. Jan pressed forward and as she started the conversation she looked into his mind for confirmation of the evil she felt. Her expression never changed and the look of innocence remained plain on her face.

"I didn't mean to interrupt," and she took the drink from Toby's hand and wrapped her arm around his. She noticed that Moore's eyebrow rose ever so slightly. From the information she had gotten from Jack and what she had read in Toby's mind and others here, she was prepared for Moore's reaction to her being with him, "Hi, I'm Liz."

"Liz this is Nathan. Nathan, this is Liz. I work with Nathan," that was as far as the explanation went, and would go. Toby was a bit flustered at having to introduce his date. Nathan normally would be introducing his date, of which he had none this time, instead of him introducing her. He thought it was funny though. Suddenly he didn't know what to say, and as soon as he felt a bit flustered the words seemed to just come to him. He was more comfortable than he had been in a long time with a woman near, "Liz was lost the other day. She's a visiting professor of architecture from UCLA, Berkely. She graciously accepted the offer to be my date tonight. I think she feels guilty about taking up my time," Toby wasn't sure where those words had come from, but in the back alley, Ward smiled.

"Oh," and that was all Moore said. Jan was careful not to say anything as she leaned in closer to Toby and sipped at her drink, "I expect you are having a good time."

"The banquet has been wonderful," Jan knew this was not what he meant but wanted him to drop his guard a bit more.

"I meant Peru," he seemed a bit put out having to explain himself. "Have you seen the ruins yet?" Nathan watched her intently, his true nature and training taking over.

"Yes, I was able to take a tour out there on Thursday and I'm afraid I spent too much time walking around and looking at the sights and not looking after myself."

"The town of Ica is wonderful this time of year," Nathan was looking her straight in the eye. It was a test. She knew it. Toby had checked her credentials, she had gotten the hit on her sight, and now it was Nathan's turn.

"I think you mean the town of Cuzco," she put in lightly.

"Oh yes, you're right. It's been a while since I have been able to get out of town and just do some sightseeing," Jan had made it through the first of the barriers in his mind. He knew the dead man that was going to be sent home as Golightly's double; had met with him recently. Moore had shot the man himself. She watched the scene play itself out in his mind, without sound thankfully. It was one of the men that had been sent up to kill Golightly in the surveillance tent. When they had failed and returned to talk to Moore, he had just shot him. It was quick and without feeling. The others were then instructed to take his body back up the hill and burn the sight beyond recognition. Jan kept her face set in a smile as Moore continued to talk, "What are you doing down here, is it business or pleasure?"

"A little of both," Jan felt Toby's grip tighten as he sensed that it was also a bit of a come on from Nathan. Jan could feel it to. Nathan liked good-looking women and knew that Toby himself was feeling a bit out of his league with her. It was only because Toby had a value system he followed.

"How long are you here?" She knew that Nathan was still

fishing, and his gaze was intense on her eyes.

"Depends on what I find," warning bells shot off in her head from Ward not to go any farther, but Jan quieted both him and them. She quickly shot back a thought. Not enough to interrupt the flow of information but enough to let Ward know she had to do her job and she was capable of it. If she was right, his phone was in his breast pocket and that would be where she would find all the information they would need to implicate him and get him pulled in by the Company. It would be tricky getting it, but worth the risk. Ward admittedly agreed with her and then stopped distracting her altogether.

"Toby, you wouldn't mind if I asked your date for a dance would you?" It was less of a question and more of just an assumption. Jan knew that he wanted to check her out further, in more ways than one. For some reason he wasn't going to easily accept her for what she presented herself to be. Then again if you played both sides of the field you never knew who to trust.

"Well," and Toby again hesitated. Ward filled in the gaps for him. Toby turned and looked at Jan, "As long as you don't mind Liz? Then I was thinking about taking you back to the hotel since you seem a bit on the tired side." Toby almost had a blank look on his face as he wondered just where the words had come from.

"I guess one dance couldn't hurt," she said hesitantly, "but then I'm all yours." As she said that she let go of Toby's arm and twisted her foot and fell towards Nathan spilling her drink on his pants. Toby grabbed for her and she made a quick twist to make sure that Toby couldn't catch her and she would hit Nathan square in the chest. Toby picked her up off of Nathan, and helped her to stand up again. "Maybe I should skip that dance, and," she looked at Toby with more feeling than she had all night. Most of the emotional leading was for Nathan's benefit, "have you take me straight back to the hotel."

Toby looked uncertain for a moment until Nathan leaned over and whispered something to him. Even though Jan wasn't supposed to hear she saw it in both of their thoughts. All he said to him was looks like this one's into you, and then Toby turned her around to leave standing closer together than they had all night. It was much cooler and more comfortable outside when they left and Toby nodded silently to the guard at the door as they turned and walked down the street. They walked a bit with Toby's arm wrapped tight around her before they talked again.

"Feeling better," Toby's grip hadn't lightened. Jan mused that one day he might make a good husband, if she didn't completely wreck his ego or trust in human nature and women. "Would you like me to get a cab?"

"No let's walk," she said in a low voice and leaned into Toby, "The cool air is helping." She wasn't really talking about the air around her though. She could feel it still. The cold was following them. She used Toby to brace herself as she started to look for who was following them and send out an SOS to Ward. If Moore wanted to take her out, by now he knew his phone was gone, Toby would side with him and things wouldn't go well.

Ward was up quickly. He had seen them leave and walk down past where Golightly was stationed. He didn't take the time to contact Jack. He moved out of the alley to intercept them, he had also seen the item Jan had as well. He couldn't let him find it on her. Once out of the alley he could tell that Jan and Toby were being followed, and seconds later Jan and Ward knew by whom. If Jan was discovered with the phone, and the wallet she had lifted, that would be the end of the night, the mission, and he wasn't going to think of Jan. Ward was only a block away and Nathan was a block and a half, only he was moving faster. Ward upped his pace a bit without looking suspicious. As he approached them he began to weave back and forth in a more drunkenly manner. Talking to himself, Ward looked like an old man that had drank himself half crazy, and the other half was already crazy. He was hunched over and looked to be a good five to six inches shorter than his regular height. Toby tried to steer them out of his path but failed to do so. Ward took his opportunity when he saw that Moore was only about a hundreds yards away and fell into Jan. Jan was braced for the contact and stayed upright. As he hit, Jan dropped the phone and wallet into his inside pocket as she tried to push him back upright.

"Careful man! Cuidado!" Toby shouted as he helped push the drunk away. Having already passed him the phone and the wallet she didn't do anything else but straighten her dress out while the drunk made his apologies and wobbled down the road.

"Lo siento, lo siento," and he just kept repeating it as he weaved down the street and down another alley. Nathan had slowed down a bit. Nathan's plan was to tail them all the way back to the hotel, which was a matter that concerned Ward. Jan passed a calming thought to him and they moved on down the street, letting him know that Nathan wouldn't get that far. He watched Moore pass and felt the anger inside of him as he followed the two down the street.   Ward pushed the anger away knowing that it was only a hindrance when working.

Ward knew that Nathan had discovered that his phone and wallet were missing soon after they had left the party, and he assumed it was one of the two of them that had taken it, if not both. Ward knew that Jan had this information as well and continued on with their plan. The farther Ward got from them the quicker and surer he moved. As he did so he began to change again from the drunk he had portrayed himself to be into a middle-aged man out for a stroll that night. When he reached the stand he could see that Golightly had seen all that had taken place and was beginning to close down the stand itself. Ward made his way to the front of all the people before he talked.

"He's the one," Ward handed him the phone and wallet. If anyone thought it strange they said nothing, "Do you know how to turn off the GPS?" Jack nodded an affirmative. Ward didn't have time to do it himself.

"Don't leave her to him," it was a command even though Jack new that Jan was more than capable of taking care of Moore if she needed to, and she had the advantage. Maybe it was just that innate sense that a woman needed protecting, or that he didn't want Ward to lose what he had. This, he knew, was unproductive and moved past it. A job was a job, and they all knew what was involved.

"I'll be in touch," and Ward moved off down the street standing straight up which added to his height, and he quickened his pace. His focus was Moore and what he was going to do. He trusted that Jan would do what she needed to keep safe, and at close quarters Ward himself wouldn't want to be on the wrong side. He focused looking for Nathan Moore's mind only.

Jan felt better after she dropped off the phone and wallet but she knew she had been made. She wasn't sure how, but Nathan suspected at least Toby and most likely her as well. Her first job was to keep Toby safe, and clearly out of his suspicion. As they walked along she could feel that Moore was keeping a safe distance and tailing them. His intent was to confront them in the hotel room, and probably kill them. Jan wasn't going to let it get that far. She hadn't felt Ward's presence back yet so had to keep her target on the move.

Placing her head on Toby's shoulder as they walked along she began to relax in his arm. Toby's arm tightened. She was giving him all the wrong signals, promises of something that would never come. It didn't matter. Nathan was relentlessly following them, and Toby had not picked up on it yet. How could he? Only a reader would be able to sense that far back, and why would Toby suspect him to be behind them. Way in the back of her mind she could feel that Ward had dropped the items and was making his way back.

His part in this job was to follow the suspect, if they found one at the party, and see where they went. Moore had made Ward's job easy because the suspect was now following her. Knowing that Ward's cover was just as important, Jan made a decision. Scanning the street she saw what she needed. About fifty yards down the walk there seemed to be a small side road that was hardly used. She had noticed it in her walks about town and knew that no one would be on that street at this time of night. Jan let her hand start to caress Toby's waist. He turned and kissed the top of her head. He was a bit confused at her out and out playfulness but she knew it would be the only way to keep him safe. She lifted her head and let him kiss her on the lips gently to begin with and then pulled away slightly. Flirting was easy, what she would have to do next would be hard.

As they approached the road's entrance Jan gave him a little push. They moved into the shadows of the night, and she leaned up against the wall. Toby leaned in and began to kiss her again on the lips, this time more deeply. Jan played along but all the while kept her mind on where Nathan was. Toby's hands began to explore her waist and start to move higher. Jan let her arms wrap under his arms and just above his waist. She knew enough to keep clear of the area where his gun was, she didn't want to make him nervous. Her hands came up to grip his shoulders, and she knew she was now in position. Nathan was on the move again. Jan knew it was time.

"I'm sorry Toby," she whispered in his ear as she clipped the sensitive nerve in his neck. He immediately tensed then passed out in her arms. Jan had braced herself for his weight and now she waited. She held him up against her until Nathan came round the corner.

"Alright Toby," Nathan was angry and his voice was low. She let Toby drop roughly to the ground. She felt Nathan's surprise, but she had her knife at the ready before he even thought of going for his service weapon. "I never would have guessed," he sneered.

"He thinks you're a live wire and a liability. He sent me down here to check on you," it was a chance, but one she felt comfortable in making. Jan was pretty sure she had seen another person in on this. She just couldn't identify who yet. Moore slowly moved the one hand and began to go for his weapon. "I wouldn't," and she released the black blade of the knife, moving it carefully so that Nathan could see just what kind of weapon it was. She knew the reaction she would get from him as well. It would be the same as the one Golightly had given her. Not too many completed the training, and especially not women.

"Okay, calm down. Tell him I don't plan on messing up on this one," he moved his hands to where Jan could watch them comfortably. "No one suspects me in Golightly's death. And I have taken care of those who could talk." It wasn't a pleasant thought but expected. Ward was watching from fifty yards down the road and was close to pacing the street as he heard the conversation.

"How can he be sure?" Jan knew now that Moore had been transporting illegally purchased information for a while. She could see it in his mind. What she had just said had brought it all to the surface. She could also see that he had never told his contact that it wasn't Golightly that he had killed. Nathan had been using other agents to get the information to other countries and then had it removed from them without their knowledge. But Moore only placed the information. Someone else picked it up and delivered it. Jan was beginning to see deep enough in his mind to hear his contact's voice. Moore had never seen his face. The only contact he had had with him was by phone. The voice wasn't clear, but she was pretty sure she had heard it before.

"I don't go back on my commitments. Tell your boss that the next time he wants to check up on me, he should do it himself," Nathan started to turn to leave, stopped and then held up his hands, "Unless you want to kill me now?"

"You haven't out lived your service," she paused, "yet." Nathan turned and walked to the end of the alley.

"Nice. Just remember he has to get the next shipment to me soon as the agent will be leaving in a week, and this will be my last job," he left after saying that. Jan stayed in the street with Toby as Ward walked past her. *Gutsy*, was all he said to her. Problem was that if he contacted the other man he would know she was lying. Time would now be shorter than ever. She did have something more though. There was another drop to be made, and it looked as if it was one of the most important ones before Moore just disappeared himself. With any luck, they would continue as planned, just a bit more carefully.

Toby began to stir and she had a choice to make. If she stayed there might be a lot of explaining to do, some of which she couldn't and keep everyone safe. If she left then he would draw his own conclusions. She didn't want him spending time trying to find her, so she stayed for a moment until he was able to recognize her voice. He was unable to move much, and she knelt down beside him.

"Toby, you'll be okay, just don't try to move too quickly," she gave him a kiss on the head, "Someday someone you trust will explain all of this to you. For now, just forget it and keep business as usual with the Company," and she got up and walked away as he started to blink his eyes. She made her way quickly down the street.

Nathan waited for her to leave and then went back to the street. It was what Jan hoped he would do. It would clear Toby and make him think that he had been taken in by a woman. Not exactly what she wanted him to believe, but it was what made him safe for now.

"Man you really know how to pick them," was all Moore said to him as he helped Toby to sit up. Toby leaned over and put his head between his legs to keep from throwing up.

"Didn't even see it coming, and he checked for his weapon and wallet. Everything was there which seemed strange.

"It was a good thing I came along when I did," Moore said as he now helped him to stand up, "You okay now?"

"Yah. Did she get away?" something was haunting him in the back of his head. It was what she said before he was completely conscious. It rattled in his head and something inside him wanted to believe what she had told him. She had known who he worked for, how he wasn't sure. She had given him good advice, in light of everything that was going on, to just forget it. He didn't know what it was, but something made him trust her for the moment. Toby decided to give the idea a couple of days to torment him since there seemed to be missing pieces.

Jan had went straight back to the hotel to get changed. She was only in the room for ten minutes before she was out the window and down the vine. Jack had been in the room and done another wipe down of it for prints. When she got to the safe house and let herself in she noticed that Jack was already busy working on the phone. On the table beside him he had a list of numbers written out.

"Nice work," was all he said to her, as she came in and closed the door. Jack had gotten changed as well. He had gone back to the hotel and dumped his clothes and redone his hair into a manner he was more accustomed to. He had wiped down both rooms and made sure that anything left in the rooms couldn't be traced back to them. He had watched Nathan come out of the hall and exchange a couple of words with the guard at the door. Then he went straight after Toby and Jan. The only thing that kept Jack from following was the fact that he knew Ward would meet up with them long before Nathan could catch them. He almost signaled Ward, until he had heard the phone beep in his ear twice meaning that Ward was on the move and silence was necessary.

"It did get a little messy," and that was when Jack looked up at her. His face held all the questions, no reading was necessary, but an explanation was. She didn't mince words, "My cover is gone, and I have a feeling I will find a number on that list that I don't want to see."

"Where's Ward?" His concern was real. Losing your cover was serious business, and he assumed Ward already knew what had happened. Jack figured she had a good reason for it, and waited patiently for the explanation.

"Following Moore at a safe distance. It's okay for now. Moore thinks I'm the link to his contact. Moore is the mole, both Ward and I are sure of it. We'll probably find the information we need to have him convicted on this phone somewhere. We just have to get the evidence in order. He has been the link that has illegally transported sensitive information for a while. Moore has been using agents to move the information from one country to another, and then another man picks it up from them unknowingly on the other side. You may have accidentally come across something, or messed up a drop," Jan stopped only for a moment as she moved to the couch. "Toby began to wonder about Nathan at the party. If I didn't do something then Nathan wouldn't have had any problems taking care of Toby as well, and he might not have been as lucky as you were," leaning her head back she continued, "He had sent one of his men to kill you. When that went wrong, he killed one of the men he had hired, leaving him for you, and probably the rest are either dead or scared to death. Toby will be safe so long as he keeps his mouth closed for now, which I think will happen. He knows nothing except that trusting in women may not be what he wants to do. You'll have to fix that later. If I'm right, Ward will be back here in the next half an hour."

"Should I call him?" The phones were set up only for emergencies and she hadn't foreseen one yet. If all went well and Ward was back on time they wouldn't call. Any later than half an hour and they would try and check to see where he was. He had had time to equip that phone with a GPS system for them.

"No, did you disable Moore's GPS on that phone?" She figured he had, but details needed to be seen to. Jan slipped into the room to change.

"First thing I did at the hotel. They will only be able to trace us to there if they were fast enough. If you're both right Moore wouldn't have tracked the phone yet, and now it's too late. You're that sure that Nathan Moore is who we're after?" He had known Nathan off and on for years and this came as a surprise. He didn't want to doubt Ward or Jan but it seemed strange.

"Evil has its own feel, and I think he has been hanging around with the wrong people way too long," Jan had changed into black yoga pants and a black long sleeved tee-shirt. Her hair was tied back in a pony tail and all the make-up had been removed. She looked lean, muscular, and ready for whatever came next, "Are these all the numbers?"

"Who are you expecting to find on the list of numbers?" Jack was watching her face carefully as she looked down the list. Her brows were furrowed and her face set. Reaching for a pencil she marked three of the numbers on the list. Her jaw tightened as she marked off the numbers. She was sure if she got her phone that one of those numbers would match the one that had sent the message.

"We need to check these numbers first. Compare them to the numbers on my phone that you have then work on who the rest belong to. One of the numbers may be to a bank or an account where he has stashed his money. I'll start working on that. He mentioned that this was his last job, so I expect he plans on disappearing himself. We need to check any aliases you know he uses and bookings on planes as soon as we locate where his stash is. We may be able to trace the transaction he used to buy an airline ticket, if we are lucky. Anything interesting in the wallet?" Jan looked over at Jack handing him the list back.

She got up to get the handheld she used when she heard the lock on the door start to move again. Jack looked at Jan for confirmation of who was on the other side. Looking past the door and into the thoughts of the man on the other side Jan felt Ward. He welcomed her thoughts in and let her know that her suspicions were correct. In that instance Jan knew all that had happened during his surveillance. Jan looked at Jack and gave him a reassuring nod, but there was no smile. It was getting serious. The door opened only a crack, and in slipped Ward. He quickly closed the door behind him and locked it without looking at it. Leaning up against the door he looked at the both of them before he said anything. The look on his face spoke volumes to Jack, and Jack had to assume that Ward had already explained the rest to Jan.

"Party's over boys and girls. It's time to leave."

Chapter 14

"Don't panic, she won't cause you any trouble," the voice on the other end of the phone was deep and rich. He was sure of himself and had no trouble voicing it. There was no emotion in his voice though, Nathan had never heard any emotion in it ever, "I've dealt with them before and I always win. I already knew they were on to me and they have had their warning to back off. If she doesn't I will deal appropriately with her. By the way, have you seen a man with her?" The command, not question, demanded an immediate answer.

"No," he had never even thought to look for any back-up she may have had. He had taken her word. She had seemed to know too much not to be on the inside already, "There was no one else." He knew his phone was gone and was pretty sure she had it. If she was working with Toby then she could be Agency, but Toby hadn't been involved in it. She had also attacked Toby. Maybe she had left the Company and was just a freelance agent, they did exist. He should have forced the issue and gotten his phone back, but that knife had scared him off. He had only known one other person with a knife like that; in close quarters not only was he deadly, he was brutal. Since he had planned on disappearing in a couple of weeks he wanted to do it with all his digits and parts still connected.

"I think this time I will enjoy taking care of her," his voice held a sadistic tone that made the hair on the back of Nathan's neck stand on end. It was a rare emotional moment and it chilled him to the bone, "Is there anything else I should know?" He doubted that Moore had told him everything.

Nathan had considered telling him about Golightly, but he had never been seen coming out of the jungle. He was pretty sure he had died there. It was a suitable place for him to die at least. The man on the other end of the phone didn't seem like he would be very forgiving without a body to prove it, so he had omitted this small piece of information. He had provided him with a body, not an exact match, but close enough. Moore was unsure if he suspected him of keeping information from him or not. He had to make a decision, and he knew what to say to play it safe.

"Everything else is on schedule," and he waited silently.

"I'll have her out of your hair soon. By the way, don't think about disappearing yet. You've not out lived your usefulness," was all he said before the phone went dead. Nathan put down his end of the phone and wondered why he had ever started into this. He then thought of his bank account in the Cayman Islands and knew why. No matter what happened, he would disappear in two weeks and be done with this mess. The rather large and luxurious beach house on the end of the small island about twenty miles out of town had been purchased in another name and with the some of the funds he had stored away. He had been careful though, he had transferred all the money around the world to different accounts at least twice before removing it and using it. There was no way this man or anyone else would find him.

"He contacted his boss as soon as he had Toby home. Toby's fine, confused, but fine. He has decided not to say anything for a couple of days yet. Do we have a confirmation on any names or numbers yet?" Ward was all business and his voice held a bit of urgency. Jack wondered if he was the only one who didn't know who Moore's contact was and what was taking him so long.

"Jack's on that. I'm working on getting the account numbers and the location of the bank. Do we have time to spend the night here to work?" Jan had gotten the handheld and moved back to the couch swiftly.

"It will be pushing it, but if we get good information it could be worth it," he talked and moved toward the other equipment in the room until he felt Golightly's thoughts. Ward stopped and looked at Golightly. His face was set, his jaw tight, the small muscle in his cheek jumping from the strain. He was holding Jan's phone and the list of numbers together and in plain view for Ward to see.

"I have a little clue here. Want to tell me who we are dealing with?" He showed more patience than he was feeling, and had tried to wall in the impatience from them just incase they tried to read him.

It was time for him to keep his feelings to himself and let them start to do the explaining. Jan and Ward didn't exchange looks, they didn't have too. Somehow the two paths that had seemed totally separate when they had started had now come together in a big bad ugly way. Jan went back to work and left the explanation up to Ward. It was up to him how much he wanted to tell Jack.

"There have been more than just two agents that have left the PED's," with this information Jack seemed a little stunned. He leaned back on the couch and waited.

"How many more?" It was a serious question, and his eyes held Ward's.

"Just one. And he was a bad apple. He now sells his services to anyone who pays well. I'm pretty sure he has never let anyone know that he is a reader. It would be an advantage he wouldn't want to give up. We trained together, he recruited me and we were as close as brothers at one time," Ward paused and looked down at the threadbare rug, "He framed me. The department thinks he is dead."

"I take it this was the man who sent the first message about your SUV. The one that caused all the tension between you two to begin with," Jack didn't look at either one of them. He wasn't sure who was going to answer him at this point.

"The last time I, we, dealt with him he tried to kill Jan and then Rob. He nearly succeeded. His behavior has deteriorated each time we've dealt with him. His skills though have gotten better, stronger. This time our paths crossed by accident to begin with and he told us to back off permanently or he would make sure he finished the job this time. His name is Robert 'Bobby' Malone. What he goes by these days I'm not sure. In the past he has used a lot of his old cover names, and a few new ones as well. Our paths cross occasionally but we have tried to stay out of his way. Each time I deal with him I feel like I lose a piece of myself. But this time it won't be possible to avoid him. One other thing I should let you know," and this time Ward got up and walked toward the wall and fingered the faded old frayed wallpaper absent-mindedly. He stood looking at no one and nothing in particular. Jan knew that this was going deep, far deeper than he had ever planned on going. Ward had never been able to tell anyone about what had happened to both of them in Asia so long ago now. Jan didn't know the entire story, and neither did the department.

Jan stopped what she was doing and waited. Whatever Ward was going to say she needed to be his strength. She looked at Ward's back. It had been hard enough for him to let her learn any of it. Ward had never told her himself, he had let her find his classified file, and had even planted the information so she could. The silence was long, and yet they both calmly waited. Jan was careful not to intrude on his thoughts. He didn't need her sympathy, what was done was done. It wasn't until Jan was sure that Ward couldn't continue that she silently asked him for his permission to do so. She waited until she saw his small nod allowing her to tell the rest.

"They were imprisoned together on their last official mission for the department. Tortured, and when their captors discovered what they had they were then tempted with the prospect of enhancing their abilities even more if they stayed on with them. They had some other research, experimental drugs, but no subjects. At least none as well trained as they were. Ward didn't give in and was tortured, even forced into the training and some of the experimental therapy. Bobby gave in and let them control both him and his mind, until it no longer served his purpose. Later he orchestrated his exit from the group. It was a character flaw in him that no one saw coming," Jan got up and walked over to Ward. She placed her hand on his arm before going on, "Bobby can now plant and remove memories from almost any mind, as well as devastate one's mind and sanity. He practiced on Ward at first and tried to kill him when he wouldn't surrender to him. He then later attacked me. If it hadn't been for Ward, I'm sure I wouldn't have ever completely recovered. He is dangerous." Jack sat for a moment not being able to see Ward's face at all. He was sure that neither one of them were trying to read his thoughts right then. There was too much pain in the room that he could feel. From what he had just learned the mission had become increasingly more dangerous, not just for him, but for all of them in many different ways. It was all pretty hard to swallow, but not unbelievable. Jack realized that if Bobby could do these things then maybe the fear Ward really felt was that others might view him as a monster and wonder just what he was capable of.

"Can Ward do this?" He decided it would not scare him if Ward could. He had known Ward for years, and they had faced many dangers in the past, and past week together, not once had he ever had reason to doubt his trust in Ward. Ward had saved his life on more than one occasion. He could never have misgivings about his honor and devotion to country and people.

"Yes," it was the first word he had heard from Ward since Jan had started speaking. It emerged from the depths of his very soul as if it were being pulled up out of him forcibly, and was tinged with pain, guilt and regret. Jack realized that Ward had never ever admitted this to anyone else but Jan. It was a leap of faith he was taking.

"And you?" Jack looked at Jan. Jan looked back at him square in the face as if trying to read his face, but staying clear of his mind. Jack appreciated that she was allowing him some privacy. Again, another reason to trust both of them.

"A bit. In order to recover he had to show me how to do some of it, but I haven't had any experimental therapy so it only goes so far," she let the silence fall again. Jack took a few moments to think about what he had learned. He wondered how much Moore had been influenced to begin with, and once caught couldn't get out. Jack truly doubted that Moore's change in character was solely to do with this Bobby. Even if you could plant a thought, you couldn't change one's soul. He could attest to that seeing how Jan and Ward fought for what was right, and against what had happened to them. He stood up and walked over to the two of them. Jan took a step back as Jack placed his hand on Ward's shoulder and turned him to face him. With his face calm and even he looked into Ward's troubled and paled face.

"Looks like we have our work cut out for us then brother," and with that the weight that had clearly settled in Ward's face slowly lifted. He sighed and patted Golightly on the shoulder.

"Then what are we waiting for," Ward forced a smile slowly letting it touch the corners of his eyes. It was as if a great weight had finally been lifted, and he turned to look at Jan. She smiled back at him, then at Golightly. His trust had paid off, and now everyone truly understood the perils to come.

"Two handhelds and two phones, no waiting," Jan broke the tension, "We have a lot of work to do tonight before we take off in the morning. We also have to come up with a game plan that keeps us away from the PED and you out of sight," no one smiled now. They all walked back over to the table. "If you keep working on those numbers, I'll work on the bank accounts and travel plans Moore might have."

"I'll find us a way out of here that will keep us out of sight and under cover. We need to start to work on a new plan that will hopefully catch them all. Don't know what information they are transporting, but it has been going on way too long and it looks like the largest transfer is about to take place. May have to give Rob a call," and he winked at Jan. He had come face to face with the fear of who and what he had become, admitted it, and won.

By the time the sun poked its way into the room through a small crack in the shutters they were all tired, and had finished all the cola Jan had in the frig. Ward and Jan had been through two pots of coffee, and Jack had finished off the tea he had brought in the day before. They had accumulated more information than they had hoped for during the night. Jan had found the bank account in the Caymans and the plane ticket he had purchased to leave here in two weeks time. She hadn't discovered the final destination yet, as he had planned the trip to meet up in different places and he was changing planes more often than one would change clothes. She had downloaded the information and evidence on a small thumb drive they carried with them. Jack had diligently worked his way through the numbers, most of which were for the Agency, but the others that weren't connected to the Agency he loaded on the thumb drive with the names of the people who owned the numbers. None of the numbers had Bobby Malone's name attached to it, but one had the name of Robert Mayor, a cover he had once used and this was noted as well. They had decided in the wee hours of the morning that one of Golightly's contacts here would drop this off with Toby when they notified him to do so. If it was dropped off too soon then they would lose the entire chain of conspirators. They also planned for the worst. If the contact didn't hear from them at all he was to drop it off no later than ten days from now. If not it would be too late and Moore would have flown the coop. Ward rubbed his forehead and looked up from his work. He looked at his watch.

"We'll have to drive out of here. Any other way and they will be able to trace us. If we leave by six this morning and make good time we can catch a flight out of Trujillo," Jack looked over at him.

"I can get a car, but then what? I may know of some people around here that can forge a few documents but it would take time to get good ones," Golightly seemed to be ready to do what was necessary. Jan had never asked about Jack's past, but was now pretty sure he had worked black-ops before, probably with Ward. Everyone had their own backups.

"We can take a small flight down to Temuco, Chile with a

quick stopover in Santiago. Then we can catch a flight to the Falkland Islands, it won't be direct either. Then change planes there and get into Rio the next day. That will put us traveling for about twenty hours and then we will lay over in Rio for about fourteen hours. Not a direct route and hard enough to trace as we will use about three different identities as we travel through the airports. The paperwork is already in the bag, and I assume that Jan has hers as well," she gave Ward a nod. During the entire night they had been in contact with each other as they worked. "From there we will travel on two different flights back to the states, landing in both San Diego and Phoenix. On the last leg you and Jan will travel as husband and wife, it will give you both credible cover. Just depends on who wants to follow the scientist and who wants to go after Bobby," Ward looked up at Jan, and in that instant his fears had been confirmed. Volumes were spoken with no words passing between them. Time stood still as they imagined what their futures could be; they both could see one of pleasure, and one of pain. Bobby had wanted her for himself at one time. Ward had always known that. The best way to approach this was for her to be the pawn in his vicious game. Jan knew what she had to do and so did Ward.

"This time he's mine," Jan's voice was dead serious, low and lethal. It came from somewhere deep inside her soul and he could feel her determination. It was one thing Ward couldn't argue with her about. She was just as capable of facing him as he was, almost. He just didn't like the idea.

"I'll need his file. How will we know where this Bobby is?" Jack knew he didn't need to ask the question, but felt he should.

"He already told Moore he was going to take care of her. All she has to do is put herself out there for him to find and that won't be hard," Ward's voice was deadpan. His feelings were nonexistent now, pushed so deep that no one could get to them, not even Jan. Golightly looked at the both of them. He couldn't believe what he had just heard. Even though Ward knew that Bobby was planning on killing her if he couldn't have her, or worse, Ward was going to let her become the bait.

"And you're okay with this," his voice exploded out of his chest. The disbelief echoing throughout the room and vibrating in his thoughts so strongly that neither one of them had a doubt what he was thinking.

"It's the only choice. If I go after him he will try and may succeed in killing me. He will still try for her. He wants her to lure me back in. And yes, he plans on killing us both if we don't see things his way, but if the two of you partner up she has a better chance. He won't kill her right away. You're still dead, remember, and we need more than just Bobby. He has about three guys he works with regularly. Without them, we just dent the problem. The leaks still happen and the mole gets away. If Jan can get to him, she may have a chance of discovering their identities, and more importantly we have a chance to keep any more information from going overseas. I'll follow the scientist and see if I can find out how much information he has passed on to them and what information they have been paying for. I will also try to discover the next drop. If I'm right, it will be back in Rosarito.

"If it all works then we will meet at the same time to bring them all down, including Bobby before he can harm anyone else. We don't have a choice," Ward was matter of fact and that in itself bothered Golightly. "Bro I know this bothers you. It would bug the hell out of me if I let it, but we are all trained, and trained well. We had to come to terms with who we were and what we could expect from each other a long time ago. Jan and I belong to neither world any more. We don't work for the department, and we can't live in the real world with the skills we have. I've tried, we've tried, it doesn't work," he sighed knowing the pain Jack was feeling.

"But," Jack opened his mouth to say more and stopped.

"This is our life, and what we do, we just do it independently of any system. We pick and choose the people we want to trust. We both know what we signed up for, and we have accepted it. You're the one that needs to get over it. We promised each other only the present from the time we started this affair. If we get tomorrows, all the better, if not we have given our lives for what we believe in," his eyes now ablaze with his fervor. "If we all keep our heads no one will get hurt," and he turned to look straight into Jack's eyes now, "And we all knew what we were signing up for when we joined these little country clubs. Even if Jan and I don't work officially for the government that doesn't mean we forgot the commitment we made many years before to our country, to the people we serve. If anything, we are more dedicated now than we were before."

Jack stopped for a moment and thought. It had been many years since Susan's death. She had agreed to marry and move to Peru. She was going to become an Agency man's wife. She had never known all the risky jobs he had done over the years and how close he had come, so many times, to losing his life. He wondered now if she had known that, would she have chanced getting involved with him. Losing himself in his own thoughts, he had to question if he had been unfair to Susan? With Jan and Ward, they had both joined up first, devoted their lives to the cause, and then stumbled into a relationship and then a commitment. It was a very different situation than he had been in, they had both known what could be, or couldn't be, in their futures. Jack had seen their unconditional devotion to each other, and the depth of their love. He had felt that once before himself, and Ward, more than any one else, had known what it was like for him to lose it. He didn't doubt that if one of them got hurt or worse, it would be hard, but not the same as it had been for him.

"I understand," and Jack looked over at Jan, "Then I guess I get to play the role of your devoted husband." Ward's fingers flew over the keyboards again and tickets were booked.

Golightly slipped out the door to get a car while Jan and Ward prepared to go. By the time Golightly had acquired the old car that would safely take them away from Lima, Ward and Jan had packed up the safe house and wiped it down. As they worked their way through the apartment they didn't speak. Occasionally they had wandered into each other's minds only to find that all their emotions had been safely tucked away until an undetermined time when they would both have time to deal with what was coming. In Rio there would be time, Ward had arranged this. The layover there would provide them some needed time together. It would be enough for them to connect for one night before life got tough. Ward had booked the hotel there, one they had used before. The mission may come first, but they planned to work in one last today.

The sun had come up fully now and the city was waking and starting to move. It wasn't a pure light like the day before but a light tainted with pollution that included deceit, evil, and traitors. Sitting in silence they drove down the coastal highway with the windows down and the smell of the sea whipping into the car. Each one quietly prepared for the journey that lay ahead. Jan watched the ocean when it came into view taking solace in the movement of the waves toward the shore as her ponytail whipped around in the wind. It was a constant to her, what was given to the ocean would again return to the shore with the changing tides. It may not be the same as when it had drifted out, changed in a way that may be good or bad, but it would return to the shore at some time. Jan found comfort in that, and in the fact that they would all return to each other as the ocean returned to the beach. They may be changed, different, but they would all drift back to where they should be. She was sure of it now; they would win. She held on to that thought as her breath mimicked the ocean waves.

Ward and Jack had taken turns driving the winding road. It was taking most of their concentration when they were at the wheel as fast as they were traveling. When he wasn't driving Ward's eyes were turned up to the skies and he watched the birds circle and dive into the ocean for sustenance. He marveled at their elegance and skill. He watched as they spun in graceful circles and plunged willingly into the ocean. It didn't matter what type of bird it was, seagull or pelican, they made it seem effortless, and he took in their strength with his eyes. They continuously challenged the ocean over and over again, and sometimes got the reward of food, sometimes they came up empty. Determined they would try again and again until they succeeded. He watched those that floated on the waves enjoying the meal they had just finished. He watched the two merge together as the bird landed and floated on the waves, the bird and the ocean moving together as one, as the waves caressed and soothed the bird. Jan was his stability and his calm, his ocean. Even if they were separated for a while they would again comfort one another once this was done.

They had left without any incidents, and they had expected none until they reached the airport. Jack had met with the contact before he had gotten the car, and given him all the instructions. With luck they would stay one step ahead of the group they were hunting. When Ward was at the wheel, Golightly watched the hills and reflected on what it meant to be part of the Agency. It had been his home, his aspirations as a young man. He lived off the adrenaline highs, like he suspected his companions did as well. His life had never been uneventful. Sometimes it had not been what he wanted either, but he had been luckier than most. He had never lived under the same restrictions that the rest of the world had had, and he wondered what he would have done if he had been forced to. He had been free to love, marry, and live a life that if it wasn't normal, it was at least not a prison sentence. He began to wonder what his life would have been like if he had been accepted to the PED.

His eyes trailed off to the hills that dramatically rose out of the landscape. On the hills he could just barely see two animals standing together. They were too far away to be positive what type they were, and Jack let the identity of the animals wander from his thoughts as he began to imagine them to be two wolves. He let his mind drift and slowly he began to have a vision. He allowed his vision to continue as he blankly stared at the hills. The female wolf pushed at the male encouraging him to move on, to make his way south through the rocky and sparse hillside without her. It was not an easy path, and the male struggled. As the male pushed on through the harsh terrain; the female wolf turned, looked back once toward the male wolf and left, silently moving away from him and fading from the picture. Golightly wondered what it all meant, but was afraid to face the fact that he might already know. It was time to move on, to change and let the future take him where it may. He had never had to hunt down a mind reader before. The challenge was one that enticed him and petrified him at the same time. It was his turn to be there for Ward, to even the score. The vision was clear and he wondered if his blocking skills were good enough to keep them safe.

It was late afternoon. They were now only an hour away from the airport. Ward pulled the car to the side of the road. The view was spectacular. The ocean was a brilliant blue and through the open windows of the car you could hear the cries of the seagulls, the crashing of the waves, and the smell of the salt water. A large rocky hill loomed off to the side of the car with crevasses that kept the sun from their depths no matter what time of day it was. The power of nature converged at this point bringing the water, sky, and land together. He picked up Jan's phone and began a text message. Jan knew who he was texting and as Ward typed it, she read, "J and W are on their way back to base. J is target. G will assist. W will work with the test tubes. Only seven days left. Animal found and trapped. May need your assistance to keep others clear of J and G until needed. W out."

Chapter 15

The flights seemed to criss-cross the South American continent. The planes were small, not more than a fifty seater at any time, and even though they didn't sit together they had a hard time distancing themselves from one another. They studied the people on each plane with Ward and Jan scanning the minds of everyone. When they had each decided everything was clear Ward was able to relax a bit. Indulging, he sat and watched his wife, not his partner or his coworker, as the details of the plan floated again and again in his mind. What she was facing scared the hell out of him, not that his job was a piece of cake. She was actually planning on confronting Bobby. With any luck he would never see him. Trying to keep from agonizing over what Jan was going to face, he tried to focus on what he had to do. He would need to get into the MedLab center and do a little looking around, but it wasn't as if Bobby would be there. He had hacked through to some of their computer files and had been impressed with the types of research projects he had found. If the information that was being passed and sold was only half as good as what Ward had accessed, then the government could be in trouble.

Their current focus was on the genetic engineering of fruits for faster inoculation of a population against a wide spread biological attack. There was also genetic engineering that went the other way, but it wasn't discussed much. All Ward had been able to access were the general files; none of the experiments had been logged into the data base that he could hack into. Whoever was managing the security had it down pat. He would need direct access to the guy's office and especially those computers that were not online to access the damage already done. That would be tricky. A break-in was too obvious, it would take a long time to plan in order to make sure no alarms were raised, but it might just be the only way in. He would spend a day or two shadowing the guy before he made his final choice.

Ward wished that he could have gotten two different flights out of Trujillo, but that had been impossible. He hoped the route was choppy enough to cause confusion if someone got wind of them and tried to follow what they did. He had chosen the back of the plane so he could keep his eyes on Jan, for pleasure purposes only. With each flight, they had changed their appearances just a little. When they landed on the Falkland Islands they looked completely different than when they had begun the trip. They were tired and ready for a rest, but no one would be able to tell by just looking at them. They each looked as if they had just had a good night's sleep and were ready for a day's work. Shoulders squared and eyes constantly scanning the area for threats. The Falkland Islands was just a gamble. Not many flights came or went from here. A Bonus was that it wouldn't be a place that anyone would look for them to book through. If they had been tracked to Chile, then they would have lost the tail by now. Walking off the flight, they turned and walked across the concrete to the next plane that would get them into Rio before the day was finished.

Joining the line to board the plane they stood in silence, no one acknowledging the other. Once on the small but comfortable hundred seat jet, they all leaned back and one by one closed their eyes once again after they had done their checks of the crew and passengers. Since the flight would take a few hours they wouldn't be in any danger until they were back on the ground. It was the perfect time to recharge the cells.

As hard as Ward tried, he couldn't fall asleep, even once he felt the landing gear click into place. He checked the minds of those around him again and found nothing. He watched out the window as the sun began to fade into the background of the blue sky. Not knowing what else to do, he looked at Jan and her mind was open to him, welcoming him. He crept into her thoughts effortlessly and allowed her to guide his thoughts with hers as she started to fall asleep. He could see Jan's mind drifting slowly into a dream like state. It was a heady feeling to know that he could just stay in her mind and allow himself to be absorbed by her, wrapped up in her dreams, lost with her. But as intoxicating as it would be he knew it would serve no purpose to stay, so he made himself pull out slowly enough not to wake her, and they each drifted off to sleep, alone.

Jack had been the first asleep; he was also the first awake an hour and a half later. He didn't look back at Ward. They had not spoken or acknowledged one another since they dumped the car hours before. It would be like this until the end of the trip. Golightly took the time to think as the others slept on. He looked out the window and down at the ocean. Ward had partnered him with Jan and he had a responsibility to take care of her, to be her backup. In reality, they were a team and they would function as such. But Ward knew Jack's history in the area of relationships almost better than he did. Ward had been there at the beginning and then at the end of his relationship. He had called for Ward during that most difficult time, knowing that if anyone could help him save her, it was him. Jack made a silent vow to himself and the team, that he would do everything in his power to keep them all safe and assure the success of this mission. He owed that much to Ward. When they got off this plane Jan and Jack would proceed to the hotel and check in as husband and wife. From that moment on they would be working undercover in order to draw Bobby into the web. His thoughts were interrupted when in the distance Jack could see land coming into sight.

Ward stirred when he felt the slight change in air pressure as the plane started to drop altitude for landing. He felt Jack's thoughts enter his head. The other people on the plane had not been a cause of concern when they started the trip. Now that they were approaching landing things may be different, so after one last quick read and finding nothing he left them each alone to their own thoughts again. Ward gently reached back into Jan's mind and woke her up. They stayed together for only seconds before the announcement came on in Portuguese to prepare for landing. With their gear stowed and the plane slowly dipping to land in Rio, they all waited, ready for anything. If anyone had been able to trace their plane trips they would try to pick them up at the airport before they could disappear again. If they were clear, it would be the last chance to relax, and catch some sleep. The landing was smooth and the sights from the window breathtaking as they came into the airport. They could see the many lights from a city that seemed not to know it was night. Up on the hill, the gigantic statue of Jesus beckoned them to come enter into the city as nothing else could.

Jack was first off the plane. He did a quick scan of the area and saw nothing out of place. He left his mind open, knowing that

Jan or Ward could be working through him as well to check the area. Jan followed behind with about fifteen people between them. As she made her way into the airport she could barely see Jack and she could only feel Ward's presence behind her. She had looked through Jack's mind and wandered through the terminal among the many other thoughts there. She limited herself to the right side of the terminal and Ward went left. That way they could cover the area quicker. It worked the same way as if you were visually scanning an area. They had no luggage to pick up, just what they carried with them in their duffle bags, their go bags, as they walked from the airport terminal out to the curb. With each of them catching separate cabs they would arrive within fifteen minutes of each other at the hotel. Jan and Jack were registered as Mr. and Mrs. Lightner at the Ibiza Copacabana. Lightner was a name Ward had used at the department for cover many times and if Bobby traced their travels back to here then there would be no surprises. It was the worm for the hook. Ward had taken a room in the same hotel. He was using a cover that Bobby had never known; one that no one knew. From landing to arriving at the hotel it took all of forty-five minutes. They had sensed nothing, seen nothing, but never assumed once that they were safe. Ward checked in and went to the room just before Jan and Jack entered the lobby together.

Jan and Jack met in the front lobby and checked in as mister and missus. Jack placed his arm around Jan's waist as they checked in and for all purposes they looked the devoted, happy couple. Jan leaned into Jack and put her hand around his waist as well. As they walked to the room they held hands, laughed, and smiled knowingly at each other. They didn't stop touching each other until they had safely gotten into the room. In the room Jan slung her bag onto the couch and checked out the room. Jack checked out the bathroom and the closet area. Jan walked over and looked out the window. She fingered her ring, which she wore on her right hand instead of the left. Jack turned just in time to watch her.

"You really love him don't you." He wasn't asking a question, it was an observation. Jack stood, arms folded, by the end of the bed and studied her.

"Yah, I really do. He'd also do anything for me," Jan paused, "and I for him. This is where you come in." She walked over to the couch in the room and sat down. The room wasn't large, but it was good sized. It was an older hotel that she and Ward had stayed in before; well kept and a popular place. She knew the layout well and later that would come in handy. There was one queen sized bed in the room and a pull out couch. The older walls were made of plaster and the burnt orange color that covered the walls in various shades added a feeling of the setting sun within the confines of a small room. The small table lamps added a soft glow as well.

"How did you two hook up?" He wanted to know more about how she had met his friend. Jack knew the rules about relationships in their department. There weren't supposed to be any. The idea that they would stay completely clear of the opposite sex was unreal, and the department knew that, but they also made it clear that anything they started would never last; wouldn't be allowed to last. They had broken a huge rule and the whys of it made him want to know more. Jack had been trying to gather information from the moment he had learned she existed, and he thought he might have pieced some of the whys together himself figuring out how long this must have been going on.

"Guess it was love at first sight, I know that seems cliché but once we saw each other it was hard to not get together. Maybe we were more intrigued by each other's minds at first, what we saw in them. Some might have thought it was a lust thing, but that wasn't what happened. We only got our first chance to talk after a training session Ward had set up to purposely meet with me for longer than just a few minutes in passing. I suppose that's when we truly fell in love," Jan was staring off into space. Time passed but not for Jan. She was somewhere else, mentally, that she was really enjoying. She gave a small sigh, "but right now we need to make our plan of attack. I didn't want to do it with Ward around, well. . ." and she let her voice trail off.

"If I'm right, he might be near enough to know, and in the end I don't think I'll like what's about to happen much either," Jack looked at her and sat down on the bed opposite her.

"No you won't, but it will be the only way to do it, and he knows," Jan pulled out the phone and checked for messages, "I want to clear his name." There were none. "I plan on contacting Bobby when we get back. He knows I've, or we've, given him the slip and have been in Peru. He won't be easily taken in; I'm going to have to convince him to meet with me. That is where I'm going to need some information. I need to know how good you are at working with and against readers. We will have the advantage, he thinks you are dead and will be looking for Ward. But if he finds a trace of anything unusual, you will be in more danger than I could ever be."

"I was once accepted for PED training, didn't pass the third phase. I did learn enough to be considered as prime partner material and it is noted in my second file that I have reliable empathic abilities," Jack kept his thoughts on mundane things and closed the rest of his mind just in case she was trying to read him.

"Why didn't you take it?" Jan was trying to read him. She was reaching into his mind and looking for anything, it was one way of testing him. What she found was that his skills at blocking were formidable. She was having a hard time registering anything past the basics of daily life, which made his block less noticeable. This was good. Unless he was careless, he wouldn't be considered a target.

"Seemed too restrictive and I liked my job in the CIA well enough, so I went back," Jack turned his thoughts to the daily grind of keeping the bills paid and the paperwork done.

"Not bad," Jan looked at him and stood up. They both knew what she was talking about. She moved to the window and looked out. Just one more hour she thought. "You have pretty good coping skills for someone who hasn't been partnered with a reader."

"Thank you. Thought you might be checking," he smiled. "Remember, Ward and I have worked together in the past. As one who knew about the department, I was able to request assistance from them many times. Over the years it has been to my benefit to keep Ward from picking at my head at times," Jack walked over to the phone in the room, "I'll order room service for tonight, make it look like we are spending the night in."

"Good idea. Just get me something light," Jan found it hard to eat on a mission and heard Jack order a light meal for himself as well. Jan opened up the phone and connected to the web. She checked the news services and the data bases of the department to make sure that their paths would not cross. Jack spent the time taking care of the equipment they had brought with them. He made sure that everything was in order and stowed away from security scanners and X-rays. He spent just a couple of minutes looking at Jan's knife. It was just what he had thought it to be, especially made for her. It looked like it would fit her hand perfectly and balanced out well with the weight of the blade. Keeping his thoughts secure, he wondered just where her scars from the training were. Even though they tried to keep readers out of harms way most of the time, they always kept them well trained just in case. No matter how hard one tried, danger had a way of catching up with a person and it was better to have your investment well protected. About twenty minutes later, after all was done, there was a knock on the door. Jack walked over and opened it, taking the cart from the man. He slipped him a wad of cash and the man walked away with a smile on his face. Jan knew what he was thinking and if it had been Ward in this room then he would have been right.

"Supper," was all Jack said at first as he wheeled the cart into the room after giving it a quick check. He had ordered them two salads and two shaved pork sandwiches with two cokes.

"Thanks. So far all's quiet. If they know we are here, no one is saying. All the bases are clear of extra traffic for now. Rob has kept us in the clear as promised," Jan picked at the sandwich and drank the coke.

"So, what's it like?" This time Jack's question was real as he bit into his sandwich.

"What's what like?" Jan was tempted to take a quick read and see what he meant, but knew that talking with Jack would also give her insights as to who he was. It might also be easier since he was so good at blocking.

"If there is a chance that this Bobby character is going to mess with my head I want to know what it feels like," Jack started in on the salad, waiting patiently for her answer and being careful not to look up. It was a while before Jan wanted to answer. She had relived those memories many times in her head. And with each time it had gotten easier and easier, but no less painful. Now, there in front of her was a man who wanted to know just what it felt like for someone to try and rip the memories from your head. It was a good five minutes before Jack thought he should speak again, "I'm sorry, but I need to know." This time his voice was softer.

"It's not easy to explain, and a nonreader may have different experiences," she took another sip of the cola, "I have meditated on this many times, and have relived it in dreams, nightmares really, about as many. Each time the pain eases, but it never goes away. That's the worst scar both Ward and I have to deal with. At first it's like the worst migraine you've ever had and just when you think your head will explode from the pain, it gets worse. Every thought, every memory, every experience is exploding in your head as you try to control and keep them. The harder you fight, the worse it gets and when you think and pray that the pain may just kill you, you pass out and there is nothing,"

"Nothing?" Jack had stopped eating. He was fascinated as he watched the expression on her face during the time it took her to tell him the story. Her face went from one of control to one of pain and then nothing, a blank slate, as if she were living it all over again. He had to wonder how much of the effects still lingered with the both of them. It was the type of scar you couldn't see, the worst type that was the hardest to live with.

"On my last PED assignment I woke up in the hospital. I couldn't remember who or what I was. It was like amnesia, only worse," she stopped for a moment looking thoughtful, "By worse I mean I felt like a part of me had been ripped away. Ward and I were able to mentally fight him in order to keep our memories away from him. For me it was instinctual somehow. Over time, as I recovered from the many injuries I had suffered besides the amnesia, my memories started to surface, as well as the pain of it. If it hadn't been for Ward," Jan put the sandwich down and looked away. Her mind was no where near Rio at that moment. Jack could tell that she was a thousand miles away. He watched as she mentally shook herself, "let's just say I probably wouldn't be here now. He let me take it in small steps that were easy to handle as I recovered. It's what saved me, but when he went through it he had to do it on his own. That's when I almost lost him without even knowing it."

"What if he does this to you, or him, again?" Jack's concern was growing; the furrow on his brow had deepened as he listened to the pain in her voice. Felt that the pain was real and still fresh.

"He won't. He wants to use me, not control me. He may talk like he wants to kill me, but it's just a cover. This time he wants me to give myself to him," Jan could tell his next question, and she turned her head as if to silence him. "He has to be taken care of this time, cost be damned. He is too dangerous to be left out there. No one is safe until we take him in," and with that, they finished their meal in silence. Jack pushed the cart back into the hall. He hadn't bothered to wonder about the sleeping arrangements for the night. They were all professionals. Jan had gone into the bathroom. He took out the alarm and set it so that they wouldn't miss their plane in the morning.

"I'll take the couch and you take the bed," he said just loud enough to be heard inside the bathroom but not outside of the room.

When he turned around he caught sight of Jan coming out of the bathroom door. "Whoa!" was all he said. She was dressed in a black silk halter dress that clung to her shape. It gently brushed past her knee and swayed with her slightest movement. She must have a thing for the color black, either that or she knew just how good she looked in it. Her hair had been left down, loose, and it draped around her face and bare shoulders. Jack smiled knowingly.

"He doesn't stand a chance does he?" Jan returned his smile and walked toward the door.

"Why don't you take the bed and I'll find another place to get some sleep," and she cracked the door and checked outside, "Maybe." And with a devilish look she was gone.

Jan made her way down the hall and toward the stairwell. She entered unseen. It wasn't the first time she had been in this hotel, and she knew the layout well. She had chosen the back stairwell as it was hardly ever used. She could hear people talking as she passed the next level on her way up to the sixth floor. With each step up she opened her mind more and more. It was a time that they had prearranged, the last time they would be, could be together on this mission. Three floors up, she left the stairwell and walked down the hall. Three doors down she saw the door to room number six hundred and six open just a crack. Jan smiled and heard the soft music coming from inside and she could see a hint of light outlining the door. Ward was hiding his thoughts; she could only feel the quick beating of his heart and his constant and steady breathing. No one was in the hall and no one saw her as she slid inside the room and closed the door.

Jan noticed the room was dark, with only a small lamp lit in the corner. She could feel the breeze coming in the windows and hear the rustle of the curtains as they moved with the wind. There was a faint sweet smell of tropical fruit in the room and there was a large vase of exotic flowers sitting on the dresser. The colors complemented the room, what she could see of it, but she didn't really need to see it, she had seen the room before. Jan walked into the area three more steps and stopped. She felt him behind her and she waited. He hadn't even touched her and the electricity between them could light all of Rio itself. Jan's eyes closed and she soaked in the feeling. He was near her now, but still the only thing that was touching were their minds, and they allowed their thoughts, feelings and impressions to mingle until they were unsure of just whose thoughts were whose.

Moving up behind Jan he was close enough to touch her yet he only allowed their minds to mix. Once both of their thoughts were reeling, and all their nerve endings were vibrating with anticipation he gently touched her back with his fingertips letting his hands spread slowly and then wrapping around her. Together they began to move through a slow and methodical tai chi routine. Each movement brought them closer together in both body and spirit as their muscles relaxed and tightened. Inch by inch they wrapped around each other during the slow and steady movements, becoming one in both mind and body. When they stopped and stood quietly in the resting position with their bodies resting on each other they were finally one, finally relaxed and ready to enjoy each other's company. Ward let his hands move from her waist towards the straps of the dress around her neck. She could feel his gentle pull on the ties. Ward let the straps slip through his fingers and he moved slightly away from her for a second to allow the dress to slip to the floor. At that moment, the only thing that existed was the present, the night that they would share before they separated; the future and past were nonexistent.

He sat in the dark, in a modestly comfortable chair. He had come in the back way, unseen. It had been a long time since he had climbed in that way. When he had entered the apartment he hadn't switched on any lights. He didn't need to. Every piece of furniture in this apartment he knew well and where it was located in the room. He had spent a lot of time here when she had been part of the department and later after she wasn't it had been comforting at times to spend days and nights here as well. It had helped him heal. He should have let the apartment go a long time ago, but he wanted her to have a place to come back to if things didn't work out. Rob chuckled at the thought that he would have been an over protective father if he had ever had kids. She wasn't even his daughter and he was treating her like a child when it came to her relationships. All of her experiences over the years should have assured him that she was capable of knowing what she wanted, and how to get it; more importantly, how to protect herself from the unwanted as well. He had spent a week in the hospital recovering after she had saved his hide the last time they had worked together. His thoughts had spun around wildly trying to figure out when they had gotten married, to being a bit angry at not being invited, or even trusted to be told. It had been a while now and all that was over. It was the past. They were happy and they did work well together. If any two people deserved each other's love and respect, it was those two. They both deserved this happiness.

When he had gotten the text message yesterday he was furious. Rob had left the department in a hurry and without informing anyone where he was headed. He didn't even know. Driving around the city he had calmed down and realized what he was really mad at. It wasn't the fact that they had again put themselves into a position of danger, it was the fact that they were in danger from all sides, not just one, and there was nothing, absolutely nothing, he could do about it he had thought. He couldn't get the department off their backs, and Bobby wanted Jan and Ward dead, none of which made anything any easier. Yet they still pushed on to do the job they were trained to do. They did it now for some internal sense of right and not just because their government employed them.

He had gone into the department for only two hours today. Organized his presumed search for Jan and Ward for Gregg to see and approve. He never filed those papers though. Rob then did a little looking for Bobby. After an hour, Rob realized that Bobby had hidden himself so well that only Jan or Ward would be able to drive him out. For that matter, Ward and Jan had hidden themselves pretty well. He couldn't find anything on where they lived, or spent what free time they might have. He had a general location now. He had done a basic search of property owners in the northern Baja and come up blank. They weren't using any aliases he knew. The only benefit to this would be that Bobby wouldn't be able to trace them to that part of Mexico either if he was trying.

He had gotten lucky early on. He was able to get a bag to Jan in Peru. All the items in the bag were ones she would normally be issued, or have. Being unsure of just what would be available to her, he wanted her to have access to some of the best equipment. Besides, they were all her things. Getting it to her was another problem. He would have liked her to have taken it with her when she left, but without diplomatic connections there was no way the bag would make it through. Contacting their middle man he found that he was on vacation in Hawaii. With just a few little changes he had him going through Peru just in time to meet her and give her the bag. So far everything had worked out.   It was what was to come that bothered him and made him sick to his stomach.

Earlier today he had come to a very dire conclusion.   There was a knock at the door.   Rob didn't look at his watch, she was on time.   She was always on time.

Chapter 16

The plane arrived without incident in Phoenix and they looked out the window during the final approach. Six days, that was all the time they really had to solve this. The back wheels hit the ground and they were again connected to the world. The area was no different than when Jan had taken off from here a few days ago. The sky was a clear bright blue that nearly hurt to look at and the horizon promised the same for tomorrow. The deep red and orange rock that made up the mountains stood out in contrast against the blue of the sky. The city sprawled aimlessly out around the airport. Once the front wheels touched, Jack leaned over to her and said almost silently in her ear, "Are you ready?"

"Yes," was Jan's only reply as she squared her shoulders. It wasn't long before the plane pulled up to the jet way. They disembarked and walked down the corridor in Sky Harbor among all the other travelers gently moved along by the general bustle of those around them. The sights and sounds were always the same in airports. There were travelers on their way to somewhere or coming back from somewhere else, an occasional beep coming from the security checkpoint and the rumble of words, as well as thoughts, coming from every direction hung in the air like the noise pollution it was. They had no checked baggage so they went down the escalator and straight over to the rental car stands. Jan pulled out an identity card she had used many times and approached the counter. While Jan handled the rental car, Jack watched the airport looking for anything out of the ordinary. It took five minutes for her to get a car and they were on their way out to the lot to pick it up.

"Is he here?" was all Jack said once they were clear of the terminal. He had seen nothing inside the terminal, but as the cars passed by outside and they waited to cross, he knew it would be easier for Bobby to hide than most people. So far Jan hadn't tensed, but he had to be sure.

"No," she had been searching the area for anyone who may be looking for her, or them. They were disguised so it would be hard to physically pick them out of the crowd. Mentally was another matter, "I haven't felt anyone, but that doesn't mean no one is watching."

"Understood," Jack had also been scanning the airport parking lot that they were about to walk into. Jack had had a chance to read as much as anyone could about Bobby before they had left for Phoenix. Jack had said nothing and only committed the face to memory. What could he say? Some agents went bad; they couldn't ever get the filth off of them that they had seen and been through. As they got to the lot Jan pointed to the blue Ford Focus at the end of the row. Without even speaking Jan went to the driver's side and Jack to the passenger. The doors closed almost at the same time and Jan started the engine.

They pulled out of the lot and both continuously checked for a tail. Jan didn't expect one at this point. She figured that Bobby would make her come to him now. He didn't seem worried about finding her. She easily pulled the car onto the freeway and into traffic heading north. She knew exactly where she was going and reflexes seemed to pull her in that direction. Pulling off Highway Fifty-One on the Thomas exit she drove down the streets until she came to the apartment complex she had once lived in. As she looked again at the simple two story structures, it seemed to her that she was looking at another person's life and she realized just how much she had changed and grown over the past few years.

She had been here just a few days ago but she hadn't had time to take a good look at the place. It was still no different than when she had left. The trees were full grown desert trees and created just a bit of shade for some of the apartments on the lower floor. They were the usual desert trees that spread wide and stayed lower to the ground with full foliage that both covered the area, and with the small leaves let sunlight through. She had chosen an apartment on the upper floor for security and privacy in the back building of the three that surrounded the small courtyard and fenced pool. Her balcony backed onto the edge of the property and the parking lot and was partially hidden by a Palo Verde tree and a snail vine that had long gone out of control on that corner. As of yet the apartment manager still had done nothing with it. It also was the only corner apartment left open when she had moved in.

When she had been involved in the department, she had spent very little time here. It had merely been a stopover between assignments. By being on the corner she had been able to escape most of the people in the building and their thoughts most of the time, which provided her some escape from the world. She noticed that Jack was intently taking in the area as well.

"So, what do you think?" Jan directed her attention to the parking area. She also made sure to park in the visitor's area.

"Not what I thought," he grabbed both bags as the car came to a stop, "Not sure where I thought you would have lived before."

"Does seem pretty generic now. I need to tell Rob to get rid of it in no uncertain terms," she got out of the car and Jack followed, "This place belongs to someone I don't know anymore. Right now though, it can be very useful." They walked into the courtyard and up to the patio of one apartment.

"Up there," Jack looked up to the balcony of the apartment above this one. The climb would be easy and as he looked around he also noticed they would never be seen as they climbed up. The Palo Verde trees were well placed and full enough giving them enough cover to enter and leave the apartment at any time of the day or night in relative secrecy, not to mention the huge snail vine that clung to the bottom of the balcony like a curtain. They entered the apartment quickly through the patio door. Jan had taken the key from Rob when she left for Peru. Things were just as they had been. There was the small brown couch and a chair with the little kitchen table off to the side. There was a note on the kitchen counter as well. Jan picked it up and read it silently as Jack just took it all in. Her face never changed as she read it, but he watched as her skin tone paled momentarily and then returned to normal. Jack watched her neatly fold and place the note in her pocket before turning around. He put his bag on the couch and folded his arms on his chest. Before Jan had a chance to say anything, her cell phone rang. Pulling it out she looked at the number and frowned. He stood watching her and waited knowing the game had just begun.

"Hey cutie. Glad to see you and the boss back. Didn't think I'd be stupid enough not to have the apartment covered, did you?" His voice sounded like molten lava and it burned at her soul. She had expected Bobby to contact her, but this was quick, so she didn't hesitate, she just hung up.

"Was that wise?"   Jack sat down on the chair, his one eyebrow slightly raised.

"He wants me. He won't let a little hang up discourage him. Besides he saw, or someone saw us come in. I'm assuming it's not him because he would have known you weren't Ward and we would have known he was here. All I do know is that he'll call back," and as she said that the phone beeped with a message. She held it up as if to punctuate the fact. Jan looked at the message and read it in quiet. Her face didn't betray any emotion as she finished reading the message and put the phone away.

"Well," Jack waited for an answer.

"All it said was, 'That wasn't very nice. You'll want to see me soon enough.' We should be fairly safe tonight, but after that," Jan sat down on the couch and looked out the balcony door. Her eyes scanned the area to try and see who was watching them. "I'll take the first shift and you get some rest. I'll wake you in about three hours and then take a nap myself. In the morning we will go over the game plan."

"Okay. Don't take any chances. If you need me, wake me," he walked into the bedroom and removed his shirt as he closed the door. Loosening his belt he removed it before he stretched out on the bed. It took him only moments to fall asleep. Three hours was enough, but not much to work on unless you were trained to do it.

Jan sat staring at the balcony doors. She was constantly scanning the area as the sunset and the colors danced across the sky around the scattered high clouds. There were no sounds as she thought about what was to come and what had already happened, and she had found the flunkies watching the apartment. She had picked up the note from the counter and pocketed it when they had first come in. She hadn't shown the note to Jack and he hadn't asked about it. Rob had left it, last night. She didn't know whether to be happy about the contents or nervous. They had obviously been in the apartment last night. Rob never said exactly who the help he had enlisted was, but some how Jan knew who it had to be. Pat. With this new development she wondered if she should break the silence she and Ward had agreed on. Then, decided against it. She was probably too late to warn him and if Rob thought this was a good idea, she had to trust him. Ward's plane had landed two hours earlier than theirs had. Not letting her mind dwell on what might be in

00

the future she again scanned the area to make sure she hadn't missed anyone and then linked the phone to the Internet to get work done.

    After thirty minutes she wasn't any closer to finding answers than when she began. She tapped her fingers on the table and glanced around the room. Taking in a deep breath she stood up and started her tai chi routine. It was slow and her eyes and mind stayed focused on the world around her, but her muscles released the strain and prepared her. When she finally stopped she stood in the starting position, still and focused.

    The plane landed at LAX on a perfectly bright and breezy California day. He walked off the plane and up the jet way with the crowd of people from the plane. One crowd merged into another in the airport, and he could hardly wait to be out of it. As he approached the security check point he saw a young mother with two kids standing and stretching to look for someone on their way to them from the gates. The oldest girl couldn't be more than five years old and the little boy in her arms looked to be about two to three years old. The little boy must be heavy because she had to continuously adjust him on her hip as he squirmed to get down. He took a glance back and saw that there was a tall young man dressed in uniform out pacing him and looking right at this woman and the kids with a large smile on his face. He gave a wave and the woman waved back accidentally letting go of the five year old girl's hand for only a second. When the girl saw who her mother was looking at, she darted toward her father running the wrong way through the security gates. The officer that saw her dropped his wand and started running toward the girl. This was about to turn into something ugly and it was the last thing this newly reunited couple needed. Ward was closer than the father and dropping down on one knee he stopped the girl until the father was able to run up and beat the TSA officer to her by seconds. He swept her into his arms and swung her around. The guard stopped when Ward smiled at him, his eyes locking onto him for a second. That second was just long enough though for Ward to gain access. Slowly a smile appeared on the guard's face and he turned and walked back to his station. The crisis was over.

    Ward walked past security and the rest of the family that waited on the father and the girl. Not once did she glance at Ward, she only watched her daughter and husband as she held the squiggly child in her arms, a small tear of joy slowly made its way down her cheek. That was fine with Ward. He had spent years, in fact most of his life, living as the gray man, not being noticed by anyone. Following the mass of people that pressed into the baggage claim area he looked at his watch. Not wanting to leave a large trail behind him, he went out the front of the baggage claim area like most people would and grabbed a cab. Traffic was awful. The noise of the cars surrounded him and filled the air. The tranquil look of the sky was in sharp contrast to the sounds and clamor of the city. The temperature was pleasant enough and the cabby was the typical California type, blond hair, surfer's cut, and a tan. If he had wanted to confirm his guess he could have, but most people who looked like him in Southern California were looking for their big break. Ward just didn't think it was worth the effort to read his mind.

The cabby said nothing to Ward as he drove him toward the Amtrak station. He probably figured that Ward wasn't worth any conversation and sang along to the music on the radio. Ward looked at his watch and knew that if he was lucky enough he would get to the station just in time to catch the commuter train back to San Diego. That way there would be a lot of people and he would be just one of the crowd. The closer they got to the train station the more traffic there was. Ward began to wonder if he would make it in time. He gave the cabby a little green encouragement to get him there on time and he complied. The cabby took the next corner a little faster and leaned on the horn. Making it through the last light on an old yellow before the station, he just missed the car turning left. The cab skidded up to the curb just five minutes before the train was scheduled to leave. He got out at the station and paid him. Walking over to the ticket booth, he noticed the people around him and took an interest in none. Getting his ticket he walked back to the platform. Leaning up against the trashcan he stood waiting for the train. Ward was a cautious man and when he got a funny feeling he seldom ignored it. Right now he was getting that feeling and he started to look around. He could see businessmen just standing and tapping their toes, looking at their watches and waiting to get on the train back to home. Some had papers and others were hanging on to briefcases just looking annoyed. There were also business women standing and waiting but they were a bit more anxious than the men, looking down the tracks as if they could make the train appear at will and get them home five minutes sooner.

Ward didn't notice anyone he knew and he started looking into the minds to see where the feeling was coming from. Not being able to pin it down, he stayed alert to his surroundings as the train pulled into the station. Ward climbed into the first cabin that stopped near him, moved toward the back of it and sat down. He watched the people board around him, so far, so good. Nothing seemed out of place. No one took an interest in him and all were busy looking for seats and storing their stuff. The train slowly began its exit from the station and the whistle blew as it left. Ward watched out the window as the town and the surroundings began to move increasingly faster past the window. The large city began to vanish and the ocean once again came into view, again that uneasy feeling poked at him. Only this time it was worse.

Scanning the compartment he could see that most people were reading papers, talking on cell phones, or working on laptops. They had stored their briefcases and various other packages on the racks overhead and were self-absorbed in their own worlds. Some had even made themselves as comfortable as they could on the thinly padded seats and were nodding off to sleep. What he didn't see was her coming up behind him and sitting down; when she touched his shoulder every muscle in his body tightened in both shock and anger. His first response was to run because he knew who and what was causing this feeling now, but just as quickly he quelled it. He remained still, his face set in stone as his mind acknowledged the person before he even turned to look at her.

"Don't jump and run. I'm here to help believe it or not. I thought you might need a little help on this one," Pat was in the chair right behind him. "Don't worry, I don't want to turn you in, but I do want to put this Bobby thing to rest for the good of the department." Pat got up now and gracefully placed herself in the seat next to Ward. Ward noticed that Pat had changed her hair. It was darker now, not quite black, but with streaks of gray. It was cut short and in such a way, that care would be easy. She had dressed in navy slacks and a short sleeve sweater that matched. He never would have picked her out of the crowd without being able to see into her head. She was dressed for a mission as a businesswoman, but Ward wondered just what her mission really was. Pat had never believed that Bobby was still alive. What she had believed was that Ward had lost it when he died. Even if Rob had told her that he had seen him, she would have demanded more proof than that.

"How much do you know?" Ward looked straight ahead again, shielding his mind from her. And he couldn't help but notice that Pat did the same. She fiddled with some papers in her hands.

"I got a whiff of what Rob was doing and approached him. I convinced him to tell me just enough to know that the picture that Jan supplied him makes things so very complicated for the both of you, and you need an easy in with the labs," Pat relaxed for a minute and placed her hands on the armrests. When she did that a newspaper with an envelope containing a wad of papers gently dropped into his lap. Ward picked it up and moved the pile into his other hand. It was odd. In many ways it was like the old days. She was here to drop off an identity; a well prepared one, with him so that he could enter the lab without suspicion. The motion of the train vibrated through him as he gently and discreetly held on to the envelope. A little corner of him somewhere missed the old days when things had been this easy, but there had to be a catch.

"What is it you want in all of this?" There was nothing like the direct approach. He looked out the window again enjoying the smooth sway of the train and waited for her answer.

"Simple," she paused. "I go with you. We need what you already know and your expertise to solve this problem, and we both know a leak like this is a problem," and with that she looked at him directly. She waited for him to turn and answer. She didn't try to read his mind; he would have it locked away, just like hers. She respected that.

"Then when it's over you go away just like that, huh?" Ward turned now to look directly at her. Their faces were only about a foot apart. Ward looked into the eyes of one of his trainers, a coworker, a friend, and saw the years of experience she had. He also realized what she might be giving up if caught with him.

"Yes, sort of. If he is still alive as you swear he is, I take him in tow and leave both of you alone," Pat looked at Ward, "Then again if you are wrong. . ."

"I'm not."

"Then you have nothing to worry about," Pat guessed what he was thinking, "If we are caught together you'll have to knock me out," and she paused for emphasis, "and make it look good. I'm not ready to give up everything like you two did. Think you can do that?" Pat smiled. Ward relaxed and leaned back in his seat.

"With pleasure," he closed his eyes and smiled at the thought.

"You don't have to enjoy it you know," and she saw Ward's grin grow. "Grow up. Now, you might want to read the paper to see what I have planned and if we need any modifications." Ward opened the paper and started to read her plans completely aware that she had used the word 'we' and not just him. She was unwilling to open her mind up completely to him, and he was also unwilling to let her read his yet. Trust would still have to grow between them.

Ward noticed the plan was simple. They were supervisors sent in from the Chicago offices. By keeping to the supervisor role then they wouldn't be expected to know too much about the research itself, more of the business side of it. Ward looked at his identity card and noticed that the picture bore a resemblance to him, but wasn't his picture. The hair was a bit too dark and the face a touch short in the chin. It would be close enough to match as long as no one took too long of a look. He figured she must have created the picture from memory and his old files.

"Best I could do on short notice. It was made for Rob so I had to make your picture fit the profile. Familiarize yourself with the bio. We are expected to show up at the plant tomorrow morning, but I figured you just might want to visit some people first," she leaned back in the chair and pretended to be looking straight ahead.

"It'll be late," he mentioned as he read.

"Our target likes to work late. Never leaves until seven and then goes straight home. His bio is also in there," her voice barely carried to his ears. It wasn't a safe way to communicate especially when they could read each other's minds, but there was still a trust issue.

"Why?"

"Why what?" and she turned her head slightly to look in his direction.

"This," was all he said as he held out his fake identity papers.

"If you're right then we have more than one problem that needs to be solved. Not only do we not need files being sold; we don't need any rogue agents and networks out there working against us. If he exists," She stopped and Ward just waited, "I want him back, bad." She didn't wait to continue, "Plus, in all the time you've been gone you've never done anything that would worry me. Well, except take Jan, but I think that was mutual. I feel that we've, or I've, been just a bit hard on the both of you," she paused not looking in his direction but watching the people on the train around them. Sarcastically she continued, "Is that what you wanted to hear?"

"It's a start."

He sat in the dark. Jack had woken two hours ago and he sat waiting, hoping for nothing. There had been no signs of anything, no lights, no sounds, nothing. He was good at waiting. Like Jan had done earlier, Jack also checked for information on the databases that he was able to access. They hadn't given him all the access they had, but he had a fair bit. Soon it would be morning and the games would begin again. The stakes were higher than they were when he had first started and the time short. He knew that chances would be taken and that he would need to be on the ready. The more he thought about Bobby, the more he worried about how Jan would handle him. If he truly was as bad as they said, and Jack had no reason to believe he wasn't, then it would be a battle of minds. He hoped Jan's was strong enough. He reached for his bag and slowly and methodically checked his gun and clip. Everything was ready to go and he strapped it on. He heard her stir in the other room and looked at his watch. It was still an hour too early for her to be up, and he hoped that she was just turning over in her sleep, although he knew better. Even he had felt the energy change.

Jan turned over in the bed. Her dreams had taken a turn for the worse. She had seen Ward and she had seen the accident so many years ago, only this time her vantage point was from the top of the cliff. Shaking herself partially awake she turned over again. This time the dream refocused on the gash that Ward had gotten by his eye. She saw the knife come at him. Ward sat, unable to move and, as if she were inside of Ward's head, she felt the point of the knife touch and draw blood. Like the accident scene it started to fade and then it was gone. When her dreams refocused she could see her own swollen face. Jan could feel all her pain, the broken bones and the tenderness of the new bruises. Then as if she was attacking herself she could feel her mind being prodded, drained, and flushed of all she was. She felt her silent scream of pain as if her mind was turned inside out and drained from her head. Her feelings and everything about her were being ripped painfully from her head. Making herself wake up she shot straight up in bed covered in sweat trying to catch her breath as she gulped in air. Ward had never told her the story of that scar before and only one other person could know about that and about the accident. Bobby. Her head throbbed and she knew that he was near, in her mind almost too far into her mind to keep him from leaving. Taking a deep breath she pushed out his thoughts and her headache decreased back to a dull thud.

"That sick SOB," she thought she could hear laughing in her head. Getting up she grabbed her clothes and went into the bathroom. She didn't turn on the lights. He already knew that he had gotten to her and he wanted her tired so that she would make a mistake. She splashed cold water on her face to help bring her back to reality.

Jack heard the movement in the other room. A moment later, he glanced at the door to the bedroom and in the light from the moon he could see the door open with her standing there holding her head. She rubbed it gingerly on one side and looked back at Jack. He didn't have to be told; it had begun.

"He near?" Jack asked the question even though he was sure of the answer.

"Too near," was all she responded as she turned and walked into the kitchen still rubbing her head. It was the first time Jack had real questions about the sanity of the plan they had. "Let's move," was all she shouted from the other room. As Jack stood up, he unconsciously touched his gun at his waist.

Chapter 17

Pat hailed a cab when they got off the train. The cab pulled up to the side of the curb and Ward opened the door for Pat. She climbed in and slid to the opposite side of the cab placing her bag at her feet. Ward got in the cab and placing his bag on top of his feet he got to the business of opening his bag of goodies. When he began to take out small pieces of equipment and place it into his pockets for easier access, Pat was silently surprised and impressed. As she watched, Pat was just a little disconcerted at the type of equipment Ward had in his bag and available to him. It wasn't equipment a civilian should have access too. She gave him a quick look and then turned away, not wanting to know any more; after all she had promised she wouldn't take him in after this and so far that was a promise she intended to keep. Ward ignored her as she gave the name and address of the hotel they were to stay at to the driver. He gave her that much trust and thought how ironic it was that he was now working with departmental monies again.

It took the cab only ten minutes to get to the hotel and it pulled into the loading and unloading zone right in front. Pat told the driver to wait as she ran into the hotel lobby. They were only making a quick stop at the hotel on the way to the labs. She handed the nearly empty bags to the desk clerk and was back in seconds. As she got into the cab again she handed Ward a pin with his cover's name on it. Ten minutes later the cab pulled up to the entrance of the laboratory. This time she didn't tell the driver to wait. Walking up to the gate they showed their identity cards to the security guard.

"If you could wait one moment while I check on who is available to show you around," not knowing exactly who to contact he called in the night security supervisor. Their information had been sent earlier today about their arrival but the consensus had been that it would only be tomorrow when they arrived. This visit was a big deal and the information had just been sprung on all of them like it was a surprise inspection making everyone in the complex a little nervous, "I'm sorry the director isn't here right now. They were under the impression that you would arrive tomorrow."

"We arrived in early enough to come and just take a quick look around," Ward continued to explain in a very business like tone that they only wanted to familiarize themselves with the building before the morning, and that they had nothing to worry about from this visit as it was for new monies allocations. They wanted to be able to accurately and quickly complete the efficiency reports they were to file.   This seemed to settle well. With that said the night supervisor was more than happy to walk them through just about every part of the complex.

The lobby was generic, a couple of chairs and a reception desk. Ward ignored that area as they were taken back through the double doors. He only had so many mini-cams available and he wasn't about to waste them on just any old person. They walked down a hall, passed the offices and then were keyed into the lab area itself. It was a complicated system, retinal as well as fingerprint scan, and would be hard to by pass. Hopefully the devices Ward had would keep them from having to have direct access to this area. This was the first time he was happy that Pat had actually shown up when she did. When they entered the labs and research areas, Pat played the decoy, drawing the supervisor's eyes away as Ward planted his little devices. Off of the main entrance there were at least four rooms that were environmentally controlled as well as having their own air systems.   Each room was encased by glass and had a double entrance system with an airlock. Not much of a chance that they would be taken in any of those places and he saw no reason that he would need to go into any of the experimental rooms just yet. If he planted the small camera over the entrance to the entire area he would be able to record who came in and out of each room. He might have thought to hack into the already existing system, but if the traitor hadn't been caught yet it seemed a pretty good guess that he knew how to circumvent them. The night supervisor was proud of the fact that there were still two scientists working, making a comment about them being the most dedicated ones on staff. They were in two of the sealed rooms and Ward looked over the set up. Of the two scientists still at work both Pat and Ward noticed that one was the guy in the picture Jan had taken. With that information they could determine which rooms they needed to pay more attention to.

Keying them through the next set of locks, the supervisor took them through and into another office area. There were many doors that led off of the one hallway. Walking down the hall they noticed that each door had the name of a different scientist on it, private offices.

"Since the research we do here is in the interest of national security you can see we are serious about the security," he was pointing at the doors, "Not only do the labs have a common security pad they have individual ones that require both a hand and a retinal scan. The office area where their findings are recorded and mulled over are given another keyed pad as well as the whole system having a constant visual recording of what goes on. Each recording unit, twenty four hours, is then stored to DVD and filed away in a vault," he was almost as proud of his security as a father would be of his newborn son. Too bad for him, all the bells and whistles still didn't stop the traitor in his midst. Pointing to one of the office doors he continued, "Would you like me to get Doctor Ross, he's still here?"

"It won't be necessary to interrupt his work. We only want to see the type of office set ups that have been allotted here. If we could get a quick look inside his office then we could make sure they have adequate space and if not, we would like to recommend expanding them," Pat was a quick thinker as she replied with a very simple request and a smile at the supervisor.

"I don't see a problem with that; they all complain that they want more space. That's all you hear them talk about," and he leaned in and opened the door for them. Obviously he had access to the high security areas. He allowed Pat and Ward to enter the room first.

Once in the offices they looked around with what seemed to be very little interest as he explained the types of security used to keep the computer files safe from hackers. Ward listened and looked casually at the name plates on the desk to double check. He silently read the name, Dr. Ross. He gave a silent nod to Pat and she walked in the opposite direction redirecting his attention and asking questions on the speed and timings of the downloads, square footage of storage space available to each scientist, and the time each one spent on average in both the labs and their offices. As he stumbled for an answer, Ward quickly leaned down and planted a small transmitter in between the computer and modem. This would allow him easy access to the machine and the network.

"They may need an upgrade on their computer system as well," Ward added to the conversation as he stood up. Now any contacts, downloads, and e-mails would be sent to him as well as to Dr. Ross. Escorted out of the office they were then led around a bit longer and into a couple other offices. Once they left the last office they yawned and thanked the supervisor for his comprehensive tour. They walked back to the entrance of the building and were taken to the hotel that Pat had booked earlier in another taxi.

They were still up at four in the morning going over records and setting up traces on the man that had been seen with Bobby. Pat still wasn't completely convinced that Bobby was alive, but Ward had to admit she was being a trouper on this one.   Whatever happened, she would be the winner. Ward worked at the small table with the light from an inadequate desk lamp. Pat had set up on the one bed and was using the light from the night stand lamps to read by. Pat had downloaded the plans for the building and they had both reviewed it. They had been given a tour of the labs and were suitably impressed with security. The night supervisor had looked at their credentials and was more than happy to give them the grand tour. It was no surprise, the best people in the department had set up their aliases, and Pat had later used her skills to change the picture from Rob's to Ward's. The corporate office of MedLab Tech in Chicago, who had been approached by the PED, was more than happy to cooperate and keep it secret. If someone was selling their research, they needed to find out and deal with it. Routine governmental security checks were normal. Losing government contracts was not something MedLab Tech wanted to do. They had dealt with the CEO himself with this matter.   "Nice," Pat was impressed as Ward connected to the lab's machine. She had walked up behind him and was watching him look through all the information he was now receiving. "Makes me miss what you can do so easily at times," she paused for a second, "It also makes me worry about which side you're really on. Remind me to never get on your bad side."

"No worries yet," and he smiled as the files continued to download. "Just remember you are looking the other way on this one."

"Not a problem," she moved closer, "yet," and started to look closer at the files he was receiving. "He's accessed research on all the biochemical weapons as well as the quick response plans to prevent mass deaths," she paused, "Damn."

"He could be involved in this area of the research as well as selling it or anything else they do. When we download his e-mails, yes even the deleted ones if they haven't been securely deleted, we will know more of what he has been selling hopefully," Ward's fingers flew over the keys again and another set of downloads started to appear. "I wish I had had the time and opportunity to get to his cell phone. If I had his number I just might be able to track his calls down and see who he has been talking to."

"How often do you break into computers?" Pat put her hand up to stop Ward before he had a chance to answer, "Never mind, just being nosey and I really don't think I want to know."

"If I told you, I'd have to kill you," and Ward snickered feeling almost too comfortable with this more human side that Pat was letting him see.

"Then save yourself the trouble and don't tell me," Pat pulled out her handheld and Ward gladly connected the two together. While the rest of the e-mail files downloaded he copied the first files onto her handheld for her to review. "Will you be able to tell if any of this has been sent via e-mail?"

"Might be able to, but I doubt that the information has traveled through these wires, too easy to trace," Ward let his fingers fly over the keys again and the e-mails from the last year appeared on his screen. First he sorted them according to date and looked for any sent or received around the time that Jan had seen the transaction in Rosarito take place. That narrowed it down to about eighty. Ward then looked for addresses that repeated throughout the e-mail list. He grouped these and saved them as a separate file. He then began to recompile the list and go through each address to see if there were any similarities.

Pat was looking through the research information that Dr. Ross had downloaded onto his machine. It listed procedures and experiments that had been tried to minimize an attack with a biochemical agent. There seemed to be a general theme to the information downloaded. She opened up the last piece of research that had been downloaded just today. As she read it she began to tap her foot. The more she read the more nervous she got. Ward was noticing the twitch of her foot and the deepening creases on her face. He waited, and slowly he started to look into her mind. She was allowing him some access. It was a test, for both of them, and they passed. She allowed him to read the thoughts she wanted him to and he went no farther. When he came to what she was thinking he stopped what he was doing.

"Damn," was all he said as he breathed out a sigh.

"You could say that. He has access to almost everything. If he passes this information along then the whole program is doomed and so is everyone who might be exposed to these biotoxins," Pat stopped and looked back at Ward.

"Look what I found," and he paused a moment, "The damning bit is that he knows an Agent Moore in Peru. From my sources, Moore seems to have been involved with the transfer of information and even arranged for Golightly's death," Ward paused.

"But he's not dead," Pat waited. Ward had allowed her that much information himself.

"So you know most of it. We left the information with a trusted source in Peru that implicated Moore. According to Moore's travel plans something was going to happen in the next seven days and then he would be gone. The information will be turned over in three more days to the authorities there. This gave us time to come back here and try to do some clean up," Ward leaned his hand on one knee. "We want the whole ring, not just the small fries."

"Agreed." Pat looked down at the screen again, "Any way to tell if he mailed this to anyone?"

"Not that I can find. He has saved a lot of the files to disk or thumb drives and I believe this is how he is transferring the information," Ward pulled up the files just recently copied.

"Those are the ones I was just looking at," Pat read through the list again. "Try looking in the files at the lab for his cell phone number."

"Good thought," Ward switched screens and broke into the database for MedLab Tech. He felt Pat mentally bite her lip. Ward just kept working through the database until he came up with the files for Dr. Ross. Ward made a mental note of the cell phone number and closed the files and severed the connection. To do what he just did through the department would have taken an extra day or two. He knew they didn't have the approval of the office to break into these files even if MedLab had given them permission to investigate, "Are you sure you want to watch now?"

"No, but go ahead," and Pat sat back down on the bed. Ward

could tell she was impressed at how easily he accessed the information. "I suppose it makes life easier not having all the rules to keep you under thumb."

"Truthfully, I probably follow the rules just as much now as I did then, it's just that I have no one now to ask permission for me to get into the files and look up information," he shrugged his shoulders, "I have to make the call and I don't take that responsibility lightly. On this one I think it's a necessity."

"You're right, but I'm glad that Rob is covering our backs."

"You and me both," and Ward clicked two more keys and got into the cell phone records for the company he used. Connecting up Pat's printer to his handheld he printed out the records for the last year. He then did something that surprised Pat more than every other thing that had happened that evening. Ward connected his phone to the printer and printed out a list of his numbers for her. He grabbed the papers and handed them to her and she could read what was in his mind. He trusted her not to take advantage of the information he was giving her.

"Any reason you're giving me this?" She waited for the answer with the papers in her hand. She didn't even look at them.

"If I'm right there should be a match to one of my numbers somewhere on his list. Because I don't know what number he is using I have given a list of numbers that could be his as well as the rest of my contacts. I want to make sure that I am not under any more suspicion than necessary." Ward watched her look down at the list and read through the numbers, "By the way you might recognize a few other numbers on my list and it might be better for you if you don't."

"Okay. You're that sure that Bobby is still alive aren't you?"

"I'm betting Jan's life on it," Ward was deadly serious and Pat could tell by the set of his face that he wasn't in a mood to joke.

"Then we better keep it from coming to that," and she started to compare Ward's list of numbers to Dr. Ross' cell phone bill. Ward switched his screen back to the e-mail list. It only took her a few moments before she sighed and then said, "Shit."

"Found a match right," Ward didn't even look up from his work.

"Yah and you have it listed as Bobby," Pat stopped and didn't say anything for a moment.

"It's okay; I've been fighting the odds for years. Why should you have believed that he really wasn't dead? He did a good job of making sure it looked like he was. I also know you won't be completely convinced until he shows his face," Ward stopped for a moment and then continued his work, "Looks like they don't communicate via the e-mail system."

"This isn't good," and Pat stood up and walked over to get a glass of water. She wasn't sure who or what to believe at that moment as she tipped the glass of water to her lips and downed it.

"I hate to be the one to tell you this, but the news doesn't get any better," Ward turned off the handheld and looked up at Pat. "Want to hear the rest of the story?"

"There's more?" Pat tried to look surprised. She placed the empty glass back down on the counter by the sink. The rooms they had gotten were adjoining and the doors stood open now. This allowed them to work together without the rest of the world knowing just what was going on.

"We've come a long way in our trust issues in under twenty-four hours but will you trust me a bit more?" Ward sat back in the chair. His arms were relaxed on the sides of the chair and he looked up at Pat. When she gave him a slight affirmative nod he continued, "Open your mind just a bit to me. Not enough to make you feel uncomfortable." With that being said she did. Ward could sense that she was a bit wary of what was going to happen next, but she wasn't going to let it stop her. He had thought long and hard about this. If he were going to plant a thought in her head it would have to be one that she either didn't know at all or one only she would recognize. He decided that one she had no prior knowledge of would be better. It took Ward only seconds before he had her attention. Slowly his escape from the hired thugs in Peru came into her thoughts, and just as quickly it changed to the vision of the mother and child in the airport, and then to the face of the cabdriver. Pat's eyes widened and she shook her head. At first it was a slight shake and then the movement increased. Ward stopped. It had been enough to convince her. When she stopped shaking, she looked straight at Ward and he sensed that there was just a bit of fear in her next statement.

"You did that. You placed your thoughts in my head," her voice was no more than a whisper and her face was pale, as she stood motionless.

"Yes. It affects you more because you are a reader and can

sense when the thoughts are not your own.   With others there is virtually no effect.   When we were captured and tortured years ago it was more than for what we knew as agents, it was for what we could do.   Bobby succumbed to the greed, I didn't.   That doesn't mean that I went unaffected, just that I stayed loyal to what I believed in," Ward faced her now with his face set; the feelings that had plagued him all these years had now vanished.   Somehow all the fear, hatred, resentment, and depression had left him.   All he had left was the disillusionment of what had happened afterward, "Bobby has spent years practicing it and even trying to erase or more correctly scramble memories.   He experimented on me first when I was still with the department.   All of that didn't help your diagnosis on me being totally screwed up.   When Bobby was finally convinced that he couldn't recruit me, he tried to kill me.   I somehow survived the crash and the poor dope that was his substitute was already dead before he was in the SUV.   That's when you finally classified me as crazy and that's why I couldn't stay with the department.

"Then later he went after Jan.   It wasn't intentional at first and then it became personal.   His skills had improved, and I thought when I saw her in that hospital bed that I had surely lost her for good.   Had I left her with the department we might have.   He wanted her; was fixated with her for a long time and I finally came to realize it.   It took a lot longer for her to recover the memories she had salvaged from him," Ward stopped and let the new information sink in.   "He's come close to killing us in the past, but somehow couldn't manage to bring himself to finish us off.   Each time he has come closer to doing it, as you have seen, I believe he means what he says.   He plans to take us both out if he doesn't get what he wants."

"I wished I would have believed you back then," Pat's voice was soft, caring and her posture, as well as her mind, was open.

"Get over it, we have.   No regrets.   We never wanted to leave, but how could we stay?   We now belong to neither world and live on the edge of both most of the time.   At least we have each other, and what we love to do," Ward now stood up, "We now choose our own battles and who needs our help the most.   Usually no money exchanges hands as the people we help don't have any to begin with."   He was surprised just how much he was willing to tell Pat.   Somehow he hadn't thought she would believe him, ever, but she seemed to.

"How do you fund it?"   Pat was still soaking in all that she had just learned and what the implications were. They had lost good agents because they had refused to listen the first time.

"I have my ways and my sources, all legal. By the way, I even help your crew out at times," he paused, "like this. Rob's been my unofficial contact for a while now."

"I don't know what to say," Pat moved back over to the table and stood by Ward.

"There's nothing to say. We are happy. Don't ask us to come back, we won't," Ward sat in the opposite chair, "And by the way, sorry won't work. Just forget it and let's get on with the job. I just needed you to understand what you might be facing if we get him. It starts with a headache and as it progresses it feels as if your head will explode. If you totally shut down, you will be able to keep him out to begin with. If he gets a hold, even a little one, well then you will have to battle him out and I have no good ideas on how to do that.

"Would you look at the time," Ward pretended to look at his watch, "Think we need to get some sleep before we have to go back to the labs tomorrow." Ward stood up and walked into his room. Pat watched him walk off and didn't try to stop him. She had things to think about. He didn't bother to close the door between the rooms. It took him only minutes before he was under the covers and deep in sleep. The clocks had all been set and his mind was now at rest. Only one thing bothered him, it plagued him even in sleep, a fitful sleep. Jan was going to face Bobby and it would be soon.

Pat had seen some research go past her desk a year ago on mind control and passed it off as uninteresting, and even a little bit out there. If she could believe her own thoughts; Bobby was still alive, dangerous, and it was now going to be a battle of minds once they found him. Obviously both Bobby and Ward had skills that went past what she had ever learned to do. Hooking up her handheld again she got into the files in her computer. She looked up all the research she had stored on the process of mind control. The original experiments went way back to the sixties when the CIA had first tried to control minds with drugs. Some were experimental drugs, some readily available on the street. Most of the unofficial tests had been conducted in the California area. When the project had been dispersed, not all of the research had been turned in or all the scientists accounted for. Some had continued their experiments, government sanctioned experiments, others had left the country and most likely been employed by other governments. Pat called up the last article she had placed in the file nearly fourteen months ago.

Slowly she read through it looking for anything that might be helpful. This opened up a whole new kettle of fish. If he could control minds, just how much of the information transfer was Dr. Ross's fault and how much was Bobby's? How about the agent in Peru? The article did nothing to answer her questions and just left her with more. All she could determine from the article was that it was far more draining to control a mind than to just read it like they did. It was also created by not so ethical experiments. This may come in useful if they were all able to be there when he was caught. Bobby may have a chance to control or wipe one mind, but with three of them present there should be no hope for him. Pat closed up the files and walked over to the sink.

Staring into the mirror, she brushed her teeth. Looking at her reflection, she suddenly focused on the gray streaks that she had put in her hair yesterday. She could also see the crow's feet that were beginning to standout around her eyes and the frown lines on her forehead. It had been years since she had been active in the field for longer than a couple of days. Mostly these days she was a trainer and stayed behind. It was only on larger, more difficult reads that she was ever included. When they discovered the photo, she had been called in to try and read Rob. Pat now knew the photo had been a plant and where it had been taken.

With one hand she played with the gray streaks musing over the fact that they might also be present when her hair wasn't colored, she had just never stopped to look. She was getting older and there were still things to learn and battles to be waged. Battles the PED had created. She spit the toothpaste in the sink and washed her face. Tomorrow they would tail this man and stop the transfer of information. In a few days she would be back in the office and she intended to become more active in the department. Too many mistakes, costly mistakes, had been made. As Pat crawled between the sheets she decided that she would also report Gregg's behavior to the correct people. Vendettas should never be a part of what the department did and over the last few years he had carried out his own personal vendetta against them. Pat slept soundly knowing that she was finally going to be able to right some of the wrongs done in the past. She owed them a gift. When she had a chance, she knew exactly what she would do. Her conscious was finally clear.

Chapter 18

"There's some stuff in the frig if you're hungry," Jan walked into the room and looked out the window avoiding his glare. She looked over at Jack and knew that he had some major reservations about what was to come. It was one of the main reasons she hadn't told him everything. Jan had pulled her hair back into a loose ponytail. She had on a pair of jeans and a v-neck tee-shirt that matched in color.

There was no more rubbing of her head Jack noticed. That had ended about as quickly as it had begun. Jack stayed sitting on the couch and just looked in her general direction. His arms were folded, his face set, and he was determined to get the answers he needed.

"Is he still around?" Jack didn't move. He kept one eye on Jan and one eye on the outside. He leaned back just a bit as he waited for the answer.

"No, he just wanted to let me know he could get close to me," she walked into the kitchen area and pulled out a juice from the frig. Opening it she took a long drink of the tangy orange liquid. As she set it down she noticed that Jack's gaze was relentless.

"So why didn't he just come up here and get you?" The muscles in his face were tense and his arms were still folded in front of him, "He must know that I'm no challenge to him in the mind department."

"He wants me to come to him, not him to me," Jan took another drink and noticed that the quizzical look hadn't let up yet, "Something else you want to know?"

"I saw you rubbing your head earlier, are you up to facing him? I don't want to go into this half prepared. I don't plan on losing another agent on this one," Jack's gaze never faulted, "or you."

"If you're worried about him getting control over my mind, it won't happen. Over the years Ward worked on techniques to keep him out and has shared them with me," Jan threw Jack a juice. He caught it and waited, "You have nothing to worry about, just keep me in your sights. I can't avoid the headaches though."

"I think I'm going to hate this," and he opened the juice, "Any idea when we'll hear from him again?"

"Should be any minute," and as Jan put down her empty juice container the cell phone rang. She turned it over and looked at the number. Looking back at Jack she gave a quick nod of her head before she answered it.

"Yah," and she then waited. He didn't respond right away, but she could hear him breathing.

"Was it nice to have me back inside your head?" Bobby teased.

"Let's just get right down to what you want from me," Jan was in no mood to play.

"Whoa, Wart been treating you badly lately, or is this mood just for me?" Bobby called Ward Wart, his own personal nickname for him. This had started soon after Bobby had framed Ward in some illegal activities in the department and then left him to suffer the consequences.

"No, this mood is especially for you. I want you to leave us, especially," and she stressed the word 'especially', "him, alone," Jan was blunt and hoped the game would play out the way she thought it might.

"Really now sweetheart, I don't think I can do that. You see, you two just happen to be interfering where you don't belong," Bobby's voice was sickeningly sweet, "Remember, neither of you work for that big old government dinosaur anymore either, so you don't have their protection services. Not that it would do you any good. Until now what you two have done hasn't really bothered me, but right now I'm feeling like I need to deal with this intrusion like I should have back then. Only this time I won't mess up."

"Somehow I thought it was you who was doing something illegal, not us," Jan matched his tone. Deep inside her she knew he was referring back to the time he had tried to kill Ward and things had gone horribly wrong. Whether it was on purpose or subconscious it didn't matter now.

"I keep my threats sweetheart. If you two don't back off, I'll take care of the both of you this time," he paused, "Then again, I may just take care of Wart for old times sake."

"No!" Jan said this with all the emotion she felt.   He was playing into her trap, but it was a trap set up on the truth, so easy for her to maintain.

"Really," his condescending tone cut into her heart, "Wart isn't that good is he?" and when Jan said nothing he continued, "I may just have a deal for you."

"What?" she had expected this, even planned for it.   Jack watched in disbelief as she continued to maneuver the conversation in her direction.   She knew she wasn't the only one playing at this game.

"I'll leave your precious Wart alone if you come to me, alone. You see it's simple, your allegiance and companionship for his life. Sounds like a fair trade to me.   Think about it.   I'll call back in an hour, unless you can't wait to have me all to yourself and then you know my number," and he hung up.   She put the cell phone down and looked over at Jack.

"We have him," it was both a curse and a prize.   And with any luck she would walk out of this alive.

"It's what we do with him that worries me," that being said, it just hung in the air in deadly silence.

An hour later they were ready to roll.   They stood waiting for the phone to ring.   Jack had watched her put her side arm on and also her back-up but they both knew that Bobby would quickly take those away from her.   He looked at her and wondered just how she would hold up against his continuous onslaught.   For that matter, how was he going to manage to keep up the pressure?   Jan was reading his mind and looked at him.   Slowly she reached for her belt and pulled out the knife she had hidden in the buckle showing him her one and only trick before putting it away.

"He won't find this one.   It's new and specially made," and she secured it in the belt once more.   Jack smiled.   He then tied back his hair and covered it with a cap.   Then he threw on a jacket to cover his weapon.

"We need to meet in a place where I have some cover," Jack leaned on the counter.

"I'll try.   He will probably have the area being watched as well, so be careful of those around you," neither one said anything more as the cell phone rang.   Jan looked at the number again and nodded.

"I'm alone," was all she said.

"So you're going to give yourself to me to save his life? How romantic," Bobby said it half in disbelief. He wasn't sure he should believe he had won.

"You will keep your promise won't you?" She kept her voice even, low and soft.

"As long as you keep yours sweetheart," this time his voice held a sinister quality.

"Ward has left for Chicago. It'll be just you and me," she knew if Bobby was half as talented as they were and he was, then he would probably check her story before they met. The labs had an office in Chicago and so it would be a plausible place for him to start. It also helped that that was where they had booked a ticket to in one of his aliases.

"Oh sweetheart, if you only knew how happy we will be," and that sickeningly sweet quality was back, "Meet me at Patriot Square at ten. That should give you time enough to get there and don't forget," Bobby paused, "to leave him an extra special good-bye note. We don't want him getting the idea that you'll be coming back or that he should come rescue you," Jan disconnected the phone and controlled a repulsive shake that had tried to overcome her.

"Where?" Was all he had to say. Jack watched intently and only noticed the slight change in the set of her chin and her eyes as she hung up the phone.

"Patriot Square at ten. Ironic huh?" Jan looked him straight in the eyes, "I should have been able to guess that one."

"I'll leave in five minutes and find a place to watch the area. It will give me time to leave the car so that I can follow easily," Jack picked up the keys. "Stay in view, don't let him get you out of plain sight."

"I'll do my best," Jan looked at Jack, "Don't shoot him. The information we can get from him will be of more use than what will happen to me." Jack gave her a disturbed look. There was definitely something she wasn't telling him.

"Next time stay out of my mind," Jack half smiled.

"I didn't have to read your mind to know what you thought or what you wanted to do," and as Jan finished talking, Jack walked out the door. The door closed and Jan was alone. The silence surrounded her. She would need to leave in about two hours. She had nothing to do but think about the upcoming events and she didn't want to think about it. This played in his favor. Bobby had made sure that she would be working in less than perfect shape when he woke her earlier this morning. She moved to the center of the room. Soon she was in the middle of the tai chi routine and her mind began to refocus and relax. It might be the only thing that could help.

The two hours passed faster than she expected and she was out the door in time to be down to Patriot Square hopefully before Bobby would be. It was a beautiful day, as usual in Phoenix. The sun was shining and the sky was blisteringly clear. Jan didn't need a coat and didn't notice the weather. She got off the bus and walked mechanically toward the Square, which was still two blocks away. She had a small bag slung over her shoulder. It was about the time of day when people would be taking their morning breaks and she noticed that the coffee shops, small delis and bakeries that surrounded the area were all busy. It would be good cover for Jack. She walked up to the Starbucks and ordered an espresso. She thought about ordering a pastry, but her stomach wasn't feeling in any mood to tangle with food. Taking her coffee, she walked into the center of the Square and sat down. The copper colored arched entrances to the park like area were just as she had remembered them and flags of both the United States and Arizona flapped in the breeze. Looking at the flags she remembered just why she was doing this.

Suddenly she felt cold. It wasn't because of the outside temperature, but this feeling came from within. She didn't need to turn around to know he was there. He wasn't trying to force himself into her mind. He truly wanted this to be her giving herself to him, and although it disgusted her on so many levels she had lost count, a feeling that he would also expect, she knew it was the only way to bring an acceptable end to all of this. His arm brushed against her back and she steadied herself. He let his finger play with her ponytail and she worked hard not to recoil from his touch. He hadn't said a word, but he had spoken volumes. Bobby was letting her know that he was now in control of her and he was also testing out the theory that Ward was nowhere near. Even Bobby knew that if Ward was near, this would have put him over the edge.

"So, you're as good as your word, just like Wart. Too bad for you," and he moved around the bench and sat down beside her. He held out a small bag marked with the store logo of Ma's Bakery. It was one of her favorite places to pick up pastry. It surprised her that he had remembered.

"What's this?" Jan refused to take the bag from him.

"There is a bit of nice guy left in me," and he set the bag down in her lap.

"Highly unlikely," Jan moved the bag to the bench and sipped at her coffee.

"I'm not as bad as Wart makes me out to be," his tone was harsh.

"No," and she paused, "You're worse, so much worse and I have no delusions about it."

"Maybe you're right and maybe I'll keep my end of the deal just to prove it," Bobby leaned back, "If you're good." Jan had sensed the thoughts in a mind so close that it almost scared her. "Yes, I have you covered in case you didn't keep your end of the bargain," his fingers traced the side of her face and around her ears, as if he could think of nothing better to be doing at this moment. "His orders are to kill you if you don't leave with me."

"What do you mean you might keep your end of the deal?" Jan stayed still and stared straight ahead. What he had said really hadn't surprised her.

"Now, do you think I'm that naive? If I don't go after Wart he will continue to try and find you no matter what, and I can't have that," this time Bobby glanced toward Jan to see her reaction. He had tried to get into her mind and found that this time the barriers were well placed, so he stopped pushing. "Plus, I don't think he would give up on this job even if I had you. Now, if you were in danger, like last time, maybe he wouldn't be in such a hurry to do the right thing," Bobby smiled and the corners of his eyes crinkled as he spoke, enjoying the torment he was bringing to her, "At least he showed some promise then."

"So, now I am a hostage until you finish selling out your country?" Jan could feel his hand move up her back and she couldn't hold back the involuntary shiver.

"Don't worry sweetheart, you are so much more than a hostage to me; when I'm done with you, you may still want to live," and then he grabbed her ponytail and twisted her head toward him. It was forced, but without a scream from her, no one took notice. He leaned in and kissed her. It wasn't passionate, or romantic. It was a hard and cruel kiss. His freehand moved around her waist and under her shirt. He vigorously and aggressively let his hand move along her skin and up between her breasts and then around to her back once again.

"Enjoy yourself," she said when he moved away from her lips, and she spit on him.

"You'll change your mind or die in the process. You might even decide my way is better," he leaned back again but didn't release her hair. "So far you have been a good girl and you don't have a wire on. Give me your weapon and your back-up," he waited for her to secretly hand over the items. Instead of putting her weapon away he placed it under his jacket pointed right at her. "We are going to stand up in a moment and walk over to Third Avenue. You are not going to fight me, or even try to escape, otherwise your dear Wart in San Diego will be killed and so will you. Yes, I found him; it was a nice try to hide him in Chicago too bad it didn't work. I hope the note you left him will be good enough to keep him out of the way or it might just get you both killed. In any case, he will be blamed for your murder and all that you hold dear will be in tatters. Do you understand?"

"Yes," she whispered. So far her basic plan had panned out. This was the part where it got dangerous; it made her nervous and Jack just plain panicky. It was based more on patterns than on knowledge.

Jack sat under an entrance arch in old, tattered clothes watching. He had gone to great pains to grease up his hair and to smell himself up a bit. Dressed as a street person he would just fade into the background. No one ever looked too long at street people, and Phoenix, because of the climate, was full of them. He hadn't even told Jan how he was going to dress. When Bobby had assaulted her with that kiss; Jack had almost taken out his gun and shot him on the spot just for breathing. He knew that Jan and Ward were right though, all the information that they could get from Bobby was worth what they were going through, but as he saw it, Jan was in for the worst of it.

Watching them stand up and walk toward the west, he rolled through the entrance and moved slowly toward his car. As he got closer to his car he stood up straighter and let the old coat fall off his shoulders and then into a nearby trashcan. No one noticed and no one cared. Jack got in the car and drove down the street in the same direction. He was about a block behind them when the traffic light turned red. He stopped and didn't let his eyes leave her for a moment as he tapped his fingers on the wheel. They crossed the street and went north. As soon as the light turned green Jack gunned the car and moved over to the left lane. The road they had gone up was a one-way and it only went south. He parked on the side of the road and waited.

Bobby held Jan tightly by the arm and forced her into the parking garage. They took the elevator up three floors and walked over to the silver 350Z that sat by itself on the outside of the loop. It was parked so he could make a quick escape if necessary and Jan was now sure that he hadn't trusted her to come alone. He opened the passenger side door for her, pointed for her to get in the car, and she complied.

"Now, I really hate to do this, but I don't take any chances," and he handcuffed her to the interior of the car as well as to the door. "and this will keep you from doing anything stupid," she felt the prick of a needle. There were a variety of drugs he could have used, all of them a dangerous mix for mind readers. He then frisked her to find the phone and do one last check for weapons. He pulled the phone out of her pocket and shook his head, "Really can't have you with one of these. Knowing Wart, it has a tracking device." She watched as Bobby placed the phone under the front tire.

Whatever he had shot into her veins, most likely some date rape drug to be named later, was already taking affect as he climbed into the driver's side of the car. She was having a hard time understanding him and keeping her eyes focused. Jan's last thing she heard was the crunch when Bobby pulled out of the parking space and crushed the phone.

When the light changed again Jack noticed a silver 350Z leaving the parking garage. The windows were tinted, but on the passenger side a tiny slip of cloth was caught in the door. Jack recognized Jan's shirt. He didn't ask any more questions. He pulled out behind the car and followed them through traffic making sure to stay at a safe distance.

The 350Z pulled onto Interstate 17 and headed north. Traffic wasn't heavy, but it wasn't light either. It made it easier for Jack to follow them. Bobby wasn't traveling fast; in fact he kept to the speed of the traffic around him. Jack dropped back another car and moved over a lane. Jack was getting nervous that he had been spotted. They went about six more miles on the road before Jack got more than just a little worried. They were getting closer to the outlying areas and he would be easier to spot as a tail. It was at that moment that Bobby made his move. The 350Z swerved across two lanes of traffic and took the Dunlap road exit. Jack adjusted as fast as he could and just made the exit in time to see Bobby turn toward the Metro Mall area. Silently he cussed himself out for being made.

Just before Jack got to the light it turned red. He had a choice to make. If he ran it then Bobby would be sure that he was being tailed. As it was now he may not really be sure. If he let them get into the mall area then Jack could lose them too easily. It took him only a split second to make a decision and he ran the light nearly missing a white Mazda 323 with its horn blaring. Scanning the area he thought he caught a glimpse of the car going through the next set of lights and he hit the gas on the Ford Focus. Just making that light he tried to catch up with the car. This time the car did a U-turn on a divided road at the lights and headed back toward the freeway. Jack looked at the traffic and knew at that moment he wouldn't be able to keep up. There were three cars in front of him in the turn lane and a line of cars in each of the others. The Ford wouldn't be able to jump the curb. He was dead in the water and Bobby knew that. As the 350Z passed him the horn sounded. Jack was sure that the horn was signaling a victory for Bobby. Jack forcefully hit the steering wheel a couple of times shaking the entire car and put his head down on the wheel. A moment later the light changed and he spun around the divider and headed back toward the freeway.

It was a lost cause though. He couldn't see the car at all now and didn't really know which way it was headed. It had gone back under the freeway and that was where he had lost sight of them. Opening up his cell phone Jack turned the GPS tracking system on, looking for Jan's signal. Nothing came through. Not surprising. Even though he hadn't seen him remove her phone, he couldn't imagine Bobby being that stupid.

Jack spent the next hour combing the neighborhoods just in case he hadn't gone too far. He didn't expect to find them, but before he called Ward he had to be sure. It was now noon and there was no sign of them and the traffic had picked up. Jack stopped his search and pulled up to the nearest Circle K. It was the last thing he wanted to do. Without getting out of the car he picked up his cell phone and dialed Ward's number. He knew that just by calling, he would be signaling that something went wrong. It only rang twice before Ward answered.

"Yes," the tension was thick in his voice, the word a bark.

"Can you talk?"   Jack wanted to know how much freedom Ward had before he told him anything.

"No, but if you have a problem, I may be able to help you solve it," Ward had moved away from the group at the lab and over to the corner of the conference room where he had a little more privacy, his hand so tight on the phone that his knuckles were white.   He quickly sent a message to Pat to let her know that something had happened and to keep them occupied as he worked on it.   Pat acknowledged the thought as he slowly backed away.

"Ward, I lost her," there was no easy way to say it.   He knew Ward well enough not to try and sugar coat it either.

"What?" Ward could just hold the fury in check, but the cold feeling that rushed through his veins at that moment he couldn't shake.   Jack wasn't supposed to lose sight of her.   It wasn't his fault and Ward knew that, but all the anger and hatred he had for Bobby began to bubble to the surface.   Quickly he put his feelings back in place, but not before Pat had felt the energy shift in the room.

"Everything was going and then I must have been spotted.   I had to make a choice.   Either way I was going to lose.   It was around Metro Center.   I've spent the last hour looking and have come up with nothing," Jack closed his eyes.   He could imagine the type of torment that was going through Ward's mind and how much it was taking to control it.   Jack had been through the same hell.   Everything was silent for a while.   When Ward's voice came back over the phone, it was calm and collected in a scary sort of way.

"I have a feeling he will be calling me.   Don't worry, just be ready, I may need someone here as well," he paused and then continued, "You may want to contact Rob and let him know what has happened.   You have the number."   The phone went silent after that.   He was scared for Ward, for Jan, and for whoever was with Ward right now.   Jack looked up the number for Rob on the phone and dialed the cell number he had been given.   He had known that Rob had been working in the background to keep things clear for Ward and Jan, and he was also pretty sure he wouldn't take the news any better than Ward had.   Rob answered on the first ring.

"Go," short and sweet that was Rob.

"Rob this is Jack, we have a problem," he waited for Rob to acknowledge who he was before he continued; "Jan met with Bobby this morning at Patriot Square.   After a short talk she went off with him, under duress. I followed his silver 350Z and then lost sight of them in the Metro Center area. Her GPS device is not working so I haven't been able to find her. I lost them both."

"YOU. DID. WHAT!" Rob's tone of voice conveyed all the feeling that Ward had not. Rob had not been told that Jan was meeting with Bobby. He was rubbing his head. If he had known this he wouldn't have ever agreed to run interference. It had been his understanding that she was going to follow Bobby only. He remembered how hard it had been on her just to get to Phoenix the first time and now he was with her. Rob was not only afraid of what Bobby would do to her, but how he would use her against Ward. Ward had only one weakness, his Achilles Heal, and that was Jan. This could destroy the entire mission.

"I wasn't supposed to lose her but I got made. I've spent the last hour searching the area and have found nothing. All I know is that he drives a 350Z, silver, plate number AZ FGQ 655, but I have a feeling that the plate is a phony," Jack had never met Rob before and was unsure of just how he was going to react now. He heard him mutter some explicative under his breath and then he directed the conversation back at him.

"Does he know?"

"Just told him and he told me to stand by," Jack knew who he was. The emptiness of Ward's voice still pained him.

"Do you know where the Five and Dime is on Seventh?" Rob was busy writing down some information on a notepad in front of him.

"Yah."

"Meet me there in thirty minutes. We'll both stand-by on this one," and Rob disconnected the phone. Jack started the car again and pulled out of the Circle K into the traffic. As he drove toward the downtown area, he thought about what had happened. He was getting a strange feeling that Jan knew that this was what was going to happen, even planned for it, but never shared it with anyone and he kicked himself for not picking up on the signals.

Chapter 19

Ward stood unmoving for what seemed to be a lifetime, Jan's lifetime. Then he dropped the phone back in his pocket and moved stiffly and silently back into the mix of people around the conference table, everything seeming so surreal. The room had been filled with platters of sandwiches and cups of brown tinted water that tried to resemble coffee. It had been a long and informative tour this morning; they had both gotten a better look at the facilities and what they were capable of producing. It had scared them both. If any of this information had gotten into the wrong hands, and some of it already had they knew; the world was going to be a far less safe place. They had sat and visited in the overstuffed chairs with both the board members and the scientists about the accoutrements that would be needed if the facility here were to be expanded. Pat and Ward had taken turns reading Dr. Ross as well as the others in the room and both had gotten the same information. Tomorrow was the day that Dr. Ross would pass on the last bit of information. Ward got the impression that this was happening a lot faster than it had been planned to begin with. With the information he had just received from Jack though it didn't surprise him, and for the life of him, he couldn't put all the information together. He had to get his head back in the game for both his sake and Jan's. It wasn't something they hadn't discussed. He just thought that Jack might have had a better chance at tailing them than he would. He hoped that mistake didn't cost him what he loved most.

Both Pat and Ward had been able to read about the same information from Dr. Ross' mind. Even though outwardly he didn't seem to be nervous, inwardly he very much was. Ross had taken the next few days off and was planning on taking a road trip. Ward had discovered a bit more of where he was headed, but not why. By knowing the destination, Ward had guessed what was to happen though. He had checked his phone all day for signs that Ross was getting an e-mail or sending one. Nothing had gone out or had come in. He could only assume that the business had been conducted over the cell phone. Risky, but if no one was tapping the line then it would be safer than e-mail. Ward couldn't tap his cell phone as it would have required a bit more equipment or it would have meant that he had to have Ross's phone for a few minutes.

Pat was surprised at how open Ward's mind was to her right now. She had a feeling though that he had no idea how open it was. Ward had been anxious all day to get back to the hotel and look at the camera feed he had set up, but now he was numb. The mission had taken a turn south and it wasn't a good one. They had discussed the possibility of Jan being kidnapped by Bobby, but he had never expected it to happen. The last time he had to choose between Jan and the right thing to do, he chose Jan. Deciding not to pry in that direction anymore she continued. They had agreed this time that she would never be made part of the choice in a mission again, or at least he had. Pat realized that this time the stakes ran too high and deep. Pat just hoped that she had most of her equipment yet. If she did, she had a chance.

Pat looked in his direction and suddenly felt a large void of any emotion from him. It was a self-defense mechanism that all readers used at times. She had taught it to too many readers and used it more times than she could count. And although she wasn't surprised by it, she knew instantly that something had gone wrong, seriously wrong and he had no idea how much he had given away in his thoughts. Ward gave a slight wave of his hand as he moved toward her signaling her to stay in the chair. He leaned over her shoulder and whispered in her ear. Pat's face didn't betray anything. She nodded and continued the genial chatter with the other board members in the room. Looking at her watch, she stood and moved over to the chairman and said something Ward was unable to hear and didn't even try to read. It was only a couple of minutes more before the chairman interrupted the party.

"Attention everyone. We have had a wonderful opportunity to meet and impress upon our colleagues here the necessity to expand and upgrade this facility. I have just been informed that they plan on recommending expanding the facilities by twenty percent to the CEO upon their return," the room erupted with clapping.

"Thank you. All of you do a wonderful job here with what you have," Pat spoke with authority and assurance as she addressed the group, "We will be happy to recommend expansion and we will look forward to bigger and better discoveries from all of you. Something has come up that we need to address; we will need to return to Chicago this afternoon. Please keep up the good work as we hope to receive many more governmental contracts in the future due to your dedication," and Pat walked over to Ward gently taking him by the arm so that no one noticed it. Together they walked toward the door of the boardroom with the chairman in tow. He had a driver take them back to their hotel and he had instructed the driver to then take them to the airport. Pat quickly dismissed the driver and said they would take a cab once they were packed and had changed their flights. As they watched the car drive away they turned and walked into the lobby of the hotel. Pat didn't say a word, but did look a little deeper into Ward's mind. What she found there shook her to the bone. His mind and emotions had started to thaw. She got a glimpse of what had happened then and now, and that he was forming a plan. She waited until they were on the elevator.

"Do you know what happened?" Pat watched as the numbers flashed by on the LCD screen above the doors of the elevator. She had been told that Jan and Jack were chasing leads in the Phoenix area, but had never been told just who or what those leads were. Rob had told her a lot about the job at hand but he hadn't told her about this part, need to know and all that stuff that supposedly keeps agents safe. Pat wondered if Rob had even known what Jan and Ward had planned. When they reached the fifth floor they both carefully scanned the hall before exiting the elevator. Ward knew that if Bobby had Jan then there was also a possibility that he would know they were here.

· "Jan and Jack arranged a meeting with Bobby as planned. Bobby took her as a hostage I assume and then Jack lost the tail. End of story," neither Ward's face nor body language let on how upset he was about what he had just said.

"Can you finish the job?" Pat opened the door to her room and Ward followed her in.

"I'll finish the job alright," there was a slight pause, "and Bobby if I have a chance." This time his voice betrayed a bit of the emotion he was hiding, "Then if I have any energy left, I'll give her a good spanking myself for what she did."

"Ward," Pat waited until he looked at her and the door was closed, "we will get her back." Ward knew that she meant what she had said. If it was at all possible she would get Jan away from him, but somehow that didn't seem to sooth his nerves at all.

"Thanks," was all he could muster for the moment and then, "Thanks for believing Bobby is still alive." Walking over to the dresser drawer he pulled out his equipment. Calling up the feed from the camera he had installed last night he started to play it from the start of the day. Doing something, anything, was better than just sitting and thinking. "From what I could get from Ross there is something happening tomorrow. His mind was pretty tight, but I'm sure this is going to be the big drop."

"I got the same thing from him. I wasn't able to get a location on it so unless you have one we will have to be up early to tail him," Pat had her eyes on the feed as well, looking for any indication of foul play.

"I don't think that will be a problem. I know where he is headed," Ward stopped the tape and then replayed a part. Pat's phone signaled a text message had come in. Not seeing anything unusual the second time around he continued with the feed, "We will, or you will, need permission to cross the border into Mexico and work from there." Pat picked up her phone and read the text message. When she finished she was smiling even though Ward couldn't see it.

"Not a problem, Rob just put it through. Something more you want to tell me?" Pat was looking over Ward's shoulder again. The feed he was now seeing was just before the start of the reception in the boardroom and the last scientist had just left the area. It was minutes later when Dr. Ross entered the far left lab again and stayed for only about five minutes. When he left the lab it looked as if he had a brown paper lunch bag.

"No, but look at this," and Ward rolled the feed back again. Both watched as Dr. Ross again removed what looked like a brown paper bag from the lab. Ward stopped the feed and pointed to the lump under his arm.

"Could be lunch?" Pat was studying the screen carefully.

"Why would you go get your lunch when you know you are headed for a reception with food available? Also he arrived in the boardroom without the bag only five minutes later," Ward looked at Pat and his smile was pure satisfaction. Ward saved the piece to his machine and then hooked up Pat's and made a copy there.

"Supposing that is part of the drop, where is he going to take it tomorrow?" Pat sat back and looked at Ward. Both Ward and Pat knew this was another hurdle to get past. Ward had the place of the drop and now he would have to share it. Pat could be an asset to both of them knowing what had happened today. Bobby would be expecting him, but definitely not Pat. The plan that had started to form in his mind in the elevator went a major step further. What he was about to tell Pat would come close to exposing their secret life. On the other hand, it wasn't enough for her to really find them.

"Rosarito, about thirty minutes south of the border," Ward looked at his watch. "We should cross the border at around four in the morning and watch for him on the other side."

"What about Bobby?"

"He won't be so easy. He may cross tonight, or tomorrow. I'm betting on tonight when things are slower on the border. But I do know one thing," and Ward paused, "I haven't heard the last of him. He'll use her."

"How can you be so sure?"

"He needs this deal to go through for his customer and," he paused, "he wants me. He wants me dead, he will do anything to make it happen no matter what he told Jan and she knows that too," Ward said it so flatly that Pat didn't know how to take it. In the area they worked it wasn't unusual to have people want you dead, but to carry it on for years and years, planning it, dreaming about it, was more of what a demented soul would do, not what she would expect of any agent, even one that had gone bad. She could also sense that Ward wasn't completely opposed to dying a horrific death for Jan, and that was just a little too scary for her to comprehend.

Ward's phone signaled a message for him. He looked at the phone for only a second before he picked it up. His hands were steady at first. Pat watched as Ward's jaw tightened and his hand that held the phone trembled slightly. If she hadn't been looking for the signals, she would have missed them. Without saying a word she walked around behind him and read the message. He didn't try to hide it from her. Pat wasn't even sure if he was still aware that she was in the room. The message was simple and to the point. As she finished it she noticed that there was a picture Ward had scrolled away from. As Pat took the phone from Ward and scrolled down to look at the picture, his head landed in his hands and for a moment she could feel a wave of torment pass from him. The sudden burst of emotion surprised her and yet was gone as quickly as it had come.

Pat looked at the picture clinically. In the picture Jan lay sprawled on a bed. She was in only a bra and underpants with her hands handcuffed to the headboard and her feet to the bottom of the bed. She was blindfolded and had a piece of duct tape over her mouth. Most likely she had been drugged and that in itself was dangerous enough. Looking closer at the picture she saw something shiny lying beside Jan. On closer inspection Pat could tell that it was a ring and looking at Ward's hand she got the confirmation she needed. On Ward's right hand, there was also a ring, probably the same kind that now lay beside Jan on the bed. It was foolish to wear a wedding ring at all in this business, yet they took a chance by placing it on nontraditional fingers to look just like a normal piece of jewelry. Bobby had known though. Looking into Ward's mind, Pat could tell that he had pushed away that emotion he felt, relying on the training all of them had had at one time or another. It was a struggle and when Ward discovered Pat in his head he only ignored her.

"What did he mean by 'You know what to do to keep her safe? Just like last time. See you there.'?" Pat handed him the phone back and moved her thoughts and demeanor back into mission mode to try and help him through it.

"I'd rather not discuss it," Ward's voice was low and barely audible.

"I think we need to," Ward's eyes were empty when he looked at her. She had trained and helped many agents through a lot of things, but she had never seen the look he was giving her now. It was so barren, that by looking into his eyes one felt as if they were falling into a vast, dark and bottomless pit. Pat hoped Ward was not lost in that pit himself.

"He's telling me that my only chance to save her is to let him finish what he was hired to do, like I did before, and no, I won't go into that," and with that Ward stood up and walked over to the sink. He splashed cold water on his face and then toweled it off. He had the choice. He could do nothing, but that wouldn't stop Bobby and it would condemn the mission. If Ward chose that route he would lose her and himself forever. He turned back around looking at Pat. The emptiness was still present although he seemed less tormented, "Let's get ready. We need to move out early in the morning. We have a job to do."

Half an hour later Jack pulled into the parking lot of the Five and Diner. He noticed a man with blue jeans and a yellow polo shirt standing by the entrance to the restaurant talking with a woman. She was Hispanic and about his age, average height and on the slim side. Her eyes were focused on the handheld she was working on. She was talking to him and taking notes. He wasn't looking at her at all. Jack could assume, because of the man's dress, that this was Rob and the woman was an associate of some kind. Rob looked to be middle aged with his eyes hidden behind sunglasses. Jack stopped the car and got out, leaving the door to the car open. He didn't move away and leaned casually on the car's frame. To Jack, it seemed like a bad movie, two men meeting in a parking lot outside a sleazy diner, even though the diner wasn't all that sleazy.

Rob had watched the Ford Focus pull into the parking lot and had looked the driver over long before Jack got out. Rob recognized Jack immediately, even with the cap on. He had called up his file and looked at his picture after he had secured approval for Pat and him to cross into Mexico. He had been working from home in order to keep suspicions off of everyone. As far as everyone was concerned he was with Pat in San Diego. Up until an hour ago things had been relatively easy to manage. Ward, Jan, and Jack had kept a low profile. Now he had to abandon this task and was on his way to help out. In order to do that, he had to enlist some help from Maria. She had worked as his secretary for the last six months and was beginning to comprehend the nuances of the job. Maria glanced quickly at the car and noted the plates. She entered the plates into the handheld. Rob had also given her keys to his apartment and a secured cell phone to communicate with him on. He may be leaving his post, but he was not going to give Jan and Ward back to the department or to Bobby this easily, and neither would Maria.

Grabbing the bag that sat on the small wall, Rob walked over to the passenger side of Jack's car and got in. Jack followed suit sitting back down behind the wheel of the car saying nothing until the doors were closed. They both watched as Maria turned off the handheld and pocketed it in her purse. It was so casual that no one would have known that she was about to keep up surveillance and communication back at Rob's apartment. Jack noticed her casual walk and the smile on her very pleasant face.

"There's coffee and a ham sandwich in the bag for you if you want," Rob pulled out his sandwich and cup of coffee.

"Thanks," Jack took out the coffee and food. They sat and ate quietly for a while and then Jack started the conversation up, "Who's the woman?" Jack had watched her walk down the road and get in another car two shops down not more than five minutes before, but the car stayed there.

"She works with the department, for me. She knows Jan, not Ward. They helped her out at one time," Rob watched the car pull away from the curb, "They saved her life. She's holding the fort here while we're gone."

"That trustworthy huh," Jack had already committed her face, and the rest of her, to memory.

"More than you know," Rob looked at Jack's face. Not much escaped Rob as he raised one eyebrow at the way Jack was looking at her. He took another bite of sandwich while Jack's attention was on the empty space where the car had been.

"Do you know where this is going to go down?" Jack turned his attention back to the task at hand when he was sure that Maria was really gone.

"I've got a good guess and you?" Rob was the ever careful agent, not ready to give out any information until it was necessary.

"Mexico."

"Yup." Rob was silent for a minute, "Tell me everything that happened."

"They arranged to meet at Patriot Square at ten this morning. I was already there. They exchanged a few words and he had another person covering them. Bobby took her gun off of her and used it to encourage her to leave. I followed. Sometime, once we were on the freeway, he made me and purposely lost me. I spent a long time searching the area," Jack took a sip of coffee, "That's all there is to the story."

"Probably made you long before that and just played with you for a while," Rob's voice was flat. He had suspected that Bobby would also have people in place. He was continuously looking for anyone tailing them. "What about the other guy you saw?"

"Just one other guy, no more. Walked the opposite way," Jack had seen him watching her intently and suspected that he had a gun on her from the beginning. When he left though, he had gone the opposite way as if he were finished with his part of the job.

They sat in the car drinking coffee in the parking lot and waiting. They were waiting for Ward to call, to say that he had heard from Bobby. After an hour of silence the strain of what was happening was beginning to take its toll. Rob decided to break the tension.

"Are you thinking what I'm thinking?" Rob turned to look at Jack. Rob didn't want to think it, but he knew with Jan's life now in question, Ward may need back-up closer to him than Phoenix. It was also not overly impossible that Ward would go off on his own, as he'd done it before. He may need someone to remind him of what Jan would want him to do.

"Yup. Will we need anything?" Jack looked back over at Rob.

"No, it's all in my car. Leave your keys under the mat. Maria will be back to take care of the car five minutes after we leave," and they both opened their car doors and walked over to Rob's light blue non-descript sedan. As Jack got in and closed his door Rob started the car. They pulled back onto the main road and into traffic at the light. Jack took out his phone and Rob held out his hand, "Let's wait until we are well on the way before we call him. I don't want him to tell us to turn back," and Rob just smiled broadly. With that said Jack closed the phone and put it back in his pocket.

Two hours into the ride the desert loomed in front of them dry and barren. There was a beauty to the desert that only one who lived with it could appreciate. The subtle shades of reds and browns mixed with the greens made for a unique and stark contrast against the bright blue sky. As the evening approached, the desert colors would capture the sky turning it into a remarkable color palate. Right now neither one of the men noticed it at all. Jack had put his head back and drifted into a light sleep. In two more hours they would change drivers and Rob would get the chance to rest. Jack's phone rang and he was instantly awake. Rob was quicker though and had grabbed the phone and placed it to his ear long before Jack had a chance to grab it.

"Here," was all Rob said. If it was someone looking for Jack they would be hard pressed to tell that it wasn't him on the phone with just the one word, but Rob had figured few people really tried to call a dead man.

"Rob?" Ward's voice was on the other end of the phone.

"Yes and Jack is right beside me," Rob waited again.

"Good you're both there. We are going to need you to go

down to Rosarito.   Everyone will be there tomorrow for the last installment," Ward's voice was matter of fact, completely focused on the mission.   If Rob took the time to think about things, he knew he would realize that his emotions were mixed about what was going on. He was both glad and sad to hear this, but as this was a job, their emotions didn't, or couldn't, come into play.

"We're halfway there.   We'll be on the main strip and watching out for all of them," Rob continued to drive.

"Glad to have you on board," there was a small pause, "and by the way thanks," Ward hung up the phone.

"We're headed to Rosarito," and he smiled, "It goes down tomorrow.   Pat and Ward will be there sometime tomorrow," Rob waited for the question.

"Pat?" Jack's tone was serious.   No one had told him of this other person involved in the mission, and even though information was only given on a need to know basis, he really hated being surprised.

"Last person in our team, I brought her in to help Ward.   She's a reader, old school, and met up with Ward in San Diego.   If they are still working together then things must have worked out," giving himself a mental pat on the back.   Rob answered Jack's question before he could even ask it, "Yes, she's on our side.   More importantly, Bobby will be looking for Ward and me, but he won't be looking for a dead man and a die hard PED agent on his heals."

Chapter 20

Jan started to come to and knew she was against the inside door of the car. She was still blindfolded and had little clue as to where she was right at the moment. The vibrations of the car had been soothing at first and now only served to help wake her up. She did however know where they were headed. Bobby had allowed her to see just why he had done it in his mind. They had been in the car for about six hours from what she could tell and she was ready for a change. Her body ached and the area around her mouth felt tender. She started to move about. Her head began to pound as Bobby tried to reach into her mind but couldn't get past the blocks she had set up. Ward had taught her too well and he had to concentrate on driving too much, so he gave up. As she continued to squirm against her restraints he got increasingly more annoyed. She couldn't help but wonder if he had read anything in her mind while she had been under the drug.

"Just stop fidgeting. You're not getting out anytime soon," his voice was rough and the words came out harsh.

"My arms are asleep, my legs are going to sleep and I feel car sick from having this blindfold on and from whatever you gave me," none of that was true but he didn't know that. She had matched his tone of annoyance. Jan was hoping that if she complained enough he would at least take the blindfold off, she knew that getting the restraints off wouldn't be that easy, "and you really don't think I don't know where we are going."

"All right," and he ripped the blindfold from her face along with a few strands of hair. He flung it into the nonexistent backseat of the car. "Happy now?" It wasn't a question. Jan blinked and looked at the setting sun to confirm her assumption. They were heading south, on their way through the desert. Not only was it desert, it was a route she knew well. The car was just going past the old diner that Ward always stopped at. They were on their way to Mexico. That didn't surprise her, but the route did. Jan thought back and remembered she had felt a cold and disturbing presence the last time they had crossed the border. Bobby must have been selling information for a long time. Whether he had always used Rosarito as his base or not was a major question for her. Her head began to ache.

"Get out of my head and stay out!" she yelled as the pain increasingly got worse.

"Don't worry, you'll see it my way soon, and if not, well no matter," and his smile made her skin crawl, "I'll have you both out of my hair soon enough."

"I thought it was just me you wanted," she pretended to be surprised, "that was the deal. You leave Ward alone."

"Oh course I want you," and he leered in her direction. Taking his eyes off the road for way too long, "in my bed, wanting me."

"Who are you selling the information to?" Time to change the subject, before she threw up. Jan had maneuvered herself so that she could see Bobby's face, or the side of it, as he drove. She wasn't even going to argue the issue about Ward. Going into this she knew that giving herself up for Ward would never work. She wasn't sure why he was thought she was that green though. It was her only hope that by doing this, they would be able to bring him in easier.

"Why should I tell you?" He didn't even bother to look her way.

"Humor me, will you? After all you just said that if I don't see it your way you will kill me and probably Ward. If that happens then we are both out of your hair forever," Jan watched his face carefully, "Let's just say it's my dying request."

"Glad you have no delusions on what will happen," Bobby was getting closer to the border. Jan noticed the beautiful reds and oranges and pinks that painted the sky, "But I really hope you might change your mind and join me. There are benefits," and he smiled ruthlessly.

"Why would you keep your word even if I did? It's not something you're used to doing," and as she finished the sentence he flung out a hand and it caught her on the mouth.

"If you two had taken my advice in the first place, I wouldn't have to kill you," Bobby was disturbed by this thought. Jan noticed the nervous tap of his finger on the steering wheel. She had pushed him just a bit too far and could taste a small amount of blood that trickled from her lip into her mouth from the punch he had given her.

"Who is buying this information?" Jan tried to get this piece of the puzzle again.

"Why the hell not, you probably already know," he spoke to no one in particular as one hand waved through the air, "I have a couple of buyers interestingly enough, one in North Korea and one in Libya. Happy?"

"Ecstatic," he went to hit her again and thought better of it. Glancing at her quickly he noticed that her lip had started to swell a bit. He dropped his hand back to the wheel.

"I didn't mean to hurt you," he sounded surprisingly remorseful; "We will be crossing the border in about ten minutes. I suggest, for the guard's sake, that you keep your mouth shut," and with that Bobby pulled his coat back just enough for her to see her gun tucked in his waistband. His mood was changing almost as quickly as a second hand did on the clock. It was a sure sign of mental illness and it was a cause for concern, "I wouldn't mind implicating both of you in more crimes, but it could get a little messy. Just imagine the headlines, 'Rogue Government Agents Go On Killing Spree Before Killing Each Other'."

"I won't give you a problem," and she paused, "at least not yet," and this time she chose to smile at him. He lovingly straightened the blanket he had placed over her restraints with one hand as he drove with the other. Closing her eyes she tried to keep her mind focused and away from him. She hadn't realized just how unstable he was when it came to her, or to Ward.

She pretended to be asleep as they crossed over. She wasn't interested in being saved, at least not yet. That would come later. Jan recognized the voice of the agent at the guardhouse. She had made sure her face was obscured and she could tell that Bobby was using his skills to make crossing the border easier. There was no way she could tell for certain just what he was making him think and no way she was going to try. It was only about two hours later when they pulled into the hotel he had stayed at in Rosarito. He left her in the car as he went to check in. Once that was done he came back to the car and quickly unlocked her. Carefully he placed the gun to her side and they walked in together looking like a loving couple.

They walked down past the pool and to the suites that overlooked the ocean. Jan took a deep breath as the ocean breeze brushed her cheeks and filled her soul. Somehow he managed to get the same room that he had before. She recognized it as they walked up the nearly deserted path. It was, of course, the most secluded one. He pushed her into the room and pointed to the bed. Jan looked defiantly at him. Calmly she walked over to the only chair in the room and sat down folding her arms in front of her. Bobby laughed roughly as he sat down on the bed.

"You might want to change your mind. I'm not that bad they say," and the malicious smile on his face and the way his eyes trailed over her betrayed what he was thinking. Trying at all to read his mind would just be plain stupid and open up her mind to his assaults.

"This will do me fine," Jan didn't move. Bobby shrugged his shoulders and walked over toward her. Out of his pockets he took the handcuffs he had used earlier.

"You do your legs," he paused, "and remember, I'm watching very carefully." After she finished securing each ankle to a chair leg he took another pair out of his pocket; he tossed them to her left wrist. Once she was finished with her wrist he walked over and inspected the cuffs. He was impressed and there was a smile of satisfaction. He put the gun down and did the last wrist himself as well as securing the chair to the old and very sturdy radiator in the room. When he was satisfied that she was incapable of getting away he put the gun back into his waistband. Picking up the phone he dialed a number. He sat back and let out a sigh as if the job itself was getting to him. His back was to her as he tried to hide how tired he was.

"Want anything to eat?" and it seemed like the voice had come from the old Bobby, the department's Bobby. It was the first time she questioned if there was anything left of the old persona they once knew. Ward had struggled with this question many times and had come up with the same answer each time. She was sure now, that if there was anything left of that Bobby, they would never be able to reach it again; even though she knew Ward would continue to try and try. Jan couldn't help but feel an overwhelming wave of pity for the man that stood before her.

"I'm fine," was all she replied.

"Suit yourself, but you need to drink something," and he ordered a meal of lobster and steak with a glass of white wine for himself and bottles of water and juice for her. He hung up the phone and looked at her. Slowly he walked over to her. First he just looked at her and then he let his finger trail down the side of her face, "It's not too late to make this evening more romantic," and he bent over to kiss her.

"I'd rather you kill me now," and she looked him straight in the eye daring him to. The soft loving look in his eyes cooled and hardened. She knew the man that was standing here now was not the one she had known as the tender kiss he was planning on delivering became rough and possessive.

"Not yet my dear, but soon," and he walked toward the bathroom, "Of course by that time you will be begging me to kill you."

She watched him eat his meal and then he walked over to her and forced her to drink about half the water. He set the bottle out of her reach before he stripped down to his boxers and crawled into bed. He didn't ask her again about joining him and he didn't try to read her mind. She was being very careful with her thoughts, which made it impossible to read him. As the night dragged on, Jan occasionally drifted into short uncomfortable bouts of sleep, but never deep enough to let him get a jump on her. It wasn't until the light of the morning crept through the window and gently danced under the closed curtains in the front of the room that Jan had finally slumped down in the chair and fallen asleep for more than ten minutes. Dawn made it safer because he had to make his connection today so he couldn't allow himself the luxury of having her.

The alarm didn't have to ring for Bobby to wake at six thirty that morning. Propped up on the pillows, Bobby had watched her sleep for a while before he got out of bed. Her body was in an awkward position and there was nothing more he would like to do than to lay her down on the bed and make her comfortable. Her head lay in her lap as her body pulled against the cuffs. He got out of bed and walked over to the chair and gave her shoulder a shove. If she stayed like that too long she would risk cutting off her circulation and now wouldn't that be a shame. Half the fun would be gone if she couldn't feel all the pain he planned on inflicting on her in front of Ward. He had loved her for so long, or was it longed for her; but he realized now that no matter what happened, she would never be his and it made him livid. He had tried the love thing one other time and it hadn't worked out. She had run away from him, scared as if he were some kind of monster. It had been a long time since he had seen her. He had tried to find her at first, but once he knew that she had run to the government, he knew he would never find her. He was pretty sure by now that love didn't really exist, but just what it was he didn't know. Maybe it was temporary insanity.

"Get up," and he walked over to the window. Jan stirred and started to wake. Her neck was sore and it hurt to move. At first she could only see the silhouette of the man standing at the window. She blinked her eyes and thought for just a moment that it might be Ward. The build was similar but something was wrong. When she tried to move her arm the sharp needles of pain from muscles deprived of blood flow for far too long helped her to remember what was happening.

"I'll be out in five minutes, don't try anything or I'll have to punish you," and he walked into the bathroom. He had made sure that there was no way she could move the chair near the phone before he had gone to bed, and without the lock pick there would be no way to escape the handcuffs. Jan shook her head to clear out the cobwebs. Five minutes wasn't long but she attempted some deep breathing exercises while he was out of the room. She heard the water run and her head slowly cleared as she prepared herself for the day. At least she had been clear to Ward this time, the mission came first. If there was a way to do both, Ward would find a way to do it. In fact she planned on having it all, but if not, he was to save the mission and not her. The door to the bathroom opened and Bobby walked out dressed in black jeans and a light gray tee-shirt. He placed the gun in his waistband and a lightweight windbreaker over the top of his tee-shirt. He looked refreshed and ready for the day. Jan didn't want to think about how she looked.

"Now, it's your turn," and he started to pull out the key for the handcuffs, "By the way, don't try anything. Remember I have had most of the same training as you have."

"Thanks for reminding me I had almost forgotten," it was sarcastic and as he opened the first handcuff he then handed her the key. He stepped away and casually pulled out the gun again. He was far enough out of reach to make it risky and Jan decided to play out the game for now. There would be another chance, there had to be. She rubbed her wrist and saw the marks the cuffs had made on each one. There was no way to hide them as she would have liked to. She then bent over and did her legs.

The marks there were less pronounced, but they were there.

"Your turn in the bathroom," he repeated smiling oddly.

"Be out in five."

"Hardly. Don't close the door," and the smile grew, his eyes savoring the moment.

"You can't be serious. You don't expect me to get cleaned up and shower while you watch," even as she said it she knew that was the case. She had been held prisoner before and there was one cardinal rule; don't let the hostage out of sight. He just sat back and smiled waiting for the show. If Jan hadn't expected this behavior she would have been revolted. As it was she was still trying hard not to be ill at the thought of stripping down in front of him. Instead, she did the next best thing. Ignoring him, she brushed her hair and pulled it back into the ponytail again, washed her face and straightened out her clothes. The toilet was just out of sight of the doorway and he allowed her privacy for that moment, but that was all. She was out of the bathroom in two minutes flat.

"Sure you don't want a nice long shower?" he asked when she came out.

"I think I'll manage," and at this moment the more physically repulsive she was, the better she felt about it.

"Your call, but don't think the way you smell will help your cause," and he stood up, "When I want you I will have you," he reached behind her back and put the cuffs back on. "No fight left in you?"

"When the time is right," Jan looked him straight in the eye.

"Now let me think," and he pushed her down onto the bed and walked around the bed until he got face to face with her again, "I really wish you would have asked me to do this long before I did." His fingers grasped the bottom of her shirt and he pulled it up over her breast, "Nice bra."

"I will kill you," Jan was forcing herself to stay calm wishing now she would have taken the chance to take him out earlier.

"Don't worry yet," and from his bag he pulled out a small but clearly identifiable item. Holding it up in front of her, he allowed her to take a good long look at it as he twirled it slowly in his fingers. "I got this especially for you my dear. I think you know what it is."

"A small and relatively harmless piece of C4 unless it's attached to a detonator like that one," the relief she felt about not being sexually assaulted swiftly changed to anger over what his plan really was. "Placed on a door lock and detonated, the door would open almost instantly when blown," she took a breath, "placed on a person, close to the heart, and detonated, would mean instant death, very little collateral damage, and no other options for saving them since it would leave a big gaping hole."

"You forgot about a free red paint job for the area around you," and he peeled off the adhesive he had on the one side of it.

"You're right," she felt him push it down onto her skin just on top of the area of her heart. It wouldn't be uncomfortable because her bra would hold most of the weight and her shirt would hide the small explosive devise. Pulling her shirt down he took a little too long while he took some liberties. She didn't know where the trigger was kept and she was sure he wouldn't tell her. Flipping her on her stomach he released the cuffs, slapped her on the butt and she knew it was show time.

Looking at his watch, Dr. Ross was just getting into town at around seven, not eight like that lunatic had said. He had started off just after sunrise from his home in San Diego. He was especially nervous today. It was the last drop he had been asked to do and the most important one. This one would give them all the information they would need to recreate all of his research, both the good and bad. He would collect the rest of the money today as well. Two days ago he had downloaded the information on the thumb drive he now carried in the brown bag along with some samples that sat beside him on the seat of the car. Yesterday he had taken the samples from the lab. It had been a stroke of luck for him to have the visiting directors there. He had been able to take the sack out sooner than he had planned and with far less suspicion as they all sat and munched in the boardroom.

He was driving in his old and rusty Chevy Impala. He never trusted the way the people drove down here. It was also easier and cheaper to get insurance for this car than for his Porsche. They had paid him well over the last year. This final payment would make him a free man from everything and everyone. His tracks were covered well, so if he chose to go back he could, or he could just disappear with the money and start a new life. He hadn't decided. Close behind the Impala was a nondescript sedan, light blue that had appeared in his mirror every so often. Because there was really only one main road down the Baja, Dr. Ross never took notice of it. He pulled into the grocery store lot and got out. Walking over toward the entrance of the store anyone would have thought that he was going in. The blue sedan passed by him. Dr. Ross walked straight past the entrance to the store and then continued to walk the two blocks to the steak house. He went inside and sat down at his usual table.

On the main street of Rosarito the day had just begun. The merchants were sweeping the sidewalks and the smells of the bakery filled the air. The families were up and walking around to find a good place to have breakfast and the party places of last night were just getting cleaned up. Groups of men stood around smoking and chatting about the day, the weather, and the money they were or were not making. The hawkers, street vendors, were already half-heartedly trying to sell their goods on the street to anyone who would stop and look. Many more were just opening their cases and wandering down to the beach. A young woman and her new husband passed by a case and stopped to look. The seller had some kind of MP3 thing in his ear and he was adjusting the sound or the station. He was a Native American, a little on the heavy side, and had probably come down from the hills like so many others to try and make a living in a small tourist town. Not seeing anything she liked the couple moved on.

On the other side of the main strip a man stood and looked at a map. He wore a plain blue button down shirt and a pair of shorts. His shirttails hung loosely over the waistband of his shorts and his white socks were painfully noticeable with the sandals he was wearing. He had a pair of large sunglasses on and his skin looked as if he had been out sunbathing way too long the day before. His nose was covered in green luminous sunscreen and his Panama hat from the local market place was pulled down over the top of his head to protect his face from getting too much more sun. Placing his hand in his pocket he seemed to be fiddling with some change as he watched a car pull into an empty spot about half a block away.

The door of the light blue sedan opened and Ward stepped out. He was dressed very differently than he had been the day before. He had put on a pair of faded blue jeans with a stonewashed red tee shirt. Over the top of it he wore his light weight leather jacket which hid his gun. He walked straight over to the steak house and in perfect Spanish asked for a table near, but not next to, the man that had just entered. Two minutes later, Pat got out of the car but didn't enter the steak house. Instead she went across the street and into the small coffee house that gave her a perfect vantage point to be able to watch the entrance.

She ordered a double espresso and waited with her back to the counter while it was made. She took her espresso and walked over to the small cast iron table by the window. The cup stopped halfway to her mouth. She had been about to take the first sip when she saw them. All this time she had really believed that Bobby was dead and there, right in front of her, he stood, alive and well. Worse yet, he had Jan pulled in toward him which only meant one thing. She couldn't communicate with Ward now, Bobby would spot her, and the whole game plan from this point on was based on surprising Bobby. Carefully she put the cup of coffee down. No matter what she did from this point out, she would never forget how wrong she had been about Ward and Jan. They had given up everything, in some ways, to try and bring in this turncoat for a group of people who had long since given up on them.

Out of the corner of her eye a movement caught her attention. She watched a hawker make his way down the street with his suitcase of goods stopping in front of the steak house after Jan and Bobby had entered. Before Pat could do anything, Ward and Jack would have to disable Bobby, otherwise Jan would be killed quicker than anyone could get to her or she could help herself.

Ward sat with his back to the table at first until he felt her energy come into the room. He turned in time to see them walk in. He saw Bobby's smile widen, as he looked right at him. Ward knew that Bobby had expected him to be there and he even managed to smile as they walked past. Turning just a little, so that Ward could tell that he had a gun pointed straight at Jan's side. He even sent him a little message telepathically, each of them knowing just how much they could open their minds to one another.

I will kill her first if you don't leave me alone, Bobby smiled as he thought this and gave him the picture of the bomb on Jan's chest; a nice long look of everything he had done to her and seen. It was meant to make Ward crazy and it almost did. Jan didn't even look in Ward's direction. She kept her eyes focused on the doctor. Ward caught the significance of her actions. She wasn't there for him to save; Dr. Ross came first, and damn if she wasn't right.

I'm here to get her back after you finish. You leave, and leave her here with me, was Ward's simple reply.

You need to be a good little boy. Selling out twice for the woman you love. Seems to me that you're really no better than me, and with that, Bobby sat down with Jan right beside him at the table and placed his arm around her. Ward let the last comment nearly push him over the edge as he clenched his teeth and fisted his hands. He pushed all thoughts of what was about to happen even further away and looked over at the fireplace imagining that these were the flames of hell licking at the image of Bobby in his mind. Bobby had to believe he had the upper hand or nothing would work.

"Who's this?" Dr. Ross demanded nervously and drumming his fingers on the table. He also pulled the bag closer to him.

"No one you need to worry about. Let's just say she's here to entertain me," Bobby pulled out a small thumb drive with his free hand from his top inside pocket, "When you turn over the information and the sample you may have the key to the last transaction." The waiter appeared and Bobby looked at him quickly. Recognizing him from before, he stopped and looked at Jan, "Are you hungry yet my dear?" His hand played in her hair.

"Yes," Jan had locked her mind down tightly. No one could get in and read it. Bobby could try but the most he would come up with was garble, and he was not ready to play with her yet. Not knowing exactly what to do, she decided that she needed to keep him here as long as she could. It also needed to look like she was playing his game, "I'd like a mango juice and a piece of toast."

"That's a good start, you'll need your strength for later," and he smiled, but his eyes didn't meet hers. Dr. Ross shook his head no at the waiter. Jan's face was set in stone and revealed nothing, "I'll have a coffee and scrambled eggs on toast." The waiter walked back into the kitchen.

"I just want to get this over with and leave. I think someone is on to us," Dr. Ross played with the silverware on the table.

"You're right, but I have it under control so you needn't be worried," Bobby placed his free hand on top of the silverware to still it, "Okay, hand it over." Dr. Ross placed the brown lunch bag on the table. The top of it had been folded over a number of times and Jan could only guess that whatever was inside it was not very big, but amazingly dangerous.

"Everything is in there," and he started to play with the silverware again. Bobby took the bag and opened it. He folded the top down and slid the thumb drive on the table over to the doctor.

"By the way doctor, don't think of disappearing, we may need you again later," and he watched as the doctor stood up and started out of the restaurant.   He walked past a man selling flowers to anyone who would buy one in the restaurant and he walked past a hawker trying to sell his silver rings and bracelets to a lady at a nearby table.

"What's in the bag?" Jan looked over at Bobby for the first time today.

"What's it to you?"   Bobby saw the waiter come out of the kitchen.

"Call it professional interest," and Bobby laughed.   Jan continued, "If you're going to involve me in this, make me an accomplice to keep me in line, at least have the decency to tell me about it."

"Okay," and he pulled the bag to him again and opened it. Out of the bag he pulled an apple.   The waiter approached the table just as the hawker turned around.   They bumped into each other and the hawker kept the waiter from spilling the entire tray of food and drink.   Some Spanish words of anger were exchanged and the hawker left the restaurant quickly.

"All this fuss for a piece of fruit," Jan kept the conversation going.   She could feel a bit of tension from Ward, but had expected this, but she had also recognized the way the hawker had moved. Was something happening?

"Not just any fruit.   It has been genetically altered to administer an antidote to some of the worst chemical weapons known to man," the implications were staggering, "and the thumb drive contains the last bits of information on how it was created and what will destroy it."   The waiter set down the food and drinks at the table   Jan wasn't sure what was going to happen next, but she kept Bobby's attention on her.

"In other words you've been handing over the information for chemical weapons production and protection.   Who to?"   She asked knowing she wouldn't get a response.   After waiting about a minute she continued, "You don't have any intention of leaving Ward alone do you?"   Jan started to place jelly on her toast.

"You're right.   I plan on leaving here with you and with any luck he will try something stupid and one of you will die quickly," he picked up the cup of coffee and smiled, turned toward Ward and made a mock toast with his cup before he sipped at it.   "Of course, I'm hoping it will be him after he is devastated by your death.   But then if you want to change your mind and stay with me, I could just kill him now for you." Jan looked at Bobby and noticed that his eye had begun to twitch. It was only a split second later when his hand began to shake and the cup fell to the floor. He tried to talk, to think, his thoughts garbled and then suddenly his whole body convulsed and he followed the cup down.

Ward moved quickly and was at his side in seconds. He pocketed the gun just as fast without anyone seeing it. Jan was on the other side of Bobby digging in his pockets for the trigger to the bomb she still wore. Ward turned and yelled for someone to get a doctor. Jan opened her mind to Ward and he let her know the rest of the plan instantaneously. She smiled at its simplicity. The hawker that had been in the restaurant just a few moments ago walked back in with Pat. She turned and looked at Ward and the hawker who Jan could now see well only quickly winked at her. She had suspected it to begin with, but was afraid to hope for it. Jack, the hawker, stood there beside Ward ready to help.

"I'm a doctor. He's having a seizure. Help me get this man outside," Pat issued the orders and Ward and Jack both took an arm and picked Bobby up as if he weighed nothing. Jan turned and grabbed the bag on the table before she followed them out looking worried. Once they were outside she could see that Dr. Ross had been cuffed and placed inside a light blue sedan. The driver of the sedan leaned on the front of the car. He wore shorts and a light blue shirt with socks and sandals. He still wore the hat and the green sunscreen on his nose was close to neon in color. He looked pretty burned from the sun, but Jan knew that was just coloring from a kit. Jan stifled a laugh as Ward and Jack maneuvered Bobby into the backseat of another sedan nearby. She watched as Pat cuffed him in, more than she would have to, and then handed the key to Jack.

"Nice outfit Rob," Jan leaned on the bumper.

"Just out for a little sun and fun," and they smiled. Pat, Jack and Ward walked back over to them. Jan pulled the apple out of the bag.

"Just the type of thing that got Adam in trouble," and she dropped it back in the paper bag and handed it to Rob. She looked over at Pat. There was something in her eyes, but Jan wasn't sure what it was. Jack interrupted them.

"He'll be out for about a day. If he had finished the cup though we probably wouldn't have had to worry about him," and he sounded more than just a little disappointed.

"What did you use?" Jan looked at both Ward and Jack.

"The science station in Peru kind of let me borrow a bit of a plant they have been studying," and Ward looked over at Jack.

"Lucky huh," and Jack winked at Jan and Pat.

"I guess it's time for me to walk away like I promised," and with that Pat moved back over to the car with Bobby in it. She drove off without a word leaving Jan puzzled. Jack was riding back with Rob and Dr. Ross. He had the only key to the cuffs to make it safer for Pat to travel back to the states.

"We'll take the good doctor back and start the clean-up. Your man in Peru should be pulling in Moore right about now," Rob looked at his watch.

"Do we need to drop you two anywhere?" Jack looked at them with a knowing grin, "I can also supply you with any protection you many need from a very angry husband ma'am."

"I think we can manage from here," Ward gave Jan a very angry look. Then he looked back at Jack and smiled, "Thanks bro," and Ward slapped Jack on the back as he reached for Jan's hand. He frowned as he turned her hand over in his and looked at her wrist. "Are you really okay?"

"Never better," Jan smiled as she reached under her shirt and gently tugged the bomb free and disarmed it. It was something they could keep for future jobs. Jack just shook his head as he walked away.

Epilogue

A month later the sun was just setting on the horizon after a truly glorious day. They had spent the day swimming and then picnicking on the beach and exploring each other. Jan and Ward sat on the balcony half asleep and enjoyed the colors of the sunset as they danced across the sky. As the reds turned orange and then pink, the waves crashed against the shore. Their fingers brushed over each other's as their minds circled together. No words or artificial sounds interrupted the beauty of the moment. Ward's thoughts had touched on many things over the last month. He had thought of Bobby often, mostly with sadness in his heart. Bobby was now under observation and the rest of the time he was medicated. There was little hope for his future. Gregg had been replaced in the Phoenix branch after Bobby was brought in.

He had also thought about Jack and Pat. Pat had taken a more active interest in field work lately and Rob had worked with her. Jack had called and talked with Toby after he brought in Moore. Moore had been using different agents to pass the information on to the buyers. Jack had become a liability when his trip got canceled and Moore was using him to pass on part of the information, which was why he had tried to kill him. Toby had been surprised to hear his voice but it didn't surprise him to find out that Jan, or Liz as he knew her, was working for or with them as it was. Toby had passed on his congratulations to the group and his appreciation to them for saving Jack, and him, from Moore.

Dr. Ross had told the department everything. He didn't even wait for a lawyer. There had been a lot of information passed in the last year, but the most vital part they had been able to stop. MedLabs had shut down for a month and were redoing security so that things like this could not happen again. All the other employees were also getting thorough checks from the FBI.

Nothing had peaked their interest on the e-mail in the last month, so they had been able to take some time off. Soon, too soon, there would be another job and more danger, but for now it was just the two of them. As the sun dipped below the horizon and the night took over the day, their thoughts turned to other things, again. The simple sounds of nature were interrupted by the ringing of a cell phone.

"If it's the Commissioner, Batman, we're not at home," and Jan leaned her head back on the chair. Ward stood up and gave Jan a peck on the top of her head and went in. Looking first at the caller ID, he then answered it.

"Hey Jack," was all he said.

"Are you two working on anything right now?" Jack's voice was hopeful. Ward looked out at Jan and saw that she was dozing, the breeze gently moving her hair, and her even breathing so relaxed. He sighed.

"No, what's up?" He almost hated to ask.

"I need to meet with you to discuss it. Don't want to trust the lines, even secure ones," Jack's voice was steady, "I'm in the area."

"Let's meet in Rosarito, tomorrow at six for supper. There's a place just north of the steak house that has private rooms. Go in and look for me. I'll be there," and Ward waited for the reply.

"Bring Jan, she'll want to be in on this one," and Jack hung up the phone. Ward walked back outside and sat down in his chair.

"We have another job don't we?" Jan didn't even open her eyes.

"Yah. That was Jack, says this is one we both will be interested in," Ward let his hand play with Jan's hair, "What do you think?"

"Let's save the thinking for tomorrow," Jan picked her head up and looked over at Ward. Her eyes were rich and dark, but Ward didn't need them to know what she was thinking about right now.

She awoke in his arms completely satisfied. Whatever the day was going to bring she was now ready for it. The routine stayed the same that morning. Jan meditated and then they had both gone for a five mile run along the beach. Jan had decided to take a swim before going back up to the apartment and Ward stayed on the beach to meditate as he waited for her to return. They then moved in unison in the tai chi routine after lunch. At about four o'clock they packed a small bag and got in the Monster. Ward still needed to replace the Explorer, but it hadn't been on the top of his to do list since they had the Monster. Senor Garcia handed the keys to Ward as they left the courtyard that hid them from the world. Jan walked over to the driver's side of the Monster and looked at Ward. Ward shrugged his shoulders and threw the keys at her. Senor Garcia just shook his head as he waved bye at them. They drove out of the driveway and up to the main road not knowing when they would be back.

They drove up the coast leisurely, arriving at the restaurant at five-thirty. They went in and ordered a light meal of fish, tortillas and fresh vegetables as they went into the back room of the restaurant. Ward walked out of the room at about six and found Jack standing there and waiting. His mind was tightly closed but he noticed he had a strange look on his face. His eyes were set and his lips weren't curved up in a smile, but they weren't frowning either. Ward scanned the area before he approached him. Seeing nothing that concerned him, he walked on over.

"So, what's up?" They walked side by side back to the room.

"I'd rather wait until we get in to discuss it," his voice was way too serious. He matched his steps through the open part of the restaurant, passed the other diners, and went into the back room.

"Okay," and Ward opened the door to the room. Jan stood up and walked over to Jack giving him a hug and kiss on the cheek.

"It's good to see you," she said.

"I hope you still feel that way when you hear what I have to say," and he sat down at the table with them. Jan and Ward sat facing the door and Jack sat with his back to it. Seconds later the door opened behind Jack and Ward saw who was there. Rob and Pat walked into the room along with Maria and closed the door behind them. Ward tensed. Jan could feel it.

"I didn't think you could do it," Ward looked straight at Pat and the bag she carried. Rob had updated them on all that had happened on the case long ago and what had happened two weeks ago. There was no reason for Pat to be standing there with them except to take them into custody and back to the department. "I thought you were my brother," Ward's gaze fell on Jack. That's when his somber expression broke. Jack smiled, a wicked and knowing smile, disarming Ward a bit.

"I am," and Jack looked over at Pat, "Did you tell the waiter to bring it in, in five minutes?"

"I did," and Pat sat down at the table, not saying another word. Rob sat down on the other side of Jan and Maria sat beside Jack. Both Ward and Jan were now very confused. No one was allowing them to get easy access to their thoughts. They looked at each other as the smiles at the table seemed to be infectious, except for Jan and Ward.

"Did I miss something?" Jan asked the people at the table.

"No, but we did, and we decided to do something about it," Rob said defiantly, and as Rob finished the door to the room opened again. There were a couple of waiters carrying trays of food. They had Jan and Ward's order, except there was enough for everyone at the table and more. Another waiter carried in the drinks. The first waiter went out again and came back in with the last tray. On the tray was a cake with white icing and two small figurines on top.

"We may have missed the wedding but we thought we could give you a reception, even if it is a little late," and Pat smiled at the both of them as she pulled out a bottle of champagne from the bag she carried.

"I don't believe this," was all Ward could say as he shook his head. Jan laughed and smiled like the rest of them.

"Wait, wait, wait, before we get started with the feast, let's get the presents out of the way," and there was definitely a devilish look on Rob's face. He put his hand in his pocket and pulled out a key with a small ribbon tied to it. "Never did like wrapping things and since you just lost your Explorer I thought you might be in need of other transportation." Ward picked up the key. "It's not new, but Bill and Eddy assured me that you would like it. Speaking of them, they should be here in about half an hour. They said to save them some food."

"Rob," Jan sounded a little distressed.

"Now before you say anything Jan, I don't have any family, you're it. The Land Cruiser is about ten years old, but the engine is new. It should go for a long time. I also figured I owed you a new ride," Rob smiled at the both of them. He slid the key across the table, "and no, there is not a tracking device on it."

"I don't know what to say," Jan looked at Rob.

"My turn," Pat's simple statement drew their attention away from the key. From her bag she pulled out two manila envelopes. She handed one to Ward and one to Jan. Ward and Jan opened them at the same time. They didn't see Maria take Jack's hand under the table and they didn't notice Jack squeeze Maria's hand in return. It took a few moments for Ward and Jan to understand what Pat was giving them. They paged through the papers and glanced back at Pat in sheer amazement.

"Is this what I think it is?" Jan asked Pat, and Ward looked up from his stack of papers.

"Yes, it is. You gave the department back its purpose and its honor. Who knows what else may come of it. As of this moment you two no longer exist to any one," Pat smiled, "It's the only gift I could give you that would make any difference. It is one that is truly good enough for you and what you did for us. Plus it is what you really want; your freedom," Pat held up her glass of champagne, "Enjoy."

"You may now," and they all looked to the door just in time to see Bill and Eddy, "kiss the bride."